I0688602

Praise for The Mozart Conspiracy

"A wonderful read! Full of intrigue with interesting historical and musical connections. Follow the unusual clues which help Theresa as she struggles to solve the reasons for the conspiracy against Mozart with the help of her gypsy friends."

–Reader Review

"This is a fast paced mystery that will have you guessing until the very end."

–Kate Eminhizer

Praise for The Musician's Daughter

"… this book is a rip-roaring adventure with music, murder, and espionage. It's clearly well researched, and the level of detail in the narrative makes readers believe that this story might have actually happened. Theresa's first-person narrative reveals her to be a quick-thinking, courageous, and likable individual."

– School Library Journal

"…a gutsy, sympathetic heroine who remains true to her friends, in a fast-paced historical adventure that offers a hint of romance."

– Kirkus Reviews

ALSO BY SUSANNE DUNLAP

The Mozart Conspiracy

Listen to the Wind

The Spirit of Fire

Émilie's Voice

Liszt's Kiss

The Musician's Daughter

Anastasia's Secret

In the Shadow of the Lamp

The Académie

The PARIS Affair

a Theresa Schurman Mystery

Susanne Dunlap

Susanne Dunlap
susanne-dunlap.com

Copyright © 2020 by Susanne Dunlap
All rights reserved,
including the reproduction in whole or in part in any form
without the written permission of the publisher, Susanne
Dunlap, 88 Crescent St., Northampton, MA 01116.

The Paris Affair is a work of fiction. Names, characters, places,
and incidents are products of the author's imagination or
are used fictitiously and are not to be construed as real. Any
resemblance to actual events, locations, organizations, or persons,
living or dead, is entirely coincidental.

First Edition

ISBN-13: 978-1734919103

Publisher's Cataloging-In-Publication Data
Names: Dunlap, Susanne Emily, author.
Title: The Paris affair : a Theresa Schurman mystery / Susanne Dunlap.
Description: First Edition. | Northampton, MA : Susanne Dunlap,
[2020] | Series: Theresa Schurman mystery ; [3]
Identifiers: ISBN 9781734919103 | ISBN 9781734919110 (ebook)
Subjects: LCSH: Musicians--Juvenile fiction. | Marie Antoinette,
Queen, consort of Louis XVI, King of France, 1755-1793--Juvenile
fiction. | Libel and slander--Juvenile fiction. | Paris (France)--
History--18th century--Juvenile fiction. | CYAC: Musicians--Fiction.
| Marie Antoinette, Queen, consort of Louis XVI, King of France,
1755-1793--Fiction. | Rumor--Fiction. | Paris (France)--History--18th
century--Fiction. | Coming of age--Fiction. | LCGFT: Detective and
mystery fiction. | Historical fiction. | Thrillers (Fiction)
Classification: LCC PZ7.D92123 Par 2020 (print) | LCC PZ7.D92123
(ebook) | DDC [Fic]--dc23

Dedication

To my fellow writers in the studio of Writers in Progress,
who listened to bits of this tale as it was being created.

Thank you for your generous comments and encouragement!

Chapter One

No one was more surprised than I was to find myself in Paris at the end of October, 1783, working as a bookkeeper for queen Marie Antoinette's milliner, and living in a whorehouse.

The events that led to these strange circumstances began when emperor Joseph II commanded me to wait upon him at the Hofburg a little over a month before that. I had gone there dressed in my finest gown, thinking he was going to bestow some honor upon me for the service I had done him the previous year. Although I had been thrown together with the duplicitous Captain von Bauer and found myself embroiled in a plot whose aim was not immediately apparent, I liked to think I had had a role in saving the emperor from assassination, and that he would someday see fit to reward me.

But that was not the case.

Instead of a grand reception, when I arrived at the palace in the middle of Vienna, I was greeted only by a footman who conducted me through endless corridors into a modest office. It took me a moment to realize it was the emperor himself who sat behind the plain desk. He was engaged in writing something and looked not much more important than a humble clerk.

I curtsied and then waited, listening to the scratch of his quill and the distant sounds of footsteps and doors closing deep within the cavernous building.

When at last the emperor stopped writing, he tossed the quill into an open ink pot, vigorously scattered sand over the page and blew it off in my direction. There must have been some dust mixed in with the sand, because I immediately emitted a sudden, violent, ungovernable sneeze.

"Je m'excuse!" "Gesundheit!"

We spoke at the same time. His face broke open in a broad smile and I relaxed. It was a terrible breach of etiquette, but there, alone in a tiny office in the bowels of the Hofburg, etiquette seemed not to matter.

"I haven't got much time, so I'll just tell you quickly," the emperor said, standing and coming around from behind the desk. "This letter is for you to present to Monsieur Le Comte Mercy, who is our ambassador at the court of Versailles."

"Versailles. That's France." I realized how stupid I sounded, but at that point I was utterly mystified.

"Yes, of course. It's also where our sister is queen, facing a court that is often openly hostile and a populace that is increasingly malcontent." He paced around the room as he spoke, and I turned in a slow circle in order to keep my eyes on him. "I received intelligence from Captain von Bauer about certain slanders against the queen, which he believes ought to be investigated. He thinks the wild accusations have inflamed the common people against her, and that she has undeservedly become the focus of ill feeling against the court in general. Due to his position as a captain of the Swiss Guard, he believes he lacks the necessary anonymity to investigate on his own, and he suggested that I send you to aid him in these pursuits."

Captain Bauer again! I thought. The handsome, two-faced source of several of my most aggravating moments. From all I remembered of our ill-fated adventures a year ago, he had little regard for me, and I assumed he had been quite pleased to be sent off to another country, far away from my annoying presence.

The emperor paused and leveled his gaze on me. I felt the heat rise into my face. "He and I both agree that you—with your instinct for nosing out the most complicated and hidden conspiracies and your complete lack of social standing or renown—would be the ideal person to act as our...source of information, if you see what I mean."

I ignored the implied insult, which no doubt had originated with the captain. "You want me to be your spy. You want me to go to France and spy for you." The words escaped me before I could stop them.

"As you put it so plainly, I suppose I can only concur. You will leave tomorrow on the public coach. Here is a ticket. Take only your barest necessities, tell no one where you are going, and keep this letter hidden until you have the opportunity to give it directly to Mercy. The captain will meet you when you arrive and give you more information about where you will stay and what you will do."

I opened my mouth to ask a question, but the emperor interrupted me.

"You will be amply rewarded for your service," he said—assuming that was what I, a person of no position or importance, would ask. I noted that he did not name a sum. Such a lack of specificity about money is all too typical of those with more than they know what to do with.

"How long"— I began, but then he continued to speak as if he didn't hear me.

"If you have reasons to stay in Vienna and cannot embark on such a journey, I will, of course, allow you to decline this task. A sweetheart perhaps? Or your mother needs you?"

I said nothing, and he gave me the letter. That he thought only such personal reasons might keep me from accepting the task annoyed me, but he was the emperor, so I remained silent. The door to the office opened as by some unseen signal. I curtsied, and walked home in a state of disbelief.

Since I was leaving the next day, I had very little time to ponder this sudden change in plans. My mother accepted it readily enough. She would never think of interfering with a command from the emperor, and had become used to my unusual life as a musician and violin teacher—pursuits generally not deemed suitable for young ladies.

Whatever her thoughts on the matter, I had arrangements to make. The first and most important to me concerned my violin. My precious Amati, left to me by my father. Should I take it with me? What might happen to it on such a long journey? And would I be able to keep it safe once I was in Paris? Yet the idea of going away and not having a violin at hand was inconceivable. I wasn't certain what to do.

My other concern was much more complicated. What would I say to Zoltan? Should I write to him and tell him I was going away, even though I couldn't tell him why or where? What would he think? We had left things so unresolved when we parted the previous spring. We had promised to speak again when I was a year older. That time had come and gone, and I still wasn't certain what answer to give him. I loved Zoltan, that I knew. He was the kindest, bravest, most intelligent man I had ever had the privilege of knowing. Everyone assumed we would marry. Everyone, that is, except me. It wasn't the idea of Zoltan that gave me pause, but the idea of marriage and all it entailed.

I decided to put such matters aside for the moment, though, since there was little I could do to resolve them on my own. And I suddenly had a brilliant idea of how to solve the problem of the violin: I would leave my Amati with Danior—who would be only too pleased to have it in his possession—and borrow his excellent, but much less valuable instrument to take with me. As soon as I had gathered my few possessions and packed them in a valise for my early-morning departure, I set out with my violin for Danior and Alida's apartment in the Trattner House, a short walk from where we lived.

While I waited for the porter to open the street door, I gazed up to the familiar sight of windows glowing with candlelight. Danior and Alida must have company, I thought. I heard the strains of a string quartet as soon as the old man let me in, and the music grew louder as I climbed the stairs, hugging my precious violin in its case.

I reached the door and knocked. Hurried, light steps came toward it and Alida opened it to let me in, her face flushed with delight and wine.

"Theresa! How wonderful that you are here! Your timing is perfect. We have a guest."

She showed me through the vestibule to the elegant parlor. I saw by the long drips of wax on the candles attached to the music stands that the quartet had been at it for some time. The playing stopped, and four faces looked up from the sheets of music in front of them and fixed their eyes on me. Danior sat in the first violin chair, as was his custom. With him were a violist and a cellist I knew from the Staatsoper, and playing second violin, gazing at me and awakening a confusion of feelings, was Zoltan himself.

Could I be dreaming? I thought. And then he rose and came to me, arms outstretched. I extended my hands, not for an embrace, but to clasp his. In front of these people, we were friends only. I tried to explain with my eyes, but I could see the hurt, the doubt in his. Now I would be forced to tell him face to face that I was going to Paris, and I wouldn't be able to explain why. I told myself to be brave.

"You're surprised to see me," he said.

"Yes. Happy though." I made an effort to smile. "It's not usual for you to be in Vienna at this time of year."

"The harvest is going well. And I had a matter of business to take care of at court that could not be delayed, so I set out before I had a chance to write to anyone. Alida was just as surprised as you were when I turned up at her door earlier today! I have a note all ready to send you tomorrow."

A footman brought me a glass of wine, and I drank—rather more quickly and deeply than I usually would, hoping it would numb me enough to get through an evening that had turned unexpectedly complicated.

Danior and Alida had somehow melted away, perhaps to look for music in Danior's library, and the other musicians turned their backs, ostensibly to have a private conversation. Zoltan and I were virtually alone—or as alone as was proper for a single woman and a man, both of marriageable age. I knew I must speak to him. But I couldn't find the words to start.

"You've changed." Zoltan's voice was gentle and warm.

"Not for the worse, I hope?" I touched his arm, and drew him toward a settee by a window. Zoltan looked the same as he did the last time I saw him, his soft, blond hair drawn into a queue down his back, his languid-lidded, lash-rimmed hazel eyes still alive with intelligence and sentiment.

"You're older, more reserved. Not the impetuous, daring Theresa I saw a year ago who stayed busy solving murders and putting the world to rights. And that is for the better, I think."

He was right. I had changed. So gradually that I had hardly noticed it. Where before I'd been confident that my view of the world was unvaryingly accurate, I wasn't so certain anymore. I had come to accept that the expected didn't always occur, that people we thought we knew could surprise us, and that a heart is a fickle and complicated thing. I saw nuance where before I perceived only right and wrong. Instead of always fighting the conventions I found stifling, I had figured out more subtle ways to circumvent them. I demanded more of myself and less of those I loved. But I knew that, at heart, I was just the same, with the same desire for doing and searching, the same longing to find meaning and purpose in my life, in the world. For the sake of my peace of mind, I'd successfully suppressed my growing restlessness about the unvarying predictability of my days—days that, regardless of what I had done to thwart expectations, lay mapped before me like the course of the Danube.

And yet, the prospect of embarking on another adventure brought my desire for action into stark relief. My initial hesitance when the emperor had told me of the plan had rapidly given way to eagerness, and my mind was already busy anticipating what new experiences would be ahead.

Until, that is, I encountered Zoltan. Was he part of the old order or the new? Did he want me to let go of my ambitions, or would he support my unconventional choices? He managed, somehow, to represent both continuity and change. I gazed at his familiar face, and a vision of the kind of change Zoltan had to offer opened up before me. I could see myself on his estate in Hungary playing the hostess to local gentry. I would oversee the household, hire and fire servants, decide that the furniture needed to be replaced, tend to sick animals. And children! There would undoubtedly be children. But would there be music? Yes, of course there would, but would I be playing it?

"What's wrong? Did I say something to offend you?" Zoltan's face was a picture of concern, and I realized that I must have been frowning.

"Nothing, of course. How can there be anything wrong? And you could never offend me." I squeezed his hand. He moved a little closer to me on the settee.

"What has brought you here this evening, of all evenings?" He said. "I was hoping we could go for a walk tomorrow and settle things at last. It's been too long."

Settle things. He could only mean—"I must go away tomorrow, rather suddenly. I came this evening to tell Danior." The words tumbled out before I could think of a way to tell him more gently.

"How long will you be away?"

"I-I don't precisely know." Because, of course, I didn't. Not exactly.

"Where will you go?" He'd sat up a little straighter and leaned away from me. Of course he's confused, I thought. So am I!

"To Paris."

"Paris?"

"Paris," I repeated, with wonder. Such an odd idea.

After a pause, Zoltan said, "Is that not where Captain von Bauer has gone?"

Instead of answering, *yes, but I will not see him,* a small lie that would have enough truth in essence, I said, "Is he?"

"You know it is." Zoltan stood, walked to the other window, and stared out at the Viennese night.

"Ah! There you are! Theresa, I see you have brought your violin. What premonition led you to so fortuitous a gesture?" Danior must have noticed the tension in the air between us when he returned with a stack of music.

I wanted to run from the room, pretend the entire evening had not happened, go back outside and start again from the beginning. Instead, I drew Danior aside and explained to him about the Amati, and that I hoped to trade with him for a time. "You will make sure Zoltan doesn't think anything awful?" I said. "I'm afraid I've made rather a hash of things."

Danior assured me he would smooth things over with Zoltan. What would he say, since I couldn't tell him why I was going either?

I had to put those thoughts out of my mind, though, go home, and try to sleep. Morning would come soon enough. And there would be plenty of time to regret what I had said—or hadn't said—to Zoltan.

Chapter Two

I arrived in Paris in a foul mood after a bumpy, uncomfortable journey in a public coach that took nearly three weeks. I was glad to finally part ways from the motley assortment of fellow passengers who had slept and complained and eaten rotten-smelling cheese in the crowded coach, and with whom I had to share flea-infested straw mats at inns along the way. I scanned the waiting crowd gathered to meet the coach, a handkerchief pressed to my nose against a stench I could not identify. It took me a moment to notice the captain standing among the others, not wearing a uniform, but looking—as always—dapper, and drawing admiring glances from all the women who passed him.

"Mademoiselle!" He said with a bow as he walked toward me, leaving me to carry my own valise and my violin. "Come with me."

The captain led me at a clip I could hardly keep up with. We threaded our way along cobbled streets, some so narrow we had to press ourselves against a wall to let a carriage pass. At one point, a child grabbed hold of my skirt tears streaking his face, begging for, *"Un sou! Seulement un sou pour ma soeur aveugle!"* I doubted he had a blind sister. I called to the captain and he turned and started back toward me. At the sight of the man with the angry scowl on his face striding in my direction, the urchin let go with a "Whoop!" and soon vanished into the crowd. I clutched Danior's violin to me, now glancing right and left as I hurried to catch up with the captain. The beggars were not nearly so bold in Vienna.

At one moment, when we came to the end of an alleyway, I saw the river Seine in its resplendent state of decay. This was clearly the source of the unpleasant smell. Rotting vegetables floated between barges loaded with garbage. Brown lumps that I feared were human or animal waste dotted the surface. The water was a murky brown, even worse than the canal that bordered Vienna. At least the Danube proper wasn't quite so disgusting.

I struggled to breathe through my mouth so I wouldn't be able to smell too much. To my amazement, a row of washer-women knelt in the dirty water, scrubbing linens and clothes. "That's disgusting!" I said before I could suppress it, and in the process inhaled a breath through my nose. I gagged.

Just before we reached what looked like a vast, unfinished palace, we turned away from the river.

"That's the Louvre, and the Tuileries beyond it," Captain Bauer said as we passed. "It was never finished."

"Why?"

He shrugged. "Court moved to Versailles because Louis XIV didn't feel safe in Paris."

I could never imagine the emperor of Austria feeling too unsafe to live in Vienna. "Or perhaps he just didn't like the smell," I said.

"Parisians aren't like the Viennese."

From what I'd seen of them so far, I readily agreed. I think in my mind I picture Paris as another Vienna, only with people speaking French in the streets. I could see how mistaken I had been, and began to doubt my wisdom in agreeing to come there.

We continued our dash through the dirty streets and soon made our way to some that were not so narrow and lined with elegant shops. I slowed my pace as we passed one that sold ladies' clothing.

"You can't afford it, so there's no point looking," the captain said, walking even faster so I had to run to catch up again. "Besides, you'll soon have your fill of such things."

"I wish you'd tell me where we were going!" I was tired and out of breath, and when the captain noticed, he slowed his pace a minuscule amount. "And what did you mean I would have my fill of such things?"

He ignored my question. "Nearly there." He pointed toward a building that looked much like many others, with a shop that sold leather goods on the ground floor and residences on the four floors above. He knocked on a door next to the shop entrance. Finally! I thought, assuming he would install me in an apartment of my own somewhere on one of the upper floors.

A few moments later an elderly man, bent nearly double as though he had an enormous weight on his back, opened the door.

"Is Madame Chrétien within?"

The man—clearly the porter, or concierge, as I found out later they were called in Paris—nodded twice slowly, on the way up from the second nod taking much too close a look at me, then shuffled aside so we could enter and climb up a wide stone staircase.

On the first floor the captain tapped at the single door and put his ear to it. "Someone's in there. She said she'd be alone."

She? I thought. Perhaps a chaperon arranged for me. I confess, I was as relieved as I was disappointed.

As soon as the captain finished speaking the door was opened by a woman dressed in a gown of rich fabric with a deep décolletage. And to my shock, she wasn't alone. A man old enough to be her father stood next to her. She turned and draped herself against him and whispered something in his ear that made him run his tongue over his lips.

I turned a shocked gaze to the captain, who wouldn't look at me. To my continued disgust, the man smiled at me and raked his eyes up and down my body as though he could see right through my modest, travel-stained garments.

"Come in mon cher," the lady said and took the captain's arm, drawing him away and leaving me behind. She looked over her shoulder. "You as well, little girl."

Little girl? I was nearly nineteen. What on earth was going on! Not having any other choice I followed them down a corridor and into an elegant parlor, taking in all the details of my surroundings as I went. The wooden floors were polished to a high sheen, but I could only see the edges, because Turkish carpets in rich reds and deep blues covered them for the entire length of the corridor. They were even finer than the carpets in Danior and Alida's apartment. The lady must be quite rich, I thought. At the end of the corridor was a paneled door with gilt trimmings. Madame Chrétien opened it and we walked through into a parlor that was much larger than I expected it to be—and handsomely furnished as well, with silk-upholstered settees and armchairs. She and the captain took the two chairs nearest the fireplace and continued their conversation in rapid French that I was too tired to attempt to understand. I stood in the middle of the room, feeling like a servant waiting for an interview with a potential mistress, except that instead of a broom and dustpan, I held my valise and violin case. It was a good few minutes before Madame could peel her eyes away from the captain, who was exercising his charms on her most effectively.

"Ah, yes, you are still here," she said in slow, careful French so I could understand, and rang a little bell that was next to her on a table so small, it could only hold a candlestick and the bell.

"Would someone please tell me what I'm doing here!" I was too tired and confused to be polite.

"First of all, you are here to bathe." Madame Chrétien walked over to me, her expression not unkind, took my chin with one hand and tapped my nose with the other. "In the meantime, I will converse with the captain. You will rejoin us once you have…freshened up."

I detected a slight wrinkling of her nose. No doubt the many unpleasant smells from my journey were now embedded into my clothes and skin and hair.

The door opened and a maid in a neat dress with a starched white pinafore entered and curtsied.

"Agathe, take Mademoiselle…" She paused. Either she didn't know my name, or had forgotten it.

"Theresa Schurman," I said.

"…Mademoiselle Thérèse to Odette's room and then to bathe."

I turned to follow, but the captain's voice made me pause. "Leave the message for Mercy with me, Thérèse." He leaned on the French pronunciation of my name.

Mademoiselle Schurman to you! I thought. How did he know I was carrying a message? Well, I supposed the emperor must have told him. "I am to give it directly into the ambassador's hands."

"And so you shall. After I've read it."

"It's private!"

"Don't you want to know what it says?"

He had a point. But to ignore the emperor's instructions… "I wouldn't dare."

"Ah, but I would. Don't worry, if there's trouble, I'll say I forced you."

This made Madame Chrétien laugh out loud. "When was the last time you had to force a lady, cher Capitaine!"

He'd have to force me! I thought, becoming more and more irritated. In the short time since I'd descended from the coach until that moment, I was regretting more and more my decision to accept the emperor's commission. Time away from the captain had smoothed over some of his more aggravating characteristics. Now I recalled why I was so glad when he went away to Versailles and would no longer be in Vienna to torment me. Bringing me here, to this odd place, he no doubt sought to torment me again.

Agathe took my arm and nudged me in front of her out the door of the parlor. "Follow me," she said, and led me back down the corridor to more stairs. These became narrower and narrower the higher they went, until we were in the attics of the house. Four plain, small doors led off the landing, and there was no Turkish carpet on the floor up here. She opened one of the doors. I had to hold my violin case in front of me to pass through it into a predictably small chamber.

The room itself was furnished with two narrow beds covered in faded silk and velvet spreads, a large armoire, a long mirror that leaned against the wall between the two attic windows, and a dressing table. One of the beds looked as though someone had only recently risen from it. The other was neatly made. With these items of furniture, there was hardly enough room to turn around.

"Leave your things here and I'll take you to bathe." Agathe opened the armoire and indicated that I should take off my cloak and hat and put them on the one remaining hook inside it. The rest of the cupboard was crammed with clothing of all sorts, from vivid patterned silk skirts, to lace petticoats rendered dull with washing, to men's uniform jackets. I did my best to push my cloak inside, laid my valise and violin case on the bed with undisturbed covers, and followed Agathe back down the stairs two floors below to a small room at the back. She opened the door, and a cloud of scented steam engulfed me. I stepped in. Agathe followed me. The room held a copper tub that had been filled to the brim with hot water. Such a luxury! Agathe started untying my skirt and helped me out of my clothing until I wore nothing but my shift.

"I can manage from here," I said, assuming she would leave me to wash in the tub and then dress myself.

"Madame says I'm to make sure you're clean." She folded her arms across her ample bosom and planted her feet wide, placing herself in front of the door.

"I do know how to bathe," I said, offended.

"That's what they all say."

Who all? I thought. And why would it matter if a visitor bathed or not? I was too tired to worry about it, and slipped my shift over my head and eased myself into the tub. I hadn't been that warm since we'd left Vienna. I had to admit that it felt good to rinse off the grime of travel and scrub the nits and lice out of my hair.

Agathe, rather than leave me to my own devices, took hold of a rough sponge and scoured me until I thought my skin would rub off. Then she dragged a fine comb through my knotted hair, pulling it out in clumps I feared, and picked out a few more visitors that I had missed. My scalp was so sore I felt as if I'd been hanging off a balcony from my hair.

When I finally stepped out of the tub, she wrapped me in a large linen sheet, then took my clothing and threw it all into the tub I'd just left.

"Wait! What will I wear?"

"There's a change of clothes upstairs for you," she said, opening the door and waiting for me to walk through.

As we padded back the way we'd come, one or two of the doors that had been closed until now opened, and I saw young women, some close to my age, entering and leaving. It seemed quite odd to me. "Do these ladies rent apartments here?" I asked.

Agathe opened her mouth wide and laughed. "They all work for Madame."

Could they be maids? I thought. By the time I returned to the room I was apparently sharing with someone called Odette and really took stock of my surroundings, I finally understood. How could I have been so blind? This was some kind of Huren Haus! A brothel! How dare the captain bring me to such a place? If he thought I was going to earn my keep here—but no, he couldn't think that. Or could he?

As soon as I was dressed I stepped out of the room only to run into the stern-faced Agathe. "Where are you going?" She asked.

"Take me to see the captain."

"He's with Madame and not to be disturbed," she said.

"Take me to see the captain, or I will start screaming until the entire house is in an uproar."

She stood her ground, crossing her arms in front of her. I opened my mouth wide and sucked in a deep breath.

"Follow me," Agathe said and hurried away.

Chapter Three

The captain let me harangue him for a good five minutes before interrupting me. Madame Chrétien had left us alone as soon as she noticed the expression on my face, so I didn't hold back. "Why! Why! How dare you subject me to this... place!"

I paused to take a breath and the captain, who had maintained his faintly amused expression throughout, said, "Are you quite finished? If you allow me I will explain these unorthodox accommodations to you."

By now I was so exhausted I could hardly stand on my own two feet, so I sank into one of the comfortable chairs and glared at him.

"This, my dear Thérèse, is the safest place for you to be in Paris. Madame runs a very orderly disorderly house, but that is not her only talent." He paused to pour us each a glass of wine and handed mine to me. I didn't touch it, but he sipped his and closed his eyes in appreciation before continuing. "Madame Chrétien—like you—is an agent of the Austrian government. The girls who work for her, although they are not spies, have been trained to tease important information out of their...clients, information that has so far been instrumental in getting us to what we know about the libels against the queen."

"Are the police not likely to close down such a house at any moment?" I said, recalling what little I knew about establishments like this in Vienna.

"The police are some of Madame Chrétien's best customers," he said with a smile, raising his glass to me.

I stood and faced him again, still seething at the subterfuge and the false position I now found myself in. "If you allow any man so much as to look at me with lust in his eyes I will report you to the emperor!"

The captain threw his head back and laughed. When he had contained his amusement enough to talk, he said, "Don't worry, little Theresa. That is not why you are here. This house is your lodgings, nothing more. I think you will find the accommodations comfortable, and the food superb. Because of the nature of Madame's business, we can easily meet unobserved to exchange information."

"But...people will see me coming and going, will they not?"

He shrugged. "You won't be the first relation from the provinces to stay with an aunt, whose business may well be unknown to her family."

The sense behind the captain's arguments took the intensity out of my anger, but I was still irritated. "I don't know..."

"You have my word that nothing untoward will happen to you here. If at any time you wish to terminate your mission, I will do so without question, and send you back to Vienna on the next coach."

I saw by his expression that he was being sincere, and unclenched my jaw and felt my neck and shoulders relax. I had been gripping the wine glass so hard that my hand began to shake. The captain noticed and stepped forward to take it from me just before I dropped it.

"You'll have some supper and then go to bed. Madame will meet with you in the morning to bring you up to date and start your training."

My training. I was truly too exhausted to puzzle it out then, and nodded to him. He rang a little bell, and soon I had feasted on a delicious meal and been sent to bed. I think my eyes closed before I even laid my head on the down pillow.

When I awoke the next morning, my roommate was there, but so deeply buried in the covers on her bed that I couldn't see her. The only evidence I had of her presence was the trail of clothing that led from the door to the bed and the sound of her faint snores.

Agathe reappeared as soon as I was dressed and took me down to the parlor, where I found Madame Chrétien with a large book on the table in front of her and what looked like a map and some kind of diagram draped over another.

"Capitaine Bauer says you are smart and quick. I hope he is right. We don't have much time to provide you with the education you will need to pass as French and blend into the circles where you are likely to discover what the Emperor Joseph hopes. You have had breakfast?"

When I shook my head, she rang the bell, and as if she had read her mistress's mind, Agathe returned with a tray laden with bread and butter and a pot of coffee. I reached for the bread and Madame slapped my hand away. "You must have manners that will help you pass for a lady of refinement, if not quality."

A lesson in etiquette followed, then I was allowed to eat. After I'd finished and had a second cup of coffee, I asked her about the book and the map.

"This is the fashion gazette. One is published every month, detailing the costumes worn by all the ladies and men at court, and at the Palais Royale."

"A palace? Is that not the court?"

She sighed and shook her head. "If it were, there would be no need for you to spy. The Palais Royale is the residence of the dukes of Orléans, the cadet branch of the royal family. If all the Bourbons perished, the throne would pass to the eldest son in that family."

"Is that likely to happen?" I asked, knowing that every time I opened my mouth I exposed the depth of my ignorance concerning all things French.

"The queen has not yet given birth to an heir. She has a daughter, so we know she is fertile, but she had a miscarriage just the other day. Of course, if she doesn't produce a dauphin, the king has brothers and nephews enough to fill the void and prevent the Orléans family from reigning."

"And the map?"

"This map gives the locations of all residences of those who are either welcome at court or are sworn enemies of the Bourbon monarchy or the queen." She pulled it closer and ran her finger around it. "The blue ink marks friends. The red ink, foes."

I cast my eye over it. Blue and red were equally represented and impossible to separate by geography. Even at Versailles itself, much red abounded. "Within the queen's own home?" I asked.

"There are two factions who wish Marie Antoinette to fail. One is the Orléanist group—for obvious reasons. The other is the circle of the king's aunts, who are known as Mesdames."

This made no sense at all. "Why would the king's own aunts want to undermine the queen?"

"Because she has upset the order and flouted the etiquette at court, and she is Austrian, of course!"

She said it as if it were the greatest of insults. My surprise must have shown in my face.

"That's not the only reason. And I am certain there are people of great dignity and breeding in Austria—"

"And the house of Hapsburg has as much a claim to royalty as the Bourbons, if not more so!" I said, with more heat than I intended.

Madame looked up. "My dear, Paris and Versailles are treacherous places where nothing is quite as it seems. If you do not think you are capable of setting aside your provincial loyalties for a greater good, you had best own it right away. I could put you in a carriage back to Vienna tomorrow."

I thought for a few moments. Of course, my experience of the world was indeed very limited. Although I had encountered more deceit and treachery than most girls my age, and had been unafraid of becoming embroiled in dangerous intrigues in the interest of righting wrongs, I had done it all in the environs of the city I knew, the society whose structure I well understood. I had been to Hungary, to the Palais Esterhazy, but that was more an extension of the culture of Vienna than anything else. And the foreigners who came to Vienna did so on Viennese terms. "You're right," I said. "I don't know anything. I don't even really know why I'm here, not entirely. I mean, I understand what the emperor wishes me to discover. What still mystifies me is why the captain—with whom I have not been on very friendly terms— suggested to him that I should undertake such a task."

"You're here because the captain believes you have an extraordinary talent for observation, and because you have demonstrated to him in the past that you are fearless." She reached out and took my hand. I looked into her eyes. "I may be no one's idea of a mother, but I treat my girls well, and I know intelligence when I see it. You are safe here, and quite hidden away, and I can polish you up to pass in society high and low in this city. But you must be willing to undertake the work."

"Eh bien," I said, "Let us begin."

୧୦୭

My transformation took two weeks to complete to Madame's satisfaction. I thought it all went remarkably quickly, but the captain was impatient for her to finish knocking the Viennese expressions out of my vocabulary and concealing my lack of savoir faire. He didn't see the point of having me memorize the entirety of the royal titles in France, nor of making sure I understood the hierarchy at court that meant the Comtesse de Polignac had to be elevated to duchess before she was considered noble enough to become Governess of the Children of France. By the time we finished, I could recite the relationships among all the living Bourbons and members of the Orléans clan, tell where each of them lived and who were their closest confidants, and list the most important nobles and their level of influence with the queen.

Each night, the captain would come to check on my progress, and each night, Madame would tell him I was not yet ready.

"The pamphleteers will have gone deep underground before we can act to find the sources of their information at this rate!"

"Do you want Thérèse to succeed, or do you want her to be sent packing back to Vienna before she can find out anything useful?"

They had that argument almost every evening, but not while I was in the room. I heard it through the door when I passed from the kitchen where I ate most of my meals to the bedroom I shared with Odette, whom I'd come to know a little, despite our nearly opposite sleeping schedules. I was surprised to discover that Odette was not unlike me: daughter of an artist who had fallen on hard times and couldn't provide for all his children. She didn't have a talent to fall back on, other than being very pretty and a good listener, so she claimed. "My father tried to teach me to draw, but I wasn't very good.

One of my other sisters was, though, and she's starting to get portrait commissions, I hear."

"Does your family know... you know. What you do?" I still couldn't put a name to her profession.

She laughed. "Not really! I tell them I'm an artist's model at the Louvre. Since they aren't likely to come to Paris, I'm not worried they'll find out." She yawned and stretched her arms above her head. The loose sleeves of her silk dressing gown slid down to her armpits, and I noticed a thumb-shaped bruise on the soft flesh above her elbow. I didn't say anything. Who could tell how she would have gotten such a bruise? She said that Madame did not tolerate any roughness on the part of her male clients. Still.

"And why couldn't you be a model?"

"The pay is terrible! And it's always cold in the studios." She laughed and stood, blowing me a kiss as she left the kitchen to go up to sleep for the day.

My initial shock at being in such a dwelling had begun to wear off after only a few days. Although I had been raised to believe a girl's virginity was her most prized possession, and certainly had no intention of relinquishing mine until my wedding night, I began to understand what might lead a girl to choose differently. Clearly, it was a reasonably easy way to make a handsome amount of money. Although the girls paid rent to Madame, she did not keep the lion's share of their earnings—something I understood was often the case in such houses. I suspected that Madame received some remuneration from Vienna for her services as a source of valued information. And she must have money enough to furnish such an elegant house and keep her kitchen and wine cellar so well stocked.

If I were completely honest with myself, my own activities did not bear too much scrutiny. Or at least, they would not once they truly commenced. For the moment, I was captive in this world of feminine artfulness, learning a trade that in many ways was not dissimilar to theirs.

When I had first learned I would be confined to the house until Madame thought I was ready to undertake my mission, to act as mouche for the emperor of Austria and discover the origin of the calumnies against the queen, I was bitterly disappointed. Once she had taught me how to avoid those places where beggars made walking both uncomfortable and unsafe, and how to adopt an expression that would inhibit strangers from approaching me, I longed to go out and explore Paris, to walk the streets and gaze at the grand residences Madame had marked on her map.

My days were full and busy nonetheless, and the constant learning and rehearsing kept my mind occupied until I went up to bed. Then, I would practice the violin a little if it was early enough—Madame didn't want my playing to disturb the guests who usually arrived after nine. At first, the practice was comforting and familiar. But after a time, my mind would wander back to Vienna, and the faces of my mother and Greta and Anna would swim into my view. Soon after that, I would wonder what concerts I was missing and if Danior was taking good care of my Amati. From there, it was a short hop to wondering how long Zoltan had stayed in Vienna. I tried my hardest not to think about Zoltan, though. No matter how many excuses I made for myself, I knew I had disappointed him. I wasn't at all certain I could count on his continuing affection. And it had been my own fault. Invariably, when I finally slipped between the sheets, tears of homesickness would moisten my pillow.

At last the evening came when Madame declared I was ready to undertake my task. She invited the captain to come to dinner and ordered in champagne. Madame's cook—whose food was always delicious—outdid herself. I hated to admit it, but meals at Madame Chrétien's establishment far surpassed Greta's modest fare.

After we'd eaten our fill of that special dinner, Madame asked Agathe to bring us a bottle of brandy.

"So, now?" I asked. "Shall we discuss what is to be done? How I am to insinuate myself among the queen's enemies so that I may discover who is spreading such vile rumors about the queen?"

The captain stared into his glass, lifting it and swirling the amber liquid around as if the answer would be found inside it. After a time, he said, "I have decided—in consultation with Madame, of course—what must be done." His face clouded, and he pinched his lower lip between two fingers. "Joseph doesn't realize what he's dealing with here. If Mercy knows you've been planted, all of Versailles will have that same information within an hour. I'm afraid that, even with the excellent tutelage you're receiving from Madame, your accent will give you away in an instant."

I started to protest, but my own ear told me he was right. I still struggled to modulate the guttural consonants and force my mouth into the shape that would produce the simpering vowels of the high-class French. Like any skill, it would take practice over more hours and days than I actually had. I hadn't spoken a word of German since I'd set foot in Paris, learning hundreds of words to supplement the drawing-room French I'd acquired in Vienna. I had even started to dream in French. But an accent is a difficult thing to lose.

"Perhaps we can discuss your plan, and see if we agree with it." By we I meant I of course.

"I have arranged everything. It's brilliant, if I do say so myself. That is, it's brilliant if you know how to sew."

Sew? Of course I knew how to sew. All girls learned how to sew.

Madame took my arm in a conspiratorial way, something I'd seen her do with the younger courtesans when she wanted them to tease out a piece of sensitive information from one of the guests. "The captain has told me about this, and I'm not certain it's the wisest course. You will have to persuade everyone that you know a great deal about our Parisian modes, and that will be difficult for you to accomplish. My tutelage has given you only the barest introduction to fashion."

Fashion? I had never been one to pay much attention to it, other than taking as much enjoyment as any girl in a pretty new gown. I had scoffed at the fashion gazette Madame showed me, unable to countenance how anyone would spend so much time and money on something that seemed of little lasting importance. What in God's name could the captain be thinking?

My face must have been a picture of confusion, because Captain von Bauer said, "My dear Thérèse"—even my name had had to change, but I'd already become used to it, finding it quite charming when my fellow inmates used it. "My dear Thérèse, you look as though I just told you that you would be required to wrestle a lion."

"Well, what is it then?" The more he delayed, the more annoyed I became.

"I have arranged for you to join the establishment of Mademoiselle Rose Bertin."

He said it with a smile, as if he were bestowing a great honor on me, or at least expected me to recognize the name. I glanced at Madame.

"She is the queen's Marchande des Modes. Milliner and proprietress of the premier fashion emporium in all of Paris. It is said the queen confides in her more than even the duchesse de Polignac. This is why it could be such an excellent plan."

Here was a twist I had most certainly not expected. I felt as if everything I'd learned, the subtleties of society and rank and the court, had suddenly been rendered irrelevant. All that careful training, and I would be no more than a shop girl, or worse, a seamstress—something for which I was woefully unqualified.

My mouth was dry. I could barely utter the words, "When will this occur?"

"You start tomorrow," the captain said.

I nodded. And then the room, with which I had become very familiar during my hours of drinking tea and rising and sitting started to spin, and the carpet, with which I had become intimately acquainted from the hundreds of curtsies I practiced each day with my nose nearly touching the floor, rose up to meet me.

When I recovered myself and looked up at the faces peering down at me— the captain's with its dark mustache and that of Madame, with its star patch and circles of rouge, the captain said, "You really are the most peculiar young lady. To faint at the idea of being surrounded by laces and gowns and fans. If I didn't know you better I'd think it was an expression of overwhelming delight."

He knew me well enough. The idea flooded me with dread, and the certainty that—despite all of Madame's hours of careful tutelage—I would very soon be found out for the fraud I truly was.

Chapter Four

After some heated discussion, I managed to make the captain understand that placing me in a job as a seamstress would be a huge mistake, and would undo all Madame Chrétien's hard work with me. I could mend a seam, sew on a button, or repair a hem if it were absolutely essential, but that was all. Thankfully, he came up with an alternate plan. I was to be Mademoiselle Bertin's bookkeeper.

We hired a carriage for the trip from Madame Chrétien's house, even though we could easily have walked. It was a windy day, and Madame did not want us to arrive looking as though we had been swept in by a hurricane, so she said.

"This will be the last time you will enter through the front door," she told me as she straightened my hat, "So I advise you to make the most of it. Use your keen eyes to observe. You are working from the moment you leave this house."

The carriage pulled up to the Mademoiselle Bertin's establishment before I'd had a chance to say much more than good morning to the captain. He helped me down, and we approached the shop's blue-painted door. The captain stood at attention before rapping on it three times with a single knuckle. Unlike the shops in Vienna, the door was locked, so we could not march unannounced only by the tinkling of a bell to examine the goods within. The shop's windows—which would normally be crowded with merchandise on display—were draped with extravagant quantities of silk of a pale rose shade hung with tassels and edged in braid, rendering it impossible to see inside. The painted sign above read, "Au Trait Gallant," and in smaller letters below it, "Mlle. Rose Bertin, milliner to Marie Antoinette."

Just as a gust of wind blew dust into my eye and forced me to clamp my hand over my hat to prevent it blowing away, a very pretty woman opened the door. I was on the point of curtsying, assuming we were addressing Mademoiselle Bertin herself, when the captain put his hand under my elbow to prevent me and said, "Could you tell your mistress that Captain Bauer has arrived, escorting the new bookkeeper?"

The shop itself was more like a lady's boudoir than an ordinary merchant's establishment where people went to purchase items of necessity or want. There were no shelves displaying wares, no counter behind which an attendant waited to take one's request and receive one's money. An oversized dressing table sat at an angle in one corner, a large, oval mirror framed by elaborately carved Cupids suspended from the ceiling above it. Several hat stands of different heights were dotted around the room, adorned with what I assumed to be the latest creations.

In addition to the hats, one wall of the boudoir was occupied by an open armoire from which spilled lengths of vibrant silks in carefully arranged chaos, several trimmed with silver braid or embroidered with sparkling jewels. The effect was of a flock of massive, exotic birds flashing their tail feathers as they flew away, only something—some enchantment—prevented them from going anywhere.

But what fascinated me most of all were two headless dolls the size of grown women, standing sentry on either side of the dressing table. They had been attired in complete ensembles, from quilted petticoats to silk overskirts and velvet jackets. They carried fine kid gloves and lace-edged kerchiefs, and their rigid feet wore slippers that looked like they would not survive a walk of more than half a mile. The physical attributes of these manikins ended at a slender neck, around which necklaces had been draped. One of them wore a diamond pendant on a thin, crimson ribbon. I shuddered, imagining I was looking at a stiletto wound that circled the neck, expecting to see drips of blood seep down over the pale wax flesh. "Remarkable," I breathed.

"You'll have to learn to take it in stride," the captain said. "This is nothing to the extravagance on display at court. You must drop your provincial ways and effect an air of ennui if you are to survive in Paris."

We had no time to exchange further words, because the shop girl returned, nose in the air, and said, "Mademoiselle will see you now, but you are not to fatigue her, as she is preparing to go to Versailles to attend upon the queen."

She led us down a short corridor and into another boudoir, this one a boudoir in actuality. A very pretty older woman stretched out on a chaise in a state of dishabille, a lacy negligee providing scant coverage for her still-attractive body. I thought she looked more like one of Madame Chrétien's ladies of the night than the milliner and modiste to the queen, and I own to being faintly shocked. Mademoiselle Bertin balanced a cup of chocolate on her stomach. Before greeting us, she lifted it to her lips and took the tiniest sip, then set the cup down on a three-legged table and stretched her hand out toward the captain. "Monsieur Le Comte! I have heard of your brave deeds, and I am pleased to make your acquaintance!"

The captain stepped forward, took her fingers and brushed them with the suggestion of a kiss. "Allow me to present Mademoiselle Thérèse. She is sent to help you bring order to your books."

"My books. Yes. I used to take care of them myself, not trusting anyone else to undertake such a thing, but the queen demands my presence so often that I simply no longer have time. The first old lady I hired could hardly add two plus two… I see you are not an old lady, however, but a young and pretty one." She addressed this last to me, then turned quickly back to the captain and continued. "Are you certain she is capable?"

"Oh yes," the captain said. "I can vouch for just how capable the young lady is."

I knew he wasn't referring to my facility with numbers, but I feared he also wasn't thinking of my talent as a violinist. Did he really consider me capable, or just interfering?

"Very well. We shall try her out. You have one week to prove your worth. After that, I shall pay you twenty livres a week. You are dismissed."

I was about to open my mouth and protest at having to work unpaid for even an hour, but a look from the captain silenced me.

Mademoiselle Bertin rang a little bell and the shop girl returned. "Take her back to the workroom to meet Lucienne and Ondine." She smiled at me for the first time then. "They are my most skilled seamstresses, and they work under my direct supervision. Your desk and account books are in the same room. The rest of my girls—all forty of them—work at another location."

I curtsied and thanked Mademoiselle Bertin, then turned to follow the shop girl, expecting the captain to come as well. But he stayed where he was, and just before the door closed behind us, I heard Mademoiselle Bertin say, "So, Captain, I have heard you have become quite popular with the ladies who frequent the Petit Trianon."

How like Captain Bauer, I thought, to make himself agreeable to noble ladies. I wondered if they knew he was spying on them all the time, that their secrets were anything but safe with him. Or perhaps they knew, and didn't care.

My fellow inmates of the back-room atelier glared at me when Mademoiselle Bertin's assistant, Marie, brought me in. After introducing me, she said, "Mademoiselle Thérèse will act in an administrative capacity for now. She will oversee the orders of fabrics, thread, and trimmings and ensure that everything is accounted for properly."

I didn't understand why the two young seamstresses pursed their lips and looked away at that news until days later, when I realized they were accustomed to helping themselves to the scraps of this and that no one could use because they were slightly damaged or too small. I soon reassured them that I had no interest in spoiling their small-enough perks for a grueling job. I might well be a spy, but not for Mademoiselle Bertin.

Ondine and Lucienne said nothing to me until after Marie had left us alone. That was the last silent moment I had until the day of the Valenciennes.

"Where you from?"

"What do you know about fashion?"

"Do you know how famous Mademoiselle Rose is? Why did she choose you to work for her?"

"Do you know the queen?"

When they weren't asking me questions, they conversed with each other nonstop—everything from what some beau of Lucienne's had told her the night before to Ondine discussing her wedding plans to her fiancé Roland to the best way to knot a thread in the middle of a seam so it wouldn't show to it would be better to measure the thread first so it would not have to be knotted until the end. I was breathless just listening to them.

I pretended to be examining the ledgers, which were written in a nearly illegible hand. I understood my predecessor had been quite elderly, and her hand shook so much the ink would spray from the quill.

"We had to keep the fabrics far away from her desk or risk disaster!" Ondine said. I could see that, of the two, she was more eager to overcome the frostiness my unexpected presence had inspired.

I was struck with how like my roommate and the other young women in Madame Chrétien's employ these two seamstresses were. In many ways, they appeared to me to be variations on the same theme: young girls from the countryside come to Paris to find a way to raise themselves up and have a better life. They had all chosen to do what suited their talents best, what would make them the most money and give them the greatest chance of success. For the inhabitants of the house I was staying in, a better life meant becoming a wealthy merchant's wife, or a well-kept mistress. For Lucienne and Ondine, it was the prospect of one day having their own establishment in a modest neighborhood, or marrying a worthy artisan who could support a family.

Who was to say which way was better? The honest industries of sewing gowns and ornaments to make people feel beautiful, and giving pleasure to men to make them feel wanted, seemed not so dishonorable to me. They were, perhaps, more honorable than my own job, the one I was sent to Paris to undertake. Lucienne, Ondine, and all the girls at Madame Chrétien's establishment were wholly themselves.

I, on the other hand, was pretending to be someone I wasn't, passing myself off as an innocent, trustworthy acquaintance when all the while I was listening and remembering. The secrets and confidences I heard would not be safe with me. Although I was unclear exactly what the captain—or the emperor—would do with such information, I was under no illusion that they wouldn't exploit it for whatever purpose they deemed fit. I was also under no illusion that the people who uttered those secrets wouldn't end up in prison—or worse.

Such extreme measures might seem, on the surface of it, out of proportion with what I was supposed to discover. But the captain had made sure I understood that my task wasn't simply a matter of trying to prevent gossip and whispers that accused the queen of everything from profligacy to draining the treasury to acts of incest. Gossip—although cruel—was not in itself illegal. The act that crossed the line into a punishable offense was spreading such calumnies against the queen in written form. The Paris police could arrest the authors and the printers of the scurrilous pamphlets that anyone on the street could buy for a few sous. The problem was that no one knew where they came from. The pamphleteers worked out of sight, underground.

I was roused from my musing by a sharp knock on the door of the workroom that led out to the street—the door I would use from that day to enter and leave my place of work. I opened it to admit a man shouldering several bolts of costly fabric. He brought them in, I noted them in the ledger—with the help of Ondine who explained exactly how to describe each one—and took the man's bill in exchange for a receipt.

And so began my work for the establishment of Mademoiselle Bertin, milliner to the queen.

Chapter Five

I'd been working at Mademoiselle Bertin's atelier for a week, and still had no idea why the captain thought I would discover anything of value tucked away in a workshop with two girls who were unlikely to reveal any information about the pamphleteers. Only once, Lucienne mentioned that she'd seen a pamphlet in the gutter and had picked it up.

"What did you do when you realized what it was?" I asked. They'd grown accustomed enough to me to speak openly.

"Of course, I found a policeman and gave it to him!" She said.

I nodded. "But surely you read it first, or you would not know it was an illegal document."

She blushed and turned away. "Only enough to discover what it was. Honestly, I can't imagine who would say such things about the queen, let alone write them!"

"Such as?" I pressed her, curious.

"It said she—Oh I really can't repeat it!"

I could tell she wanted to, though. "We won't say anything, will we Ondine? I think it's best to know so we can refute it whenever possible."

Lucienne quickly overcame her scruples and told us the pamphlet was full of rumors that the queen had an incestuous relationship with the king's youngest brother, the Comte d'Artois, and that he had been the true father of the infant she had recently miscarried.

"He's very handsome, so my Roland says," Ondine said.

"Your Roland has seen the Comte d'Artois?" Lucienne tweaked Ondine's nose. "How could that be?"

"Ow! From a distance, yes. He brings the fashion gazettes to Versailles you know."

"What does Roland have to do with the fashion gazettes?" I asked.

"He's a printer, of course," Ondine said. "One of the best. He says he'll soon have enough money for us to marry." Her eyes glazed over with a dreamy haze.

"He said that last year, didn't he?" Lucienne could be cruel to Ondine.

"How lovely," I said. Did Ondine not understand that his being a printer at a time when scurrilous pamphlets were being illegally printed somewhere might be the slightest bit suspicious? "Where is his printing works?"

"I've never been to see it. Somewhere in the city, I believe."

Well, that was no information. I couldn't delve deeper without arousing suspicion, but I really wished I could have seen the pamphlet myself. Lucienne's words did give me the idea of making sure to look into the gutters to see if I could find others like it. Knowing what was said might lead me to who said it. But we said no more about it.

After that, I thought the day would pass as all the others before it had. Yet I sensed an undercurrent of anticipation as soon as I had walked through the door at seven in the morning, and the conversation about the pamphlet had done nothing to dispel it. Something was going to happen, I could feel it. Lucienne and Ondine were quieter than usual, for a start. In addition to an unexpected lack of prattle, the burly fellow who brought the bolts of fabric and mounds of delicate lace each day was late. I busied myself going over the accounts from the day before while I waited for him.

"I hope the Valenciennes for the queen's dressing gown comes today," Ondine said, breaking the silence.

"If it doesn't, surely some other lace would do," I said, stifling a yawn and turning once again to the small window to watch for the delivery cart.

After a moment, I noticed that the workshop was not only quiet, but completely still, and that this unaccustomed silence stretched on as if perhaps someone was waiting for me to continue speaking. I turned and found myself facing four round, staring eyes, and two hands poised in mid-air with their needles like birds miraculously frozen in flight. "What?" I said.

"You can't mean it! Surely she's playing a joke on us. A pleasantry. No one would commit such sacrilege!" It was Lucienne, who had a larger vocabulary than Ondine and took great pleasure in showing it off.

I was saved from the necessity of responding by the crunch of cartwheels on cobbles, soon followed by the dull thud of a fist against the outside of the workroom door. I opened the door, expecting the usual quantity of fabrics, the brilliant silks, the whisper-soft muslins and lawns, the sturdy woolens and fustians, to be carried over a shoulder or wheeled in on barrows for my inspection.

But not this time. This time, the hulking fellow who was normally hidden behind large parcels stood reverently in the doorway, holding only a small, wooden box. I reached out to take it from him, but Lucienne bustled over and grabbed it away.

"I should look at it first!" She said.

I shrugged, not having any idea what it was.

"Let's both," said Ondine, apparently deciding not to have the argument I was certain would follow.

They cleared a space on the center table, wiping away the tiny threads of fabric that made my eyes water and my nose itch, and placed the box gently in the middle of it. They gazed at each other with what I can only describe as rapture, then looked down at the box. It was Lucienne who lifted the lid, slowly, carefully, almost as if she expected something to leap out at her.

Of course, nothing did. But the two of them sighed in unison and placed their hands over their hearts. By now, I was beyond curious and stepped forward to see for myself what marvel lay in this small container that could turn two busybody seamstresses into silent, swooning girls.

The box contained a length of lace nested in velvet. A bit of lace. I looked closely. The lace was…

Exquisite. I reached past the two seamstresses and picked up one end of the three-inch-wide ribbon, draping it over my hands. I had never seen anything so beautiful in all my life.

"It's magical," I whispered.

I held it up higher so Ondine and Lucienne could see it against the daylight. The delicate knotted net was covered with intricately woven woodland creatures and flowers. But they were neither static or stylized. One rabbit was running away from a fox, whose open mouth spoke of anticipated reward. A hawk hovered above the fox, though, as if debating whether to swoop down and snatch either the rabbit or its pursuer. Ahead, a family of hares in attitudes of anxiety stood in front of their warren, urging the fleeing bunny on to safety. And the flowers that surrounded them all participated in the scene. Some bent as though waving in the wind, some were crushed under the feet of the running creatures. The scene was about a foot long, and repeated for the entire length of the lace, perhaps twenty times. Such tableaux in miniature must have taken months to create. Perhaps years. Here was something so beyond my capacity to imagine that it struck me dumb. Someone's hands had the artistry within them to work simple, straight threads of silk into a design where they not only became a fabric, but where they twined together like counterpoint. Yet unlike the notes on a page, anyone with eyes could see it all. No intervening performance was required to bring it to life. One had no need of reading to understand its significance. It was an opera in silk, a poem, a painting.

I looked into Ondine's eyes to see them brimming with tears, and I could tell that in that instant, I had gained her trust. No woman— no human being—could remain unmoved by the artistry of this lace that was so light, I barely felt it against my skin. Was it foolish to be deeply affected by something inanimate? Perhaps. But no more foolish than the way I felt upon hearing a beautiful melody, or reading a book whose story gripped my heart and took me into another life, opening to me another way of seeing the world.

A moment of clarity lit my mind like a flame. I could imagine someone committing murder to possess such fine lace. I could see as if

I were suddenly able to look into another person's heart how acquiring such things, surrounding oneself with this kind of beauty—or, more to the point, having the power to surround oneself with this kind of beauty—could drive a person to extraordinary lengths. I don't know why it was the lace that spoke to me in this way, and not a musical composition. And yet, it did. Music, books, ideas—these could all be shared by many people, high and low. Lace like this, artistry such as this, was designed to be owned by a single individual and only seen by those privileged to be close enough to that individual. This lace was destined not for a gown that the queen would wear in public, but for a dressing gown that she would wear for perhaps an hour a day. Only her most intimate acquaintances would ever set eyes on this magnificent lace.

I gently laid the lace back down in its box and replaced the cover. Ondine took it and walked slowly, as if she feared that jiggling the box would ruin its contents, or perhaps disarrange the tableau of woodland creatures so that when we next saw it, they would all have tumbled about, or the fox would have caught up with the rabbit and all that would be left of it was a bloody stain. I watched her progress toward the shelves where such items were kept and my eyes followed her hands as she placed the box on the highest one.

For the rest of the day, the three of us worked in reverent silence.

Chapter Six

I think it was my revelation about the lace, about the desire certain people might have to be close to power so that it would somehow give them access to beauty that was out of other people's reach. I think it was this blinding clarity that started me thinking and made me decide that I had to take a more active role in discovering where the calumnies against the queen originated. That same evening, I told Madame Chrétien that I needed to talk to the captain urgently.

"He will be here soon," she said. "He has a regular appointment this evening and he never misses it."

I didn't want to imagine what this appointment was for. I had made peace with the choices the women in the house had made for whatever reasons entirely personal, but I was incapable of understanding—and did not want to understand—what would persuade a young man with good looks and prospects to frequent such a house.

"I would speak with him before his appointment. Is there a way to send word for him to arrive early?"

Madame stared at me. "What has happened? What occurred to change you from the complying young lady to the demanding woman who stands before me now?" She didn't appear to be angry. In fact, a smile twitched at the corners of her mouth.

"I am not at liberty to say." It wasn't true, but I couldn't quite explain it to myself, let alone to Madame. "I simply must see the captain."

She nodded. "I'll send Agathe."

An hour later, the captain and I sat alone in the parlor, glasses of wine before us. On my way in, I had caught the smirk of one of the older girls in the house, and I knew what they thought, but I didn't care.

"I know you didn't ask me here because you suddenly realized that you thought me handsome and charming, and wished to exercise your considerable attractions upon me," he said, lifting his glass full of ruby red wine in my direction and downing half of it in a single gulp.

Only for a moment did his mention of my considerable attractions knock me off balance. I soon recovered and decided to ignore his taunt. "I think we are going about this all wrong," I said.

He leaned back in his chair and crossed one leg over another in a languid movement. "Oh? And according to your extensive knowledge of the workings of the court and the nobility of France, what is wrong about it?"

Since I had no way of knowing the entirety of the captain's plans, I couldn't answer his question directly. This was the most infuriating thing about the whole business. "I speak only of what has occurred so far, since you do not favor me with any information that could reveal what will happen next."

"And you then dare to say I'm in the wrong?"

I had to bite my tongue. The captain had a way of being, a way of behaving, that sought to put me at a disadvantage by making me doubt the testimony of my own eyes and ears. I had allowed him to control me in that way before, but I would allow it no longer. I took a deep breath, fighting down my desire to snap back at him. "So long as I am in the service of those who wish to protect the queen, I will learn nothing. None of her enemies would trust me with knowledge that could be injurious to her, or reveal to me the mechanisms by which they are spreading this information into the world and turning public sentiment against her."

The captain said nothing, but I could tell what I said sent him deep into thought. His eyes lost their challenging sparkle and softened, turned inward. "You have hit upon a truth, I dare say. But do you imagine I don't have a plan to overcome this disadvantage?"

A plan? I thought. No doubt concocted in that instant! "Why did you put me in such a position in the first place if you had such a plan? No one knows me. Instead of making me a bookkeeper for the queen's milliner, you could have placed me as a servant in the house of Orléans, a servant whom no one suspected capable of thought, let alone reading and writing. And there I could be an invisible pair of ears to report back to you with everything I discovered."

"And how long do you think this activity would remain undiscovered? You're a clever girl, but I assure you, the queen's foes are smarter than you think. The servants in the Orléans establishments are sent from their estates in the provinces. They do not hire anyone whose pedigree they do not know, and whose loyalty they are not absolutely certain of." As he spoke, he uncrossed his legs and leaned forward.

I confess, what he said made perfect sense.

"You do not trust me. I can hardly blame you, after everything that happened in Vienna two years ago. Do you not think I have at least enough intelligence to figure out a way to insert you in the enemy camp so that they will never suspect who you are and what you're doing there?"

"Why have you not told me of this?"

"I had to be certain of you first."

"Certain of me?" Indignation tinged my voice.

"Certain that you are capable of playing a role convincingly and without disdain."

He did it again, and I hated myself for allowing it, for walking right into his trap. I had indeed been disdainful in the workshop. I thought myself superior to Lucienne and Ondine. I thought that the practice of my art, my skill as a violinist, elevated me above all other women my age. But was I any better than they were simply because I had had the advantage of a father who saw my potential and gave me the care and tutelage that made it possible for me to aspire to more than the usual lot of a woman?

There was no doubt I had changed over the course of that day. I couldn't explain such a thing to the captain, however. Indeed, when I tried to explain it to myself, it began to sound silly and shallow. "Why do you think that keeping your plan from me is helpful in this situation?"

"Ah, so you understand what I'm saying. Good. As to my choices concerning what you are to know and when, I appeal to your understanding. I have been here for over a year, and I am as deeply involved with the court, the nobility, and the aristocracy as I can be. Were it not for the fact that my elevated position makes espionage risky, I would not need you to help me."

He still hadn't told me why, and I suspected his reasons were less practical than personal.

The captain leaned forward farther still and reached for my hands. I couldn't ignore him without being extremely rude, and so I let him take them, making sure they were limp in his strong grip.

"The next phase in our investigations begins tomorrow. Mademoiselle Bertin has agreed to it. Her loyalty to and affection for the queen are without question. Theresa..."

He used my Austrian name, not the French Thérèse that I had become accustomed to in these weeks, and it caught my attention—as it was no doubt meant to do.

"Theresa, you must believe me when I say that you have a very important role to play in this. It depends not only on your innate abilities of observation and deduction, but in an ability that I am not entirely certain you possess."

I withdrew my hands. "What ability would that be?"

"In most circumstances, it is a refreshing change to discover a young lady who is truly herself, who does not attempt artifice to attract or to raise herself higher in the world. But what I need from you here is that very artifice."

"I'm not sure I understand."

"You must be an actress, Mademoiselle Thérèse. You must play a role with such perfection that all around you will think you're not acting at all. Your life may well depend upon your ability to do so." He leaned back and drew a gold watch out of his waistcoat pocket. "Now, I fear I am wanted elsewhere." He stood and put out his hand to pull me to my feet.

"You must act, Mademoiselle."

The captain had a firm grip on my hand now and tried to draw me toward him. I resisted.

"Act, Thérèse."

He stepped closer and threaded his other arm around my waist. I felt the gentle but insistent warmth of his hand on the small of my back, urging me forward. Only Zoltan had ever held me like that. I twitched away at the thought, but the captain was strong. Soon our bodies were touching, and he had curled my other hand against his shoulder and brought his face closer to mine. I could feel his breath on my cheek, and then the scratch of his cheek against mine. "Act," he whispered into my ear as he took my earlobe between his lips.

I wanted to push him away and at the same time I didn't want him to move. What was I doing! I didn't even like this man, let alone desire him. Something in my body fought against my mind and melted toward him. I sensed him moving his head into a different position, and his breath teased along my cheek and toward my mouth. Would he really kiss me? Would I really let him?

"Excuse me, Monsieur Le Capitaine—Oh!"

The door had opened and one of the girls stepped in. I pushed myself away from the captain without thinking and staggered backwards, toppling the chair I had been sitting in before and nearly losing my balance. The captain had kept hold of my hand. I knew my face flamed with confusion and anger.

"Tell Mademoiselle Ange that I will be with her directly," the captain said without looking at the intruder.

I did not turn to see who it was and held my breath until the door clicked closed again.

"Hmm." The captain looked me up and down, then raised my hand to his lips. I did my best to pretend I was the coquette he perhaps intended me to act, cocked my head on the side and smiled. But at the last moment, he turned my hand over and kissed my palm slowly and tenderly, and I gasped.

He let go of my hand, picked his tricorn hat up off the table, clicked his heels together and bowed. "I think you will manage."

Before I had a chance to say another word to him, he left.

❧❧❧

The next morning, I was still rattled by the captain's behavior and what he had revealed to me. At least he had prepared me for what was to come, and I was able to act unsurprised when Mademoiselle Bertin came into the workshop at nine and announced that I was not only to be ready to accompany her to Versailles in the queen's coach in an hour, but that I was to change out of my drab brown dress and put on a gauzy white muslin gown with a pink satin ribbon tied around the waist, and cover my head with a cap edged in lace. Ondine and Lucienne's expressions went from shock to murderous anger in an instant. Neither of them had ever been to Versailles.

They remained silent until Mademoiselle Bertin had closed the workshop door behind her, and then erupted in angry remonstrations.

"Mademoiselle Rose only brings her best shop girl with her when she goes. Why is she taking you? I've been here longer," said Lucienne.

"So have I!" Tears edged Ondine's voice. "What have you done to deserve this? You don't even sew! Before the lace, you weren't even interested in fashion!"

I made up an excuse as quickly as I could. "She needs you here to finish trimming these gowns for the masked ball next week. Only the two of you are capable of such fine work. You know I'd make a mess of it." My few attempts to be helpful had been such disasters that the girls—who had more work than they'd ever be able to finish—had banished me from touching anything except my pencil and the ledgers.

I really did feel sorry for the two of them. They hadn't done much to make me feel welcome, but how could they be happy with so little beyond the confines of the workshop to give them joy? One day off a week was hardly sufficient to taste life. They weren't pretty enough to be promoted to shop girls—which I thought very unfair. As shop girls, they'd mingle with fine society, perhaps have the opportunity to go into service with a duchess or a marquise. Ondine had natural taste, and could put colors and patterns and textures together in a surprising but effective manner. Although Lucienne's tongue could be vicious, at heart I knew she was capable of generosity. It was she who stitched little dolls out of the meanest scraps and took them to the convent for the orphans.

And they both had such skill. I often watched them, fascinated, as they gathered muslin into ruffles, embellished silk with embroidery and jewels, and molded ribbon into birds and flowers, all while keeping up a steady patter of light conversation. I guessed they'd been learning their trade for as long as I had been learning mine—my real trade, that was. I sighed.

"What do you have to sigh about?" Ondine gave me a vicious pinch as she walked by. I flinched, but didn't peep. I could hardly blame them for feeling slighted.

The coach arrived fifteen minutes late, after Mademoiselle Bertin and I had been standing outside pressed against the wall to avoid being splattered with dirt as the carriages and carts rolled by. She carried a delicate silk bag with her scissors, a measuring tape, and pins. I was burdened with a sack full of the fabrics we'd just received the day before. I couldn't place it on the ground where it would get dirty—or worse, wet from the contents of chamber pots that had been emptied hours before. It grew heavier by the instant. I shifted the sack from one shoulder to the other.

When the coach finally drew up, crusted with gilded wooden trim and with the queen's cypher painted on the doors, a footman jumped down, lithe as a dancer, and unfolded the cleverly concealed steps and handed Mademoiselle Bertin up them and into the coach. I started to struggle after her, but then the other footman took the heavy sack from me and stowed it under one of the silk-upholstered benches so I could climb in more easily.

It wasn't until we were settled inside the coach with the windows closed against the noise and stench that Mademoiselle Bertin spoke. At first I didn't realize her comments were directed to me. She stared out the window the entire time, as if she couldn't stand the sight of me.

She said, "None of the rumors you have heard of the queen are true."

I wondered how she could know what rumors I'd heard, but then realized that even the basest menial in Paris couldn't help but be acquainted with the most outlandish scandals about the queen, thanks to the pamphlets put out daily by her enemies. "Non, Mademoiselle—"

"You will not speak. Not to me or to the queen. Not unless you are asked a direct question."

She lifted her gloved hand to tuck a wisp of hair under her bonnet and I noticed that it shook. The famous Mademoiselle Bertin was nervous. I had heard that the queen treated her as an intimate acquaintance, that she entertained her in her private boudoir. Yet this woman, the most sought-after modiste in Paris, still trembled on her way to visit Marie Antoinette.

My heart was jumping up and down like a nervous kitten, but somehow, knowing I wasn't alone in my anxiety, soothed me a little. By the time we arrived at the grand courtyard in front of the palace of Versailles, I had talked myself into a state approaching calm.

Mademoiselle Bertin walked very fast through the wide halls and opulent reception rooms. "Keep up! We're late!"

I scurried after her, now followed by a footman carrying the sack of fabrics and laces. It didn't seem fair, I thought. If we were late, it was only because the queen's carriage hadn't arrived on time. Not just that, but I wished we'd walk more slowly so I had time to inspect our surroundings. There were elegantly dressed people everywhere. Some were nobles, but many, I knew, were servants wearing their master's and mistress's cast-off clothing. One would have to know whether a gentleman's waistcoat sported this-season's buttons or last to determine whether he was servant or lord. Or be sharp-eyed enough to discern the trace of wear at the cuffs, or a stain that couldn't easily be covered up.

I was out of breath by the time we were ushered into the queen's private apartments. Mademoiselle Bertin sank into a deep curtsy, and I did the same.

A sweet, high voice said, "My dear Rose!"

I heard the swish of skirts and glanced up to see the queen of France take my employer's hand and pull her to her feet. "We are alone. Madame Etiquette will not disturb us here." They both smiled. I was still bent in a curtsy with my nose nearly touching the floor, afraid to rise.

"Up, girl!" Mademoiselle Bertin said, a frown creasing her forehead.

"Do not be cross with her. Poor girl has never been here before. What is your name?"

I looked to Mademoiselle Bertin, expecting her to be furious, but her face had lost all trace of vexation and she smiled. She must have been worried about bringing me instead of her accustomed assistant.

"My name is Thérèse," I answered with a bow of my head.

"Like my daughter, a daughter of France." The queen smiled.

After the appointment, when Marie Antoinette had given all her instructions to Mademoiselle Bertin and I had written them down carefully in a little notebook, we walked back through the palace at a more leisurely pace. Mademoiselle Bertin stayed next to me instead of making me walk behind her like a servant. I guessed that I had acquitted myself to her satisfaction.

This guess was confirmed when we climbed back into the coach and instead of sitting opposite me and staring out the window, Mademoiselle Bertin sat next to me, her body angled in my direction. "You're a clever girl, Thérèse. The captain was right. From now on, you shall accompany me whenever I wait upon the queen. I hope that will help you discover what it is you're seeking. You understand, I will do anything in my power to quash the gossip about Marie Antoinette."

I appreciated her support, but in my heart, I was all too worried that—rather than discover truths that would vindicate the queen in the eyes of her subjects—I would uncover secrets that would further entrench their disdain.

Chapter Seven

My first trip to Versailles had gone well, I was made to understand. Since all I did in the presence of the queen was hold the dish with the pins in it and note down the measurements Mademoiselle Bertin called out to me, it seemed that the standard for "well" was set fairly low.

The atmosphere in the atelier grew distinctly chilly in the days following the Versailles visit, however, no matter how obliging I was to Lucienne and Ondine. Where they had started, before, to include me in their conversations, afterwards, they hardly addressed a word to me, doing their best to pretend I wasn't there at all. And my evenings were also quiet. Madame Chrétien took care to ensure that the activities in her elegant establishment were far enough removed from my bedchamber that I didn't hear anything beyond the soft closing of doors and an occasional giggle.

Despite the relative simplicity of my job, my ongoing efforts to present myself as Parisian to the core and remember to speak nothing but colloquial French was exhausting. Most nights I went straight to bed after arriving home. My violin lay neglected underneath my bed, despite the fact that I had promised myself I would practice for at least a half hour every day. Sometimes I dreamt that the violin would crawl out from under my bed in the middle of the night and poke me with the bow. But when I tried to grasp it, the instrument would squirm out of my reach. I swore I heard it laugh at me. And then I'd awake feeling out of sorts and empty for the entire day.

After one such disturbed night's sleep I decided I had to do something to shake myself out of my mood. That evening, the weather was unusually mild, so I decided instead of going directly back to the house via the most direct route, I would walk a different way and refresh my senses with new sights. And I had to admit, although the captain had warned me to stay away from it, my curiosity about the Palais Royale had become overwhelming. I could easily pass by there if I chose to, and so that evening I did. I had heard by listening to Lucienne and Ondine that although the Palais Royale should have been the home of the Duc d'Orléans himself, it was instead inhabited by his son, the Duc de Chartres. This was due to the fact that older duke had made a marriage not approved by the king to a woman too far beneath him in rank to be welcome at court, the Marquise de Montesson. She was not allowed to enjoy any of the ducal privileges her marriage would otherwise have entitled to, including living in the Palais Royale.

It was this very fact that piqued my interest, for I had overheard some gossip about the duc de Chartres that involved Mademoiselle Bertin herself. I can't be certain of all the particulars, since they were gathered by means of the ceaseless tittle-tattle of Lucienne and Ondine, but in her youth, Mademoiselle Bertin had been a beauty, apparently. She wasn't unattractive now, not in the least. But what must have been a pretty, round face and flawless complexion had succumbed a little to the ravages of time and care. Her plump cheeks were now hollow; her bright eyes red on the edges with the strain of close work and the irritation caused by the tiny threads that floated through the air of the cutting room and found their way to every part of the establishment on the Rue St. Honoré.

The story of Mademoiselle and the Duc de Chartres began when she was quite young, so my workmates said, just making her way in Paris as a milliner—which, I had learned, did not simply involve the design of headdresses, but all ornamentation of gowns as well. Her superior work won the approval of the Princesse de Conti—another relative of Louis XVI in a very confusing family tree—and had been engaged to make the trousseau of the soon-to-be duchesse de Chartres. This threw her into the presence of the duke much more often than would normally be expected of someone attending to his fiancée's wardrobe.

Apparently, the duke was taken with Mademoiselle to the extent that he made her extravagant offers of patronage, promising to shower her with jewels and set her up in her own elegant household. Many less talented or less intelligent women might easily have succumbed to such temptations. But Mademoiselle Bertin knew that, once down that path, she would never again enjoy the trust of the prominent women who would make her career. And affection was a fickle thing. Or rather, I should call it lust. In a year or two, the duke would likely have moved on to another object of pursuit, and Mademoiselle Bertin would have been pensioned off—if she was lucky. So she stood her ground.

But her adamant refusal had apparently not put an end to things.

"Just imagine! The duke had his guards follow mademoiselle wherever she went. They even tried to abduct her once. Perhaps twice," Lucienne had said, as if it were the greatest compliment a man could give a woman. But after my experiences in Vienna with kidnapping years ago, it made my blood run cold.

"Abduction is unlawful!" I said, inserting myself into their conversation.

Ondine turned to me, startled, and said, "She would have had to prove it. Besides, I think it's rather romantic."

"And do you suppose either of you would have jobs now if she had let herself be taken?"

Not to mention the fact that she would never have had entree to Marie Antoinette's boudoir. As the captain had informed me, the Orléans family not only still held long-ago grudges from the time when their arch-catholic leanings made France erupt in massacres of the Huguenots. The growing unrest and rising unpopularity of the queen had emboldened them to once again try to reawaken their scheming to wrest the monarchy from the reigning Bourbons. The irony was that they were nonetheless family with rights and privileges due to royalty, and had ceremonial roles to play on state occasions with their royal cousins still, so I'd heard.

I would not be able to recognize either the duc d'Orléans or the duc de Chartres if I saw them, however. And that, I thought, was one of the disadvantages of my current position. It seemed logical that they—or their henchmen—would have some insight into the very matter I was engaged to investigate. Yet they could do so right under my nose and I would not know it.

All these thoughts circulated in my head as I headed toward the northern end of the Palais Royale gardens. The unseasonably mild weather had drawn others outdoors, and I saw many couples and small groups of people wandering around in a leisurely fashion, possibly imagining that this would be the last pleasant night until spring. The smell of decay wafting from the Seine carried a note of something that must have drifted down from far upstream, in the countryside. Beneath the rotting garbage, I swore I detected the loamy scent of rotting leaves, the absence of growing things, the snap of chill just over the horizon. Whatever it was, I didn't have to cover my mouth with my handkerchief once that evening. Then again, maybe I'd just become used to the stench, accustomed, as the Parisians seemed to be.

My mind drifted back to Vienna as I walked. I'd been so busy and mostly too tired to think much about home since I'd come to Paris. Perhaps I had been in some measure relieved to be removed from a place that held so many memories, and so many demands for decisions I was not ready to make. Whatever it was, something about that evening conjured up images in my mind of Viennese streets, and concerts at the Redoutensaal and in Danior and Alida's apartment. I sighed. My sojourn in Paris had so far lacked any music at all. No wonder I dreamt of angry violins.

It was fully dark by the time I reached the entrance to the gardens of the Palais Royale, where I paused to take a good look. I stood shrouded in darkness, but the entire, gated garden before me was illuminated almost to false daylight. Torches flared from the pillars marching down the colonnade that bordered the palace, and promenading men and women in jewels and silks caught the light and fractured and reflected it, amplifying the dazzling effect. They, too, glowed. But it was a brilliant, cold light, not like the enveloping warmth of a hundred candles in Danior and Alida's apartment in the Trattner House.

I wiped a tear away from the corner of my eye. How foolish, I thought, and turned my attention back to the display of finery on parade in the elegant garden attached to the home of the Duc de Chartres, the very man who had tried to abduct and dishonor Mademoiselle Bertin years ago when they were both young. Part of me wanted to step into the gardens with all those fine lords and ladies even though I was not dressed properly, and would be assumed to be someone's servant. The thought made me smile. I was a servant, of sorts. A servant of the emperor. A servant of Mademoiselle Bertin. Was I also a servant of the captain? I banished the thought as soon as it arose.

I knew I shouldn't linger there, bu I paused a moment longer at the gate, looking in, wondering, imagining Danior with the Amati, hearing him play one of Mozart's mournful melodies with so much heart that it made me bleed inside.

That's when I realized it wasn't just a memory. I wasn't imagining it. I really did hear a violin. There was no violinist in the gardens that I could see, yet above, amid, and around the noise of the crowds and the carriages, the vendors wheeling their carts away, the shutters being rolled down over shop windows, I heard it. The clear, singing tones of a violin in the hands of a master. The music came and went on the breeze so that for a moment now and then, I lost it. Then it would sail back, scraping away my resolve to leave thoughts of home behind and return to my bed. I was afraid to move from my spot, thinking the sound would vanish altogether. But that was silly. The sound came from somewhere nearby. I walked a few paces farther on, and the music faded. I turned, and continued back toward the palace, and it grew, very slightly. I kept going. It became louder.

Finally, I reached a point where I could hear the violin distinctly, could tell the difference between an up bow and a down bow, hear the slight squeaking glissando between widely spaced notes. But there was no violinist anywhere to be seen.

I looked up. On the top floor of the palace building near where I stood, a light shone. The window had been thrown open to catch the mild evening breeze. My ears told me that was where the violinist must be. I wanted to see him. I wanted to talk to him.

The streets were emptying slowly, people making their way home or to evening engagements, and as the chatter faded I could hear the music all the more clearly. After a bit I thought perhaps my voice had a chance of being heard by the mysterious musician. At a pause in the music, I cupped my hands around my mouth and yelled with all my strength up toward that window. "You there! Playing the violin!"

The playing started again. I waited for another break. When it came, I yelled again. "You! Up there! Who are you, playing the violin?"

I thought I saw some movement, a shadow coming toward the window, but it backed away. "Please!" I practically screamed. "I need to know who you are!"

And I did need to. The only other violinist I had ever heard who came close to exhibiting such artistry was Mozart himself. This was the most exquisite playing, and I was desperate to know the identity of this mysterious musician.

At last, someone did come to the window. I could see the sheen of his powdered wig, and a snowy white cravat and cuffs. But the face was in complete darkness. And the hands. But that was impossible. How could it be, when he held a candle aloft, and I could just make out his features? Then it came to me. His face was black, or at least, dark brown. I had seen some Antillean Blacks on the streets, but they were all servants. This man was not dressed as a servant. In the glow of the candle I could tell his waistcoat was made of silk, and even from so far away, I saw the embroidered flowers that adorned it.

"Who is there?" His voice rang out into the night. Was it fear that edged it? Or some kind of accent?

"I'm down here! I play the violin! I heard you and I had to know who you were!"

He drew his head and arms inside and disappeared. The glow of the window faded, as though he'd taken a candle away with him. He was gone. I would never know. I drew in a deep breath and sighed into the gathering darkness. I had just turned my steps to go home, when I heard the clank of metal and something that sounded like a lock being sprung.

I turned, and a tall, well-muscled man, elegantly dressed and appearing the perfect French gentleman except for the color of his skin, stepped out onto the street, holding a candelabra that must have been the one illuminating the window. "Whom do I have the honor of addressing?" He said, much more formally than necessary for someone of my station.

"My name is Thérèse."

"A foreigner, like me."

I opened my mouth to deny it, but he pointed to his ear. "I can hear it. But don't worry, your secret is safe with me."

"And you are?"

He swept a courtly bow, holding the candelabra out to the side. "I am Joseph Bologne, the Chevalier de Saint-Georges. Would you like to come inside?"

I thought about it, but I was afraid. "It's late, and I'm expected elsewhere. I would like to hear you play more, though, if I may?"

"It would be my pleasure. I shall be performing at the salon of Madame de Montesson on Monday afternoon."

Madame de Montesson! The infamous morganatic wife of the Duc d'Orléans. Here was an unexpected opportunity, not just to hear music, but to enter an Orléanist household. "But I haven't been invited," I said, my hopes suddenly fading. And besides, I would be working during the afternoon.

"There are no invitations. One simply arrives. She is on the Chaussée d'Antin. If you wish, say you are my friend, Mademoiselle Thérèse."

"Thank you, I will try, but—"

"Come. I beg you. I believe we are not yet finished with each other."

He bowed again, and went back inside, leaving me staring after him, shivering as a cold breeze kicked up and blew away the mild evening air.

Chapter Eight

I told no one that the Chevalier de Saint-Georges had invited me to a salon the following Monday, at which he was to perform. A salon. I yearned to go. I had met Mozart at one such evening at the home of Danior and Alida. He had played my violin. My beautiful violin, my prized Amati, which was even now in that very apartment being cared for and lovingly played while I was away in Paris. If I closed my eyes, I could almost hear it.

"How you going to keep the books with your eyes closed?"

Lucienne's squeaky voice jolted me out of my reverie. "I was just resting them. The atmosphere in here makes them itch." It wasn't a lie. Not altogether.

She shrugged. "You get used to it. I say, Ondine, did you hear that the comtesse de Gramont's pouf caught fire at a ball last weekend? Apparently she danced too close to one of the torches! They had to douse her, and her entire costume was ruined. She'd paid more than three-thousand livres to have her dress from last month made over and trimmed with real gold lace."

They continued their prattle—a constant barrage of meaningless gossip I'd grown so used to I mostly didn't hear it—and I returned to my private thoughts.

Madame de Montesson's *hôtel particulier* was on the Chaussée d'Antin, the chevalier had said. The street wasn't far from Madamoiselle Bertin's establishment, but how would I know which house was hers? I could hardly ask someone. What reason would I have to inquire?

And there was the problem of the time to overcome. The salon took place in the afternoon, not in the evening like the ones I had attended in Vienna. On a Monday afternoon, I would be stuck in the atelier, adding up columns of figures in the ledger, trying to keep up with the endless stream of orders for the latest models and figure out how the fifty livres Mademoiselle charged for each one could be justified, when the materials to make them were not generally very costly, and the girls in her workshop could concoct one in an hour or less.

The door from the shop flew open at that moment and the breeze it created sent scraps of silk whirling about the room—and Ondine chasing after them. "These are for the Marquise's chapeau!" She said, her voice squealing on the last syllable. "They could be ruined!"

"Never mind that," said the pretty shop girl, her turned-up nose wrinkling to an even daintier size. "We're to embellish ten costumes for the masked ball at the opera on Monday evening. No one's going home before ten tonight or tomorrow. And all three of you will have to help to deliver the gowns during the afternoon on Monday."

Monday! Could I manage it? Was there a way for me to take one of the gowns on a small detour to the home of Madame de Montesson? I couldn't carry it in its bag. I would have to wear it. I'd choose the plainest one. It might just work. Without the accompanying masks, most costumes were simply gowns with a little extra trimming.

I smiled. I would make it work. I was going to hear music. Wouldn't the captain be surprised when I also managed to circulate among a crowd gathered in a household where no love was lost for the queen.

෧ඏஐ

After two very long workdays and an early start that morning, it was at last time to deliver the costumes to their respective owners. I'd worked alongside Lucienne and Ondine all Saturday and Sunday, not doing any sewing, but fetching whatever they needed from the shelves and cubbies to save time. My enthusiasm and willingness helped to rehabilitate myself somewhat in their eyes after the perceived slight of my trip to Versailles.

"I'll take that one!" I said as soon as Lucienne had finished it. It was the only costume that was not entirely encrusted with gems and pearls and still bore some resemblance to an ordinary gown.

"It's to go to Madame de Marivaux. I don't understand why she only wanted it trimmed with lace. Something about going to the ball as a peasant. You'll have to go out of your way to deliver it. She's north of the Palais Royale."

"Oh it's no problem. I often walk that way myself." I took the muslin bag that contained the gown—it was heavier than I thought it would be. There must have been more boning in it than I thought. I hoped it fit—although the food in Paris was superior to that in Vienna and I ate heartily, working had made me shed the weight I'd put on during the weeks of my training.

I shouldered the bag and walked out on the street past the two carriages that would transport the other costumes. The largest number of gowns were destined for Versailles, where members of the court had their own apartments, so I'd heard. Mademoiselle Rose stood on the cobbles directing the disposition of the bags in the carriage.

"Do not fold it in half, you idiot!" She screamed at Lucienne.

"Yes, Mademoiselle Bertin," she said. This would be fodder for complaints and gossip in the workshop tomorrow, I feared. To be fair, she hadn't actually folded it, merely eased it to get the voluminous bag through the carriage door.

Ondine stood smugly by the much-less-packed carriage that would take three of the costumes to Saint Germain and Passy, where she would travel with them.

The one I'd decided to borrow was an oddity—Mademoiselle Rose rarely agreed to work for ladies who were not members of the queen's inner circle. I had no doubt that this simply trimmed gown would cost more than the others, and wondered what the lady had agreed to in order to enjoy the privilege of being overcharged.

I waited until the carriages drove off toward the west, pretending to wave them off. Then I turned my steps in the direction of the marquise's *hôtel particulier*. As soon as I did so, I realized I had failed to consider something important. In my mind, I'd leapt from being in the workshop directly to imagining myself attired in the borrowed gown and moving among the guests at the salon. Nowhere in my imagination did I actually change my clothes. *Merde*! I thought. I would have to return to my lodgings first, which would take altogether an extra half hour. I considered abandoning my plan and arriving attired in my simple muslin dress and plain fichu, but I soon realized that, in such garb, I would never gain admittance to the salon. Although I didn't need an invitation, I had to at least look the part of someone in the right rung of society to attend.

And so I ran, dodging carriages and sedan chairs, leaping over puddles and closing my eyes against grit kicked up by horses' hooves, my cloak flying out behind and occasionally catching on a barrow. Once it snagged on the hilt of a gentleman's sword. I yanked it out before he could even utter a "Pardon, mademoiselle!" And kept going.

I was gasping for breath by the time I reached my room. Odette was still asleep, having no doubt been awake until the sun came up. As quietly as I could, I unpinned and unlaced myself from my dress and pulled the costume out of the bag. It was someone's idea of a peasant, supposedly. As if a peasant would ever wear so magnificent a costume, I thought. The dove-gray satin shimmered in the light, and lace ribbons had been threaded with multicolored silks, sewn into the bodice in an attractive vertical pattern that nipped in at the waist and then were freed to swish over the skirt, which—thank heaven—did not include wide panniers. I had already planned to tie the ribbons into bunches so I didn't look quite so frivolous at what was apparently a very sober salon. I anticipated poetic readings and performances, perhaps a singer or two. There might be conversation about art. And of course, the chevalier. Would his playing live up to the image I had in my mind?

I shook my head to bring my focus back to the practical matters at hand, and for one awful moment, I thought for certain I would have to abandon my ludicrous scheme, undone by simple logistics. The bodice fastened at the back. Of course, the baroness would have a lady's maid who could tug the laces and smooth out the fabric, pin the sleeves in place and pin and tuck everything neatly out of sight. Such practical considerations were never part of the calculation for a dressmaker. Even young girls could depend on a sister or mother to help them complete their toilette. On any ordinary day, I could have requested the help of Madame, or Odette. But I did not want to have to explain what I was doing.

I contorted myself trying to reach around and pull the laces. They were nearly tight, but I feared not tight enough, and I had no way of telling if they puckered the silk underneath them, and then, I would need to tie them securely and hide them in the band of the skirt. I glanced over at Odette's sleeping form. Her mouth was open, and a line of spittle made its way down her cheek to her pillow. She was so dead asleep. It would be cruel to wake her.

Instead, I opened the armoire and searched among Odette's clothing to find a light jacket I could wear indoors. Anything in a nondescript color would do. But hers were all bright scarlet or canary yellow. Then I spotted something that had fallen off a hook and lay crumpled in the bottom of the cupboard, a plain jacket of an older style that used to be white, but had dulled to an uneven cream. I held it up next to the gown, and stood in front of the cheval glass.

No. It would be like marrying a frog to a princess. I would simply have to hope that, once admitted to the gathering, no one would bother about what I was wearing.

Chapter Nine

By the time I arrived at the Hôtel Montesson, I knew that the laces of my bodice were starting to loosen. Worse, the band around my waist was not secure, and I could feel the skirt drifting slowly downward. I pressed my elbows hard into my sides to grip the delicate fabric, willing it to stay in place just long enough for me to hear the chevalier play and then leave, go home, take off the gown, return it to its muslin bag, and deliver it to the baroness in time for her to dress for the masked ball at the opera that evening.

The Hôtel Montesson was nothing like the house I lived in. It was only minimally less grand than the Palais Royale, which shouldn't have surprised me. The Orléans family—at least at that time—possessed vast wealth. I followed a few people who appeared to be going to the salon, staying behind them and hoping they wouldn't notice I was there. A footman led us down a long corridor to a door that led into an enormous reception room with high ceilings. About fifty other guests wandered around, forming and then unforming small groups as they greeted each other familiarly. The presence of a clavier and a harp in one corner, and ornate plaster carvings on the ceilings and walls of putti playing flutes and lyres marked this out as a music room. I assumed the chevalier would stand near the instruments to play, and looked for a discreet corner where I might have a clear view of him. One or two people glanced in my direction, but no one approached me, which was an immense relief. I began to think I would be able to sneak away as soon as the performance ended and the hostess would not know I had been there.

"Would mademoiselle care for a glass of wine?"

The voice was just behind my ear, and I whirled to face it, keeping my body rigid so that I wouldn't loosen my grip on the bodice. The dark-skinned footman deftly swept the silver tray of glasses filled to the brim with red wine out of danger. I started to perspire when I realized how close I had come to disaster. "N-non, Merci," I said.

This was a terrible idea, I thought. How could I have imagined I would be able to carry off such a brazen deception? At any moment, I was certain the hostess—who I guessed was the lady stationed in a corner that the other guests greeted politely—would whisper in a servant's ear that he was to escort me back to the street where I belonged. My face was surely a picture of embarrassment and shame. I inched back toward the wall near the door, keeping my eyes focused up and over the heads of the other guests to avoid catching anyone's gaze. I must have succeeded in part, because the assembled company had started to drift toward several rows of gilt chairs arranged in a crescent that had previously been hidden by the milling guests. No one came near me. I was the only person standing entirely alone.

I occupied my mind and distracted myself from my discomfort by counting the guests and trying to deduce their rank in society from what they were wearing, the quality of their jewels, and their bearing. I estimated at least one or two counts, whose ceremonial épées marked them as noblemen; perhaps a duchess or two festooned with diamonds; a few slightly more plainly dressed types who might be artists or musicians; and the rest were probably wealthy merchants and their wives, judging by the smiles glued to their faces and the fact that they were being avoided by those of higher rank.

My shoulders began to relax and my breathing became slower and calmer. Yes. I could do this after all. No one would remember seeing me there, I was invisible, and I could listen and then steal away.

"I don't believe I have made your acquaintance, Mademoiselle..."

I had let down my guard for no more than an instant, and an older man who might once have been considered handsome had found his way to my side, and pressed up much closer to me than was necessary. I stepped away a little, keeping my arms plastered to my ribs, and flashed the quickest smile at him as I pretended to be looking for someone else in the room.

"Ah, you prefer to remain mysterious! But you have forgotten your mask, which I assume you will don for the ball this evening."

Was it so obvious that my gown was really a costume? It seemed not very different from those worn by several of the ladies present. But perhaps they planned to go directly from the salon to the ball, only changing their appearance by putting on a barely concealing mask, purchased at great expense from a milliner.

I was on the point of fleeing, abandoning my plan and probably ruining any chance I would ever have of blending into the elite society of the salonistes, when a young lady broke free of a group that had been tittering behind their fans and swept over to me. "Ah there you are! I don't know how I didn't see you before, you naughty girl. You promised you'd come and find me as soon as you arrived. I'm so out of my depth here among all these talented folk."

She tried to insert her hand into my arm, but I would not loosen my grip on the sides of the bodice, and I widened my eyes and gave her a piercing gaze, hoping whoever she was she might guess my predicament.

"Monsieur," she said to the old gentleman who had accosted me, "My friend and I need to discuss a matter of great importance." Although she could not take my arm, she grasped my hand and pulled me away toward an anteroom. Once we were out of sight of the other guests, she forced my arms open, and to my horror, my skirt slid down to the floor, leaving me standing in my petticoat.

At this, the girl covered her mouth and laughed hard but silently, tears squeezing from the corners of her eyes. I pulled up the skirt and started fumbling with the laces.

"Come with me," she said, once she had recovered from her bout of hilarity, and led me into a boudoir and closed the door. "This is simply too delicious. You have to explain to me who you are and why you are here. My aunt will be so entertained when I tell her afterwards."

"Please! I'll leave! I only came to hear the chevalier de Saint Georges perform. He invited me. But I can hear him another time."

"That's no kind of answer, but at least I know your connection. You have an accent. Are you also from the islands?"

"No," I said, ashamed that, in my extreme panic, I hadn't spoken French as perfectly as I knew I could. "I'm from..." I searched my mind for a reasonable excuse for sounding other than Parisian, "Alsace."

This satisfied her curiosity, I was relieved to see. "But we must do something about your attire. This gown fits you very ill. Is it your mother's?"

How could I ever explain. "No. I borrowed it."

"No matter. I have one that will fit you better."

"Please—you have not told me your name."

"Nor have you!" She said.

"I am Thérèse... Sauvé." It was all I could think of in that moment, a reference to the fact that she had saved me from an embarrassing situation.

"I am Sophie Delalande. The hostess is my aunt, Madame de Montesson. I am in Paris to find a husband, so my mother insists, and she has given me only three months to accomplish this. Alas, I'm not likely to find a suitable match at one of these salons. Nothing but poets, musicians, and old lechers here."

"Thank you, by the way," I said as she unlaced me and laid the borrowed costume across a velvet-upholstered divan.

"Not at all. I couldn't bear to see you stranded, and the duc d'Orléans licking his lips at the innocent prey before his eyes." She returned bearing a much more suitable sacque gown of pearl brocade. I stepped into the skirt and put my arms through the sleeves of the bodice and she laced and pinned me securely. We must have been nearly the same size. "Now you need an ornament for your hair..." She brought a decoration with feathers and pearls—one I was certain must have been concocted in Mademoiselle Bertin's atelier. "And slippers... I have big feet, so my mother says, but I can stuff some gauze into the toes."

My transformation was accomplished within moments. I turned to face the tall mirror in its ornate frame, and gasped.

"You're very pretty, you know. If you had not been, I might not have come to rescue you." She pinched my cheek and planted a quick kiss on my lips. "Now, shall we return?"

❧

I walked back into the reception room arm-in-arm with Sophie. We could have been old friends who had just been sharing secrets in a private antechamber. I suppose we had been, and I was her secret, a small rebellion against the pattern of her days and the hopes of her mother to have her mix in elegant society. I was her secret, but I hadn't told her any of mine. She didn't seem to mind that I was a complete stranger who had wandered in wearing the most unsuitable gown imaginable, and evinced little curiosity about what had brought me there. Perhaps she understood the need beneath my deception, that something important must have drawn me to that salon, that something essential to my soul led me to take such a brazen step.

The hostess, Sophie's aunt, clapped her hands and all eyes turned to her.

"It is my pleasure to introduce the Chevalier de Saint Georges, the artist all Paris is celebrating since his grand success at the *Concert Spirituel*, and his new triumphs at the Concert Olympique. He will perform a new composition for us today. We are privileged to hear its debut before the concert next week."

Murmurs of pleasure and wonder rippled through the room. I held my breath. This was the moment I had been waiting for.

Sophie whispered in my ear, "I hear he is renowned—and feared— as an unrivaled swordsman as well."

I flashed her a quick smile. I didn't want to be rude to the girl who had saved me from mortification, but I was also determined not to let her prevent me from focusing all my attention on what was to come. She gripped my elbow. I could feel her fingernails digging through the silk of my sleeve. I wanted to break free of her, but I didn't dare. Her touch distracted me, and I failed to notice when the chevalier appeared, only alerted by the applause that greeted him. Surely she would release me so she could clap as well?

But no. And she hindered me from doing so, too.

"I'd much rather watch his swordplay, wouldn't you?" Her breath warmed my ear, and I felt her tugging me, just as the chevalier's bow touched the first string and sent a glorious low G reverberating into the air. He followed this with lightning-fast arpeggios and a chromatic glissando that made the hair on the back of my neck stand on end and a shiver pass through my entire body.

Sophie continued to pull at my arm. She wanted to take me to another room, probably to gossip and chatter about matters I cared nothing for. I couldn't let her! I turned pleading eyes on her, hoping she would comprehend and not force me to speak over the sweet, aching melody the chevalier teased out of his magnificent violin. He swayed with its contours, eyes closed, and I could feel him tug at the hearts of all who listened. He was fully engulfed in the music, yet aware all the same of the slight incline of bodies toward him. What Sophie didn't understand was that this—this was power.

In that moment, I could have prostrated myself at his feet. Perhaps it was just as well Sophie had a firm grip on my arm.

She let loose a sigh that made a handful of guests near us turn and stare. I squeezed her hand in appreciation for leaving me to listen, aware that I would probably have to pay for her forbearance by attending with equal concentration to her when the performance was over.

And then, something utterly remarkable occurred. Madame de Montesson had said that the chevalier was performing a new composition, but I distinctly recognized something in it that I had heard before. It wasn't exactly the same, but there were echoes of the love duet from Mozart's Abduction from the Seraglio. Had it been performed here in Paris? I thought not. But Mozart had been in Paris a few years before. He must have met the chevalier. Perhaps they improvised music together, delighting in each other's skill. The question was, had it been Mozart or the chevalier who had brought that melody into being?

I decided then that I would have to find a time to quiz the chevalier about it. Not in front of anyone else though. But that simple act of recognition distracted me, and I only half attended to the remainder of the performance. It ended to uproarious applause, and the guests surged forward to grasp the chevalier's hand and congratulate him. I stared at his dark, handsome face for as long as I could, watching him reward his adorers with a dazzling smile that lit his eyes, willing him to look in my direction so I could nod to him and he would know that I had acted on his impulsive invitation the previous week.

But he was utterly engulfed by enthusiastic admirers, and I could ignore Sophie's insistence no longer. I let her draw me away and back to the boudoir where, only minutes before, she had garbed me in one of her gowns so I could lay the ill-fitting costume aside.

I was still under the spell of the music. I said, "Wasn't it marvelous? I think his violin is an Amati. It has the same tone, and the color of the varnish—"

"You strange thing! Imagine knowing such nonsense. I'd much rather talk about the court at Versailles. What do you know of the duchesse de Polignac? I hear she is the most beautiful woman in Paris. And does the queen truly have ten lovers? How can she do it when she has only recently had a miscarriage?"

Sophie required little or no response from me, although I suspected that somewhere beneath her superficial prattle were genuine concerns and doubts and fears. How could I blame her, when it was clear her education had consisted of little more than acquiring the skills necessary to attract a wealthy husband?

Chapter Ten

It took me quite a while to extricate myself from Sophie's overwhelming need for conversation with someone her age. I didn't blame her, not really. We never returned to the reception room, instead sitting on her bed and talking about—well, we mainly talked about fashion. I made the mistake of telling her that I had sneaked away from the atelier of Mademoiselle Bertin, and before I could explain that I had little to do with the actual millinery and decorations that came from the famous modiste's imagination, she quizzed me about lace, and velvet, and whether real flowers or silk flowers were more in style, and how much the latest headdress cost—something I could answer, thanks to my familiarity with the ledgers.

The one benefit of letting her in on at least that part of my secret was that instead of treating my borrowed costume with disdain, she touched it reverently, suddenly discovering how artful it was, what genius had gone into the selection of ribbon colors and laces. I didn't tell her that this costume, because it was for someone not associated with the court, had been hastily concocted, and that Lucienne had had more to do with its design than Mademoiselle Bertin.

"I really must go! Now that you know my real identity, you must understand that I have to deliver this costume to the baroness in time for her to dress for the masked ball."

Making promises that I would call on her at the next opportunity, and that if she sent a message to the atelier I would suffer her to drag me along to some of the tedious operas and ballets she would have to attend, I backed out of her boudoir, the costume safely stowed in a muslin bag provided by my new friend. I would have no time to return to my lodgings to change, so we had agreed on that expedient.

"I shall return your gown tomorrow," I said.

"Oh that old thing! It's last season's style, and I don't plan to wear it anywhere outside this apartment. Keep it. Perhaps you can remake it into something better."

I protested, but she insisted, although I knew I would never presume to alter so fine a gown myself. The satin brocade was very costly, and it had seed pearls stitched in a floral pattern on the bodice. I did, however, think that it could be quite useful to possess such an item of clothing, if my as-yet-not-entirely worked-out plan to insinuate myself into the good graces of the queen's enemies was to be effective.

Once I had safely delivered the costume to its intended wearer, I returned to my lodgings in the pleasure house, exhausted but wide awake. I took a roll and some cheese from the kitchen up to the room I shared with Odette, but that I knew would be empty now. She would be busy elsewhere in the house until long after I was fast asleep.

It was a mild night, but something in the air suggested that it would be the last one for a while. A sharp edge to the breeze that found its way through the cracks in the window hinted at icy weather to come. I did not want to be in Paris over Christmas, but as yet, I had discovered little that would be of any use to the emperor in assessing whether or not his sister was in danger, and whether there was any action that could be taken to assuage it. My plan to listen in to conversations at the salon had been thwarted by Sophie's enthusiastic friendliness. But perhaps I could make use of the connection in some way I could not yet see.

I sat facing the wardrobe in the chair draped with several of Odette's dressing gowns. I didn't mind. They covered the threadbare patch and gave the illusion of elegance, an illusion strengthened by the silk gown I still wore. Thoughts swirled in my mind, snatches of ideas and unanswered questions. The day had been extraordinary, even though it hadn't gone precisely as I'd hoped.

I don't know how much time passed before I realized I had been staring at Danior's violin, still sitting in its case below my bed where I had placed it upon my arrival several weeks earlier. I had not taken it out to play. I was told not to play it lest the sound disturb the other occupants of the house. But why? They were all doubtless occupied with more interesting activities and wouldn't care if I played quietly. As long as I didn't practice endless scales, a little music might actually be appreciated.

I crouched on my knees and drew the case out from its hiding place. I was chagrined to see that it had been there long enough for a fine film of dust to have settled on its top. I wiped it off with the corner of one of Odette's cast-off robes, laid it on the bed, and sprung the latches open.

Danior's violin was familiar to me. I had played it several times, on those occasions when I gave in to his pleading to let him use my Amati to play the singing first-violin part of a quartet we were reading through. His was a fine instrument, with a slightly brighter tone than my Amati. I tuned it up, tightened the horse hairs and spread rosin on the bow, nested the violin on my left shoulder and drew the bow slowly across the lowest string. I played a measured scale up from there with hardly any vibrato, closing my eyes and concentrating on the pitches and their tones, feeling the music spread through my awakening body.

Soon I began a melody. Quiet and mournful. And then another. And then I paced slowly around the room, becoming bolder and bolder and letting the air vibrate with music. What was that tune? I thought. The one the chevalier played that I thought I recognized from Mozart's Seraglio? I tried to recreate it, but it wasn't quite right. After a bit, though, I found it. I found it, and then continued it as I had heard it on opening night, where I sat at the back of the second violins, engulfed in the experience of performing in disguise at the Staatsoper—despite the objections of the disgraced director.

Something was different though. It wasn't simply that I hadn't been playing the melodic part, because for much of the opera the second violins merely filled in harmonies or played measure upon measure of repeated notes. I felt—different.

I stopped playing and looked down. Of course. I was wearing a dress. Not just any dress, but one that proclaimed me to be utterly feminine. The last time I'd played the violin, I had not been myself, but Thomas Weissbrot. I wore a court musician's uniform. A man's uniform, with a jacket, waistcoat, breeches, stockings, and a cravat. My hair had been pulled back and tucked away under a man's itchy wool wig.

I turned so that I could see myself in the mirror, lifted the violin, and began to play again, this time with my eyes open. Did I always pinch my eyebrows together when I was playing? Did my lips remain parted just a little, and my body sway in just that manner whenever I performed as part of an orchestra? It occurred to me that, although it hadn't been entirely necessary, when I played chamber music with Danior, I also dressed as a man, even though his friends well knew I was a girl.

It came to me quite suddenly that I hadn't performed or even played very much as the person I actually was. Was I that girl I saw in the mirror? Was it really me? If I closed my eyes, I recognized myself in the music I made, the sounds I drew from the fiddle. When I opened them, though...

My arms grew tired. It was all too much. I laid the violin back in its case, loosened the hairs of the bow, shut and latched the case and slid it back under the bed, then unlaced myself, put on my night shift, and crawled beneath the covers. I would make sense of it all tomorrow.

Chapter Eleven

"You are in so much trouble, Thérèse!" Ondine whispered this to me loudly enough so that not only Lucienne could hear, but that the man who had just delivered ten rolls of lace trim turned and looked back at the door of the atelier as I closed it, his eyebrows shooting up and disappearing under the brim of his cap.

It was true, I had delivered the baroness's dress a little on the late side. It was also true that I had torn the slightest hole near the hem when I was rushing from my lodgings to the salon. But the baroness had her costume with ample time to prepare, and I was certain no one would have noticed the tiny rip, at the back, near a seam, tinier than the nail on my littlest finger. I only discovered it when I took the costume out of its sack and laid it on the bed as instructed. The baroness was still having her hair dressed, so she didn't look at me when I curtsied and sped away home, crossing myself against discovery.

Home. What a place to call home, I thought. Yet, oddly, as soon as I walked through that discreet door and let myself into the dimly lit parlor used by the girls, I felt the cares of the day slip away. There, no one expected much of anything from me—except the captain, and he hadn't visited for weeks. Madame and the girls were always occupied by the time I returned after a day's work. And I could come and go as I pleased, as long as I didn't have to disturb the concierge to do it.

I wished, at that moment, that I was back in that place, for I heard the quick, angry step of Mademoiselle Bertin coming toward the door of the workroom that led toward the boutique, and I braced myself. I made sure I was poring over the accounts with a freshly dipped quill, brow furrowed, checking the rows and columns for mistakes, so she would see me working assiduously at the job I was supposed to be doing.

The door flew open and banged into the wall, making all of us jump. "Mademoiselle Thérèse!" Her high, sharp voice pierced the tense atmosphere. I did not look at them, but I knew Lucienne and Ondine must be stifling smiles. I had seen them cower at the receiving end of Mademoiselle's fury before, and they must be delighted it was my turn.

I laid down my quill, stepped out from behind the desk, and sank down in a curtsy. What else was I to do?

"It seems, young lady, that you have a talent for dissembling, something I do not appreciate, not in my workshop. If it were entirely up to me, you would be sent packing back to whatever provincial slum you hailed from. But alas, it is not up to me. Come."

She pointed toward the boutique, her arm straight as an arrow, all the tension she felt at whatever situation awaited clenched in that slender limb.

If only she knew that dissembling was the very skill I had been sent to Paris to exploit.

"What are you waiting for!"

She whirled around, and I followed her rapid steps into the faux boudoir that served as her shop. It was too early for customers yet, so my curiosity grew as we entered. I could not imagine what reason she could have for conducting me there.

As soon as we passed through the door, my question had its answer. The captain. He was lounging at his ease on the chaise normally reserved for noble customers. Attired in his uniform, he'd removed his hat and had a delicate porcelain cup of tea balanced on one knee. Without hurrying, he set the cup on a table hardly bigger than the cup itself and stood, nodding his head to me in the most dismissive excuse for a bow. I returned his greeting with a facetious, nose-to-the-floor curtsy.

"I will leave you to explain to Mademoiselle Thérèse what you just explained to me, although I find it very difficult to credit, let alone believe. Good day!"

Mademoiselle Bertin swept out toward the workroom again, and I feared that she would find some way to exercise her thwarted anger on my hapless workmates. I felt sorry for them.

"So, you've been flapping your wings a bit, I hear. And scratching away at your fiddle as well."

This caught me by surprise. Had he been somewhere in Madame Chrétien's establishment last night?

"I have my informers, as you must know."

"What do you want?"

"Two things. First, apparently you made quite the impression on the queen when you attended Mademoiselle Rose to Versailles the other week."

An impression? I'd hardly uttered two words. "I'm flattered, certainly, but—"

"Such an impression that she would like you to be part of the theatricals she is planning at the Petit Trianon the day after tomorrow, which means you will go there for a rehearsal today."

"But... Mademoiselle Bertin."

"She will go with you, to take care of the costumes. Including yours."

Oh, I would not live that down, not in a lifetime of living! To have Mademoiselle herself deck me out in finery was something she would consider the lowest form of insult. Yet the queen commanded it, and so she must.

"I need hardly tell you that this suits our purpose quite well. You are to observe everything while you are there—who performs, what the play is, who is the audience. See how they react. Which ones are sympathetic, which ones are simply waiting to run back to Paris and feed the pamphleteers with more lies to stir up the populace against her."

"But, I am not an actress! And I can't sing, heaven knows."

"You will sing if she asks."

"She won't ask twice!"

"And whether you sing or not, if you see any messages pass between guests, you are to do whatever it takes to discover what they contain."

How on earth would I ever be able to do such a thing? Especially if I were stuck on a stage performing—what? The idea of being in front of people and doing anything other than playing the violin terrified me. The violin, the instrument that was as close and familiar to me as my own shadow, shielded me from true scrutiny. With a violin nestled on my shoulder, Theresa—the uncertain girl full of doubts and worries—became invisible. It was the music people saw. I proved it, didn't I? By successfully performing in disguise for over two years. But this—I could see no way of avoiding it. "When is this rehearsal and costume fitting?"

"Even now. The carriage will come for you in less than an hour."

And an hour later, I found myself once again in an elegant carriage with the queen's cypher on the doors on my way to Versailles. Mademoiselle Bertin was with me, as before, but the respect I had previously earned had evaporated with the morning dew. Once again, she glared out the windows at the passing scenery, this time not even bothering to speak to me.

I was sorry it was a cold, dreary day. I understood that the queen had a charming little dairy farm and a hamlet surrounding her retreat from the formality of Versailles. Somehow I doubted her ladies would brave the wind that made me pull my cloak around me tightly just to stroll through a bucolic fantasy.

The Petit Trianon was a jewel box of a royal residence, positively tiny compared to Versailles. Not only that, but in its rooms, rather than stand stiffly by, awaiting the order of precedence to be observed, nobles wandered around casually. I did not enter through the front with the others, but the door through which I was led did not look like the usual servants' entrance either. Although smaller and a bit less ornate, care had clearly been taken to make it match the aesthetic of the rest of the building.

I followed Mademoiselle to a little theater—in all respects like its larger cousins, except that everything was on a smaller scale. Every opulent detail was there, crafted in papier-mâché and gilded, with rows of dusty-blue velvet benches stretching back about ten deep. A loge ran around the egg-shaped sides, with the same blue silk wall coverings behind. It was stunning.

"My dear Mademoiselle Rose! And Thérèse! Please don't look so frightened. Here, we are not at court. We are players, dancers, singers, all come together to lighten our lives through the pursuit of art and pleasure."

The queen had emerged from the wings. Despite the cool weather outside, she wore one of the muslin dresses that Mademoiselle Bertin had made so popular, a gray silk brocade shawl draped over her shoulders. Of course I had curtsied, but I felt her hand gently cup my elbow and encourage me to stand.

"It is so kind of you to lend me your assistant, Rose. Perhaps I could have found some daughter of one of the courtiers, but this one—her face, her demeanor, stayed in my mind. It would particularly suit the small role I wish her to perform in the play tomorrow."

The queen turned to me. "There is something so familiar about you, my dear." She took my chin and examined my face, turning it this way and that. I kept my eyes on her at all times. Was it possible she had seen me performing in Vienna? Surely not. She was ten years my senior, and had been in France since I was but five years old.

But she may have seen my father, and I have been told I look more and more like him as I grow older. Or perhaps it is simply some general feature, something to remind her of her Viennese roots.

She let go of me after giving me a small, somewhat pained smile. I recalled that only a few weeks before, she had suffered a miscarriage. No wonder she was sad. All the more so because she had as yet failed to produce the much-longed-for heir to the throne.

"I require Mademoiselle Thérèse's costume to resemble that of a Greek nymph, something that drapes across and reveals one of her shoulders. I, myself, will wear the garb of a shepherdess, but I will not be performing, only watching. I am not yet strong enough. I thought perhaps you could adapt one of my gowns to that purpose?"

"If Your Majesty thinks that will be adequate?"

I guessed that Mademoiselle Bertin thought she would be designing a new costume, and thus earn a great deal more money.

"I must be mindful of the cost of my entertainments, so my husband tells me. I am told that the price of bread is rising, and that the sages are predicting a cold winter."

I looked off the stage and at the rows of benches, imagining them peopled with indigents who had come in from the cold and begged crusts of bread, tracking in the mud from the lanes. In my mind I heard babies crying, mothers shushing them, and hollow coughs echoing in the sublime acoustics of the bijoux theater.

My fantasy was disturbed by approaching footsteps. Soon a dozen people—six men and six women—came from both wings to fill the small stage. One of them—a tall, attractive man with a confident bearing—clapped his hands to get everyone's attention. Mademoiselle Bertin slipped out through the wings and reappeared through the curtained entrance at the back of the orchestra. She did not sit, but stood right in the middle of the aisle, glaring at me, her pencil poised to note costume ideas in the notebook she pulled out of her reticule.

"Our theatrical adventure for this weekend is *Le déguisement forcé*, by Monsieur Faur."

A polite murmur of approval greeted this announcement. How apt, I thought. The forced disguise. I should be able to play my part extremely well.

I tried to stay on the periphery as the gentleman in charge sorted people into small groups and told them who they were and what they would do. Because of the social mixing of ranks in this place, I couldn't really tell who was low-born, like me, and who was an aristocrat. I had to judge by their behavior. Clearly, the gentleman at the center of it all was not lowly. A large diamond ring flashed on his pinky finger, and although he'd removed his coat, the waistcoat he wore was of the finest quality brocade. I sidled over to a woman who looked to be about my age and equally as lost, and whispered, "Who is that?"

She turned to me as if I were a spider that had slid down a filament from the ceiling to land on her shoulder. Her previously open expression became a grimace of distaste. "That is the Comte de Vaudreuil, of course."

Before I could thank her, she marched over to the other side of the stage.

For the remainder of the afternoon, we walked around the stage as directed by the Comte. I was relieved to discover that my role was merely decorative. I was to stroll slowly across the stage in my classically inspired costume carrying a small harp that was strung too loosely to make a sound. And this stroll was at the very end of the finale.

I was about to give up on being able to observe anything remotely helpful to the captain, when I saw a man and a woman half-hidden in the wings stage left. They didn't look as though they were waiting to come on stage. They paid no attention at all to Vaudreuil's direction, in fact. I slowly made my way across the stage, trying to ensure no one noticed my movement, to see if I could hear what they were saying to each other. When I reached the wings on that side, I made sure to keep my back to them and focus out on the so-far chaotic activity, so if they looked at me, they'd see I was paying attention to Vaudreuil's amusingly given directions for what seemed like a very absurd play.

The actors clustered about, rehearsing their lines in little scenes on the stage all at the same time, which made it hard for me to hear anything else. The lovely acoustics amplified the voices under the proscenium and deadened those off stage.

After a time, Vaudreuil clapped his hands and everyone stopped. He gave a few notes and bowed to the queen, who had tired, perhaps, and now sat rather than stood in the middle row of benches in the audience. Everyone on stage bowed or curtsied in her direction as well. I took the opportunity of my own curtsy to turn my head toward the wings again.

The two people who had been there were gone. I would have to wait for tomorrow's performance to see if their presence meant anything.

Tomorrow's performance. Well, everyone seemed in good enough spirits, as if this was often the state of affairs before they climbed onto the stage. For my part, I could not imagine facing an audience—invited or not—without having had many hours of practice, and being sure of every note, every nuance. Perhaps the lack of care here would be to my advantage.

The play was predictably chaotic, although I believe I managed to discern my cue in the last act and stroll across the back of the stage at the right moment, wearing nothing much more than a sheet of white muslin and a beatific smile, pretending to strum my lyre. The little theater erupted into applause that echoed encouragingly. After all, it was filled to the brim with invited courtiers and military officers. Thankfully, I didn't notice that the captain was among them until after we had all streamed out of the wings to take our bows.

There he sat, halfway back, staring straight ahead, his characteristic expression of amused detachment providing just enough mystique for him to belong in such surroundings. He was a nobleman, after all, I had to remind myself.

Afterwards, the players and the audience members went to the reception room where refreshments had been laid out by invisible hands while everyone was in the theater, the sound of laughter and applause masking any noise of clinking glasses or cutlery. I wanted to change out of my costume first—I was by far the least covered of all the cast, I imagine on purpose because of Mademoiselle Bertin's pique—but without the queen's permission to do so, even in that less formal setting, I didn't dare. Everyone else who had been on stage remained in costume, not even removing the lead-white face paint and bright circles of rouge on their cheeks. I felt as if I were at a children's party and surrounded by harlequins.

No one spoke to me, which wasn't surprising. Everyone else seemed to know each other well, and I assumed I was the only non servant who didn't have some connection to nobility. I was able, therefore, to move among the guests freely and listen.

What I heard was mostly inconsequential gossip—about the fashions of the day, upcoming opera performances where the diva refused to sing an aria as written, whispers of who had started having an affair with whom.

But after perhaps a quarter of an hour, I noticed two of the guests wander away, glancing over their shoulders at the cluster of sycophants positioned around the queen. It wasn't polite to leave before the queen did, but that wasn't what caught my attention. It was the fact that two other guests, similar looking and similarly attired, came back to the reception as if they had been there all along. Not only that, but I recognized these new guests as the gentleman and lady I had spied in the wings at the rehearsal the day before. What could this mean?

I moved toward the table that had been laden with exquisite cakes, partly because that was where the new guests were heading, partly because I was hungry. I arrived there almost at the same time they did. Another gentleman approached from the opposite direction and moved past me to speak quietly to these new guests. I saw him reach for the lady's hand and tuck a piece of paper into it surreptitiously.

Guests passing notes. That had been one of the tasks the captain set me, to intercept them if I could. Now, how to manage it?

I helped myself to a confection so light that it collapsed when I bit into it. These were nothing like the good, solid Viennese cakes, the dense chocolate tortes one could purchase in the cafes. Unlike those, I could have eaten a dozen of these and not felt as if I'd eaten a thing. But I had work to do, and so I did not take another, instead weaving among the guests to follow the lady who'd received the note.

In a stroke of good fortune, I saw her try to put the paper away in a pocket hidden in the seam of her gown and miss her mark in her effort to be discreet. I watched the note flutter to the floor. No one else noticed, at least not yet.

I moved to where the note lay as quickly as I could and bent down to pick it up.

Of course, in my ridiculous costume I had no pockets. Nowhere to hide anything, in fact. I longed to open the paper and see what it said, but I couldn't do it in full view of the company.

Which then gave me an idea. I stopped a servant passing by with a tray of dirty champagne glasses and said, "*Excusez-moi.* Is there a privy I could use? Nerves, you know!" I tried to garner some sympathy from her, but her face remained impassive, and she pointed to a door in the corner. I remembered too late that I had given away my lowly status by being polite to a servant.

I headed to the indicated door, pretending to walk with my eyes trained forward, but I could see everyone I passed out of the corner of my eyes. More than one of them—especially the men—turned their heads to watch me as I went. Merde!

I passed through the door and, instead of the privy, I found myself confronted with a corridor lined with six more doors. Now what? I started along, grasping the handles and pulling and pushing, hoping to find the right one.

Until the last two, they were all locked. It has to be one of these, I thought, relieved. I said a silent prayer, and grasped the handle of the second to the last door, and pulled. It gave way.

But I hadn't found the privy. Instead, the door opened into a small chamber currently occupied by a couple, the man with his hand reached up under the lady's skirt, the lady with her head thrown back in ecstasy. I recognized her. It was the duchesse de Polignac, the queen's closest friend, and the man who was embracing her in that intimate way was the Comte de Vaudreuil.

I gasped. They turned to me at the same time. Vaudreuil grabbed my arm and threw me in front of him out to the corridor, leaving the duchesse to rearrange her dress.

"Guards!" He called. "Guards!"

Three men in military uniforms rushed out of the reception room. I noticed with relief that one of them was the captain himself. But as he drew closer, I also realized that he showed no signs of recognizing me, and let the other two take hold of me without doing anything to stop them.

"I can explain! I was looking for the privy!" I tried to wrench my arm free, but they held me fast.

In their rough handling, I was forced to drop the note I had recovered from the other guest. The captain—who never seemed to miss a thing—bent down to pick it up. His eyes flashed with something I couldn't identify. Anger? Amusement? I only glanced into them briefly before he looked down to unfold and read the note. When he finished, he folded it up immediately and tucked it inside his waistcoat. Of course he wouldn't say what was written there, but I hoped at least he would turn his attention to securing my release from unjustified captivity. I expected he would be pleased I'd managed to accomplish the one very difficult task he had assigned me, and therefore tell the guards to let go of me.

But instead, he said, "This lady is spying on the queen. Take her to the Bastille."

Chapter Twelve

Years later, long after I'd left Paris and the queen was no more, I would remember my ride from the Petit Trianon to the Bastille, located in the eastern, Saint Antoine district of the city. Although my own journey had an entirely different outcome, I shiver even now picturing the queen, her hair shorn, wearing only a simple homespun dress, riding through the jeering crowds to the guillotine with no escape possible. I knew in my heart I was not facing indefinite incarceration or execution—the emperor would find a way to extricate me if that were the case, I was certain. Even without that fear, the experience was terrifying. No elegant, gilded, velvet-upholstered carriage this time. Just an open cart, drawn by two scarred old horses reluctant to hurry anywhere other than a warm stable.

They tried to toss me in wearing nothing but my flimsy costume. But the captain must have remembered I was not really the enemy and threw a heavy wool blanket in after me. I wrapped myself in it with some difficulty, because it wasn't big enough to cover me from my head to my bare toes. And what had started out a cold, dreary day had disintegrated into a wintry one. In another situation, I might have thought the snowflakes drifting down from the heavens enchanting. That would have to have been a situation where I was safely tucked up in a warm room, a fire blazing, and looking out as the snow gradually softened and cleansed the cityscape.

Instead, my teeth chattered and I shook from head to toe. To take my mind off the damp cold, I thought of my mother and brother and sister, wondering what they were doing that very moment in Vienna. I wished I had been free to write to them and tell them about Paris. Toby especially would have been amused. My mother would have been horrified if she knew where I was staying. In Vienna, I might have been playing in some of the upcoming Advent concerts. That brought to mind my father and the Amati in Danior's safe care. And the fact that I must try to keep my fingers warm so the frost would not bite them and leave me unable to play again.

The journey was long and slow enough for fury to build in my heart, too. What game was the captain playing now? How dare he expose me to such physical discomfort and peril? I knew from my previous experience with him that he was not to be trusted, that he could keep secrets so arcane and obscure that only he could understand what they were for. The belief that he must have had some twisted reason for having imposed this trial on me was cold comfort.

A thin film of snow coated my blanket by the time we reached the vicinity of the Louvre. I thought with longing of the workshop behind Mademoiselle Bertin's boutique, yearning to be there to hear Lucienne and Ondine pore over the latest fashion gazette and tear apart each design, headdress to shoe ornament. I ached as we passed the end of the street where my lodgings were located, thinking of Danior's fiddle in its wooden case under the armoire. The last time I'd played it was the evening of Madame de Montesson's salon, where I had heard the sublime Chevalier de Saint Georges. That had been only a few days ago.

And then, it struck me. Could it have been the captain's intention all along to establish that I was an enemy of the court? I had told him that I thought we were going about this all wrong, that it would make more sense for me to be embedded in the establishment of the duc d'Orléans or his son the duc de Chartres than at Versailles. But at the time he pooh-poohed my idea. Perhaps that, too, had been a clever trick. If I knew he planned to throw me to the dogs, I would not have been so panic-struck. I was good at disguise, but not that good.

By the time we arrived at the prison I was ready to go inside anywhere, as long as it had a roof and four walls. I could no longer feel my feet, and I was shivering so hard I could barely make it across the now-wet ground to enter the prison. The brute who had driven me there handed me off to a guard who actually bowed to me.

"Do you have the *lettre de cachet*?" he asked the driver.

To my surprise, the surly cart driver reached inside his jacket and drew out a folded letter bearing what looked like a royal seal. The prison guard broke the seal and scanned the letter before putting it inside his waistcoat and saluting his compatriot, who left me just inside a door of the massive fortress.

"Follow me. We have quarters arranged for you for your stay, which I hope will not prove terribly uncomfortable. A package arrived just a few minutes ago for you. I assume it contains warmer clothing." He glanced at me with a smirk. I pulled the blanket more tightly around me.

As we climbed not down into dungeons but up to higher floors that were increasingly well lit and warm, I became confused. Was this not a fearsome prison? By the time my escort let me into a sparely but comfortably furnished room with a fire blazing in the fireplace and a window looking west over Paris, I thought I must have had a blow to the head and was in some semi-conscious state.

"I will leave you here. Madame Fantin will attend you." The guard bowed again and closed the door behind him. The only indication that I was anywhere but a luxurious residence was the scraping of a key in the lock and the firm clunk of a bolt in its housing.

A woman rose from a stool near the fire and approached me.

"Mademoiselle Thérèse, I presume? I'll be taking care of you while you are a guest here. Let's get you into some more suitable garments." She smiled at me and reached out for the blanket I still clutched closed at my neck. Within a few minutes, I was dressed in a warm night shift, had had a bowl of rather delicious soup, and was tucked up in a bed that was more comfortable than the one I occupied at Madame Chrétien's.

I'll wake up tomorrow and this will all have been a bizarre dream, I thought, and soon drifted into a deep slumber.

❧

I woke the next morning feeling unaccountably refreshed. How was that possible? I wondered. Here I was in a fortress whose name evoked fear, that was supposedly where prisoners were taken and tortured and never heard from again. And yet, it appeared that in my chamber I had everything I needed. I was brought meals that were more than palatable, my clothing and personal effects miraculously appeared, and I even had a servant to take care of me. The only thing I couldn't do was leave.

"Might I have paper, quill, and ink?" I asked Madame Fantin, who told me she looked after me and two other women confined there.

"Of course. Are there books you would like as well? I can have a messenger sent to your lodgings to bring them."

"No books," I said, suddenly very excited to think that here, imprisoned, I might have time to practice the violin, "but there is a musical instrument in a case beneath my armoire. Mademoiselle Odette will know what I speak of."

Although it was comfortable enough in my strange new accommodations, I did find it unsettling not to be able to escape. I hoped that playing my violin might take my mind off that disconcerting fact.

My—or rather, Danior's—violin arrived later that same afternoon, and I passed two hours in the company of blissful music. I decided that here, I could take my time and practice scales, that I needn't worry about irritating anyone with such repetitive noise. My fingers felt lazy and out of practice, and I vowed never to be away from the violin for so long again.

I had to stop when my hands were tired. The last thing I wanted was to injure myself. But I had passed enough time for a day to be almost over. I heard the bells from Notre Dame and watched the pale, winter sun sink below the horizon. Another night of captivity loomed.

Captivity, but apparently not solitude. I was just finishing the supper Madame Fantin brought me when I heard the approach of booted feet echoing along the corridor outside my cell. Oh no! I thought. Could it be that they tricked me with all this soft treatment only to drag me away and chain me up somewhere?

The key rattled in the lock of my door, and it swung open to reveal the captain. He still wore his stern face with no sign that this was all in jest, something I half expected, although I could not imagine why.

"Leave us. I must ask Mademoiselle Thérèse some questions of a highly confidential nature."

"Very good, Capitaine," the guard said, nodding his head and taking care to close and lock the door after the captain stepped inside.

"Would you like some wine?" I asked, pretending uninterest in why he was there. "Madame Fantin will bring another glass if I ask her." It was a little disconcerting how quickly I had become accustomed to being waited upon.

"No, thank you, Mademoiselle. I have some serious matters to discuss with you." As he said this, he reached into his waistcoat and drew out the very letter I had picked up from the floor at the Petit Trianon the day before. I reached for it, but he snatched it away, putting his finger to his lips as he did so.

Then, he tiptoed to the door, put his ear to the hatch that could be opened to see who was outside it, and listened. My ears pricked up in sympathy with his rapt attention.

Sure enough, a few moments later, footsteps walked away from the door. The guard had stayed, perhaps hoping to pick up information that could be useful, or valuable. I gestured, palms up, shoulders shrugged, a silent, why?

He took the seat opposite me at the table by the fire and leaned close so he could speak very softly. "I think you have not been very inconvenienced by this change of tactics." He looked around him at my comparatively comfortable surroundings.

I nodded. "It would have been nice to have a little warning,"

"I couldn't do that. You mustn't think that I took your advice in particular, but I did come to see that, if you were a creature of the court, you would be unlikely to find yourself in a position to discover anything concerning the slander that is detrimental to the queen. It was the invitation to be part of the theatricals that made me realize it. The queen likes you, for whatever reason. And if I could see it, so could everyone at court, including her enemies."

At that moment, a key turned in the lock.

The captain sat up and leaned away, as if he had been lecturing me. "Your crimes are quite serious, you know. I will do what I can to have your reputation restored, but once lost…"

"*Je m'excuse, mademoiselle.* I thought the gentleman might prefer cognac to wine, and I have brought the decanter and a glass."

Madame Fantin—who was not a young woman, although still attractive—simpered into the room, her hips swaying just a little. I saw she had applied the faintest bit of rouge to her cheeks and lips as well. I looked from her to the captain, who gratified her with one of his winning smiles, and saw with disgust that Graf Edelbert von Bauer was not above using his decent looks to charm women in whom he had no interest. He took the decanter and glass, placed them on the table, then pressed a coin into Madame's hand—and winked at her.

She turned to leave, a real blush spreading beyond the confines of the blush she had applied with such care.

Once she was gone and we'd heard her footsteps echoing down the stone floor of the corridor, the captain returned to his secretive tone. "I think it won't be long before the queen's enemies hear of your incarceration and take some action to turn it to their advantage. Especially because of this."

At last he handed me the letter I had intercepted.

The queen is having an affair with Count Axel von Fersen of Sweden. The only person unaware of this at Versailles is the king himself.

"Is this true?" I whispered.

"The truth of it doesn't matter at all. Whoever wrote this note understands that the mere suggestion of it is enough to further blacken the queen's name, and cast doubt upon the legitimacy of any children she may have."

"Surely since we have the note, there is no need for such a rumor to be circulated abroad."

The captain shook his head. "Thérèse, Thérèse, for a smart young woman you are very naive. Do you think only the person who wrote this note is capable of making such a rumor known? The count has been a regular guest at the Petit Trianon, often one of only a couple invited. Such intimate, informal gatherings not only cast suspicion, but they entrench the queen's enemies, who see her disregard for court etiquette as tantamount to open rebellion."

I was struck by the fact that, what should have endeared the queen to her people, had been twisted and distorted to make her seem evil. I had not spent much time in her presence, but what I did know was that she was kind and generous. She did not deserve to be treated so barbarously. "If I can't help destroy the rumor, can't help make people understand that it isn't true, what can I do?"

"In order for such rumors to take root, they must be spread. The way they are being spread is through the pamphlets."

"Then arrest the pamphleteers!"

He sighed. "First, we have to find out who they are. After that, we must discover who prints them. People must be made to understand that spreading such calumnies is not without consequences."

I thought about this. If truth didn't matter, if people were willing to believe whatever they wanted to believe, how could I have any effect upon them, even if I uncovered an entire network of pamphleteers and printers? "I still don't see how I can help you from in here." I swept my arm around the room, with its ostensible comforts undermined by the presence of bars on the window and a locked door.

"I have a suspicion that the Palais Royale is the seat of these activities."

"Why?"

He shook his head. "As the property of the senior member of the cadet branch of the royal family, the police can have no jurisdiction there. He could be murdering people within its walls and there would be no way for justice to be served."

It seemed implausible to me, but not impossible. "And so?"

"If I have planted the seed correctly, you will not remain prisoner here for long," the captain said. "And if all goes according to plan, you will be in a position to report back to me about activities inside the Palais Royale."

"I suppose you have no intention of telling me how this miraculous event is to transpire?"

His answer was to stand and reach for my hand. I gave it to him. He bowed over it and kissed it. "If you have need of me, you may send word secretly through Madame Chrétien. But only in the case of dire necessity. From this point, you and I are no longer to be seen talking to each other, and if we are ever accidentally in one another's presence, we must appear to be strangers."

He left me more mystified than he found me.

Chapter Thirteen

The captain was right about one thing. I didn't have to wait long to have my situation reversed yet again.

The next morning, when Madame Fantin came to pick up my breakfast tray, she rather ostentatiously placed a note on the table, making a feeble attempt to mask her action by saying, "They say it will snow today, and it's likely to be a cold enough winter to freeze the Seine right over!"

I prayed that my business in Paris would be finished soon enough that I could leave before ice and snow made traveling to Vienna for Christmas impossible. "Thank you," I said. It seemed obvious that Madame Fantin wanted me to look at the note while she was there, but I steadfastly pretended not to notice it. At last, she turned and left the room, closing the door behind her, but not locking it.

Strange, I thought. I picked up the note. It was written in a very elegant hand, I had to admit.

Friends have ensured that the lettre de cachet that led to your imprisonment has been rendered void. Gather your belongings. Madame Fantin will conduct you to a secret door where you will be met by a conveyance that will transport you to a house of safety.

No wonder she was waiting for me to read it! Without another moment's hesitation, I gathered up my few possessions—a night shift, brush, and the violin in its case—and crept to the door. I half expected the handle not to yield when I grasped it, but I pulled on it anyway.

Miracle of miracles. The door opened, and I stepped out into the corridor for the first time in two days. Two days. How many poor souls were locked up for months, years? Even a prison as benign as this one had started to act upon my mind, giving me fancies of being trapped, not being able to breathe, my limbs atrophying, my mind being stultified by the lack of intelligent conversation.

A moment later, Madame Fantin tiptoed from around the corner, put her finger to her lips, and gestured me to follow her. We wound through other corridors, going down stairs mostly but in one case up again, until I was sure she planned to leave me in a maze from which I would never be able to escape. But eventually, we came to a door. Not the one I entered through, but a small one that looked more like the door tradesmen would use in any other house. She held it open, and put her hand out, palm up.

She expects me to pay her! I realized with a start. I had no money at all on me. Just as I was to start explaining this to her, a plain carriage pulled up and the driver jumped down from the box. He put a heavy purse in Madame Fantin's hand, grabbed my violin and tossed it inside the carriage before handing me up.

I had hardly settled myself when I heard him cry, *"Allez!"* To the horses and crack his whip over their backs, throwing me against the cushion as the carriage tore off.

The curtains were drawn across the windows, and I peeked through one to see where we were going, but everything went by so fast that I couldn't read the street names etched into the buildings on the corners. We sped through the narrow lanes of Paris, scattering pedestrians and splashing through puddles that left cries of *"Merde!"* And *"Saloppe!"* in our wake, until at last the driver pulled up the horses. I heard a gate open and we passed through. So, we were going to a *hôtel particulier,* not an ordinary residence.

Somewhat shaken in all senses of the word, I took hold of the coachman's hand as he helped me down the step from the carriage. We had arrived at the grand entrance of a large residence, and standing at the top of the stairs to the main door of the house was Sophie Delalande.

"Don't look so surprised! I told you we'd meet again, didn't I? And what fun. All this secrecy and intrigue. But don't stand there, it's freezing out here! Come in and tell me all about it."

The connection, I discovered after talking to Sophie for near a half an hour, was difficult to understand at the very least.

"You know, my aunt, Madame de Montesson, is married to the fat old Duc d'Orléans. But she's not allowed to be his duchess, because her own rank isn't high enough. And he's old and, well, fat. So she has her own place, in the suburbs, and this house here in Paris. They were told they had to stay out of court circles. But really, I don't see what the big fuss is about being accepted at court! Everyone who is anyone comes here as well."

"I still don't understand why I'm here, exactly."

"Remember, at my aunt's salon, when I rescued you? From the duke, who you probably didn't realize at the time was her husband."

I most certainly did not realize it. I said, "Ah, I'm beginning to see. And the chevalier…"

"He is the music director of my aunt's private theater, as well as the director of the Concert Olympique, a private concert series at the Palais Royale. And, since we now know that you are accustomed to appearing on stage"—

"I beg your pardon?" One walk-on part in a play at Versailles, and suddenly I'm accustomed to appearing on stage?

"But really, what I'm saying is, seeing that you play the violin and that I think you'd like to become better acquainted with the chevalier, this is the perfect place for you to live. Don't you see?" She took my face between her hands. "Where were you living before, that you are so eager to return?" She gestured at the surroundings, knowing I'd probably be insane to pass up the opportunity she was offering me.

"Nowhere like this, I can assure you. But my work…"

"My aunt is one of mademoiselle Bertin's best customers. She can send around a note that she requires your services here for a time."

I wondered how Mademoiselle Bertin would react to such a thing. Perhaps she knew enough, I thought, to go along with it all.

I had no doubt that the captain would have acquainted her with the circumstances of my arrest and brief incarceration. "Very well," I said, and was rewarded with a genuine smile and a warm embrace.

"You must become friends with my aunt. She writes her own plays, you know. And her dear friend, Madame de Genlis, has written operettas that the chevalier sets to music."

I misjudged Sophie. Perhaps her frivolity was as much a disguise as my adopted French identity. It seems that through the bizarre machinations of the inscrutable captain, I had been tossed on the breeze and landed like a fallen leaf in precisely the place I would most wish to be while in Paris, and that somehow Sophie sensed it as well. If only it were my true purpose to absorb what I could of the musical world here—a world that I now saw was more accepting of women than the conservative, tradition-bound Viennese musical establishment—my accommodating godfather Haydn notwithstanding.

"But what a strange name for an orchestra. Olympique?" I had heard of the Concerts Spirituel, of course. Those had been public concerts. I learned to my chagrin when I arrived that due to budgetary and other constraints, those famed events no longer took place.

"Oh." Sophie fluttered her hands in the air as if shooing away a fly. "It's because of the lodge."

"The lodge?"

"You know, the Freemasons. Don't they have Freemasons in Vienna? My aunt belongs to the women's affiliate lodge here, the Nine Sisters."

This was truly remarkable. Women Freemasons? In Vienna—despite the best efforts of the emperor and Mozart, and nearly getting myself killed in the process of trying to discover what they were doing—even Jews were not allowed to be initiated into those supposedly liberal secret societies, dedicated to the improvement of mankind. Mankind. "I must speak to the chevalier. When may I do so? Do women also play in the orchestras?" A vista of immense opportunity opened up before me.

"Of course not. Don't be so silly."

And then, it closed once again. "So, how is it that I may play my violin here? If that is what you intended."

She took my arm and walked me around the large music room as she spoke—now empty of the guests that had made it seem even bigger the week before. "You must understand a few things if you are going to get on here. I know you're not from Paris. Your accent gives you away. Are you from the provinces?"

I repeated my lie about Alsace.

"Well, then. You already know a great deal about our fashions, from being in the workshop of Mademoiselle Rose, *n'est-ce pas?*"

I didn't say that I knew more than I ever cared to about fashions, as it happened.

"We must start by polishing you up a little. I have gowns enough for three ladies. Then I will get us invited to my cousin's palace."

"His palace?"

She sighed, perhaps she was becoming impatient with my apparent ignorance of all things Orléans. "The Palais Royale, of course. It's the hereditary home of the ducs d'Orléans, and also the home of the Freemason's lodge, which hosts the Concert Olympique."

And that was where I'd first heard the chevalier! It was all starting to connect in my mind, at last. Saint-Georges invited me to a salon at the home of the marquise de Montesson because he was the music director of her private theater. And he did so from the Palais Royale, where he was the music director of the Concert Olympique. "When shall we go?" I was ready to leave that very instant.

"The problem is that the duc de Chartres—he's the one who lives in the Palais Royale— objected very strongly to my aunt's marriage to his father, and barely tolerates her as it is. There were rumors for a time that my aunt—a virtuous woman, I assure you!—took the chevalier for her lover. She was a little younger then, but she is beautiful still. And the witches at Versailles will seize upon any crumb of slander to blacken the Orléans branch. But they had it all wrong. Really, that was Madame de Montalembert who had her eye on Saint-George, who begged and begged my aunt until she eventually gave in and allowed her to employ the chevalier as music director for her own theater for a few months."

My head was spinning with the names and the gossip. Was there nothing of interest to these Parisians besides who was having an affair with whom? And was the fabric of the musical world so tied up in such intrigues that one must know of them in order to understand what was going on? "So, if your aunt is out of favor with the duc de Chartres, your uncle by marriage, how exactly does this concern me? And I still don't understand what made you—or your uncle—arrange to have the lettre de cachet that sent me to the Bastille declared void."

Finally, we stopped our restless pacing and sat on one of the velvet-upholstered divans. "You have no idea, dear Thérèse, how tedious my life here was until you turned up in that ridiculous costume. I had already planned to seek you out after that, to lure you into my own life of parties and concerts and the opera so that I didn't have to be chaperoned all the time by my aunt, when we heard that you'd been dragged off to the Bastille. You must tell me all about that, by the way! How exciting. And dangerous."

"Hardly dangerous," I muttered.

"And further, that you'd been taken directly from the Petit Trianon, where the queen had been favoring you with her attention. I haven't been to Versailles. We're not welcome there."

She appeared genuinely sad about that. "I'm flattered that you think I am worth your trouble. I assure you, I am quite common and not at all interesting as a person."

Sophie cocked her head on one side and looked me up and down, finally settling her gaze on my eyes. I noticed that hers were a fine shade of blue, and that beneath the powder her blond hair curled beguilingly. "You, common? My dear Thérèse. You are most decidedly uncommon. You have an extraordinary talent—at least, I hope so—that could bridge the gulf between my uncle and his son. The chevalier, as a much-valued but nonetheless paid retainer, does not have that power. You, as my friend—we'll make up some claim to minor nobility for you—can seek out the chevalier, perhaps let him give you lessons or share his wisdom with you—and through him, bring us all closer to the duc de Chartres."

I began to have a sick feeling in my stomach. Sophie's enthusiasm was touching. But I was even more of a fraud than she had already guessed. In trying to bring about this thawing of relations between the two houses, she would be inserting me precisely where I needed to be in order to accomplish the spying that the captain wanted me to do. Had he foreseen this state of affairs? How could he have done so?

I didn't know for certain that I would find the source of the pamphleteering in the Palais Royale, but I did know that it was a distinct possibility, from what the captain told me about its immunity from the police.

Everything was becoming more and more twisted and complicated. Why could my life not be more normal? Why did the emperor have to send me here? He could have told the captain no, that he would send someone else, someone with more knowledge of the court and of Paris. For that matter, I could have refused to go.

Yes, on reflection I realized I had myself to blame. Once again, my curiosity, my desperate need to discover everything I could about the world and music, had gotten the better of my judgment. Now, I must make the best of it and try not to do anything that would endanger Sophie.

Chapter Fourteen

I met Sophie in the small breakfast room the next morning, after her maid had come into my chamber bearing an armful of gowns I was told Sophie no longer needed and helped me into a pearl silk robe a l'anglaise trimmed with lace. Before I could sit down at the breakfast table, Sophie made me pause and turn around so she could examine me head to toe.

"It's a little out of fashion, but that doesn't matter so much for daytime. We'll get some slippers made to fit your feet, but the ones you're wearing will do for now."

I wondered how she planned to make so free with her money on my behalf, and hoped my own more modest clothes had not been discarded or given to the servants. But I had to admit, I felt very elegant in Sophie's gown. The stays were not so tight that I couldn't breathe, and I wore a headdress on my powdered hair that wouldn't have been amiss in Mademoiselle Bertin's workshop. I wished I could show Lucienne and Ondine.

"So," Sophie said after taking a bite of her roll and several gulps of coffee, "I imagine you are quire eager to deepen your acquaintance with the Chevalier de Saint-Georges."

It took me a moment to adjust my mind to this unexpected diversion. "Yes, I would, but I hardly think it's necessary—"

"Let us see if my cousin Madame de Genlis can help us."

"Madame de Genlis?" I asked. To the best of my knowledge, she was simply the governess of the Duc de Chartres's children, although of noble birth herself and—according to Lucienne—very beautiful.

"She lives in an apartment in the Palais Royale, but she is not afraid to be my aunt's friend. In fact, any rapprochement between the two houses so far has been entirely her doing."

Sophie continued to explain the complicated interrelationships between the elder duke and his son and the various women in the households, past and present, until we finished our breakfast and prepared to present ourselves at the Palais Royale.

"I wonder that the chevalier has been so fortunate to have so many prestigious musical posts," I said after the breakfast things had been cleared away.

"He would have had more if it weren't for the color of his skin," Sophie said as she rang a bell for a maid.

"What do you mean?"

"He was appointed some time ago to be director of the Paris Opera. But three of the divas there went and complained to the court, saying that it demeaned them to take direction from someone of his race."

"What happened then?"

Sophie shrugged and said, "I gather the chevalier bowed out politely and went back to the Concerts Spirituel. A pity we have to cover ourselves with heavy cloaks." The maid had appeared and draped one over each of our shoulders.

I, on the other hand, was grateful for it, having still not entirely shaken the chill I'd endured on my rough ride from Versailles to the Bastille. Besides, the weather had indeed fulfilled its promise to be fierce. It was not yet December, and several inches of snow already frosted many of the buildings in Paris, softening their contours and hiding the ubiquitous dirt. The constant foot and carriage traffic had cleared the snow from the cobbles, though, making them dangerously slick. Because of that the carriage took longer than I expected to convey us the short distance to the residence of the Duc de Chartres.

"Madame de Genlis," Sophie said to the guard as she presented him with her calling card through the open window of the carriage.

He bowed and handed the card to a footman, directing the coachman to enter the inner courtyard where we were deposited at a grand door. "Is this all the same building?" I asked, trying hard not to reveal how intimidated I was starting to feel.

Sophie didn't answer, but smiled at me, squeezed my arm, and whispered, "What I didn't tell you before is that Madame de Genlis was once the lover of the duc de Chartres."

I stopped walking. "And she lives in the house with him and his duchess?"

Sophie shrugged. "Their passion has cooled, although apparently the duke still has a tattoo on his arm that bears her name."

I thought about how such a thing would shock the more conservative social circles of Vienna. Even in the ranks of the nobility, no one would dare such a brazen act. I don't know what I expected to find when I met this femme fatale exactly, but it wasn't a beautiful young woman with eyes like a fawn and bow-shaped lips, modestly dressed in a pale pink morning gown.

"Sophie! How lovely to see you."

They kissed on the cheeks and turned to me. I curtsied.

"This is my new, great friend, Thérèse Sauvé. She is visiting from Alsace, where her relations are landowners of some renown."

"*Je suis ravie*, Madame de Genlis," I said, not rising from my curtsy until she took my hand and pulled me to my feet.

"Please, call me Félicité, at least within these walls."

I choked back a laugh, thinking how far removed she was from the other Félicité who had helped me leave the Bastille.

She rang a little bell and requested tea and cakes, and we sat in upholstered chairs near the fire in her comfortable boudoir.

"Thérèse plays the violin, and it's all she talks about, strange girl," Sophie said after pleasantries were exchanged. "But I suppose I must indulge her passion by introducing her to the chevalier, whom she heard perform at my aunt's salon a week ago. Unfortunately, he is not currently in rehearsal for anything in my aunt's theater. So I was wondering..." She let the request hang in the air, a smile on her lips.

"You want to attend this evening's Concert Olympique?"

"I knew you would understand!"

We left an hour later with the coveted badge in our hands, and assurances that we would be welcome to visit anytime.

The cold weather did not dampen the enthusiasm among society guests for the Concert Olympique that evening, nor did it reduce the size of the audience at all. Carriages queued up along the street and entered the courtyard to discharge their occupants, who had taken advantage of the cold to flaunt not only their jewels, but furs. I saw fox, ermine, marmot, miniver, and lots of rabbit trimming on collars and hoods. The men favored wolf and beaver—an expensive import from America. The cold weather also didn't interfere with the wearing of large hats with clusters of feathers on them, and I found the combination of fur and feather rather amusing.

We entered the elegant salon—there must have been a thousand people there—and took seats nearly at the back. I was afraid I wouldn't be able to see well, but the stage was raked to make it easier for those seated far away to watch what transpired upon it. It wasn't an opera that evening, but a few arias and vignettes and some instrumental works, according to the programs we'd been handed on our way in.

Programs. Printing. A short step to a scurrilous pamphlet, I thought. Perhaps a few judicious questions might reveal some useful information.

I'm sure Sophie didn't enjoy the concert as much as I did, especially when the chevalier performed a beautiful solo on the violin. It was not flashy and virtuosic, just deliciously tuneful, and I noticed that I was not the only one in the theater to have to take a handkerchief out of my pocket and dabbed at the corners of my eyes...

Then, as sighs still resonated around the audience, the chevalier did something quite extraordinary. A footman brought out a chair and a guitar, and he sat in it and strummed and sang. A guitar! He had a beautiful, deep voice, and the song spoke of warm breezes and sensual love. After the first verse, he rose, left the stage, and wandered among the audience. He strolled wherever he could find the room to pass among the listeners—the ladies, I noticed, made sure he could find a clear passage through near where they sat. He smiled at the most influential of them, and I thought he would go back on the stage once his song was finished, but instead, he re-tuned the guitar and started again, coming farther back, toward us.

"He's coming this way!" Sophie whispered so loudly in my ear that everyone around us turned to stare.

But she was right. He was coming toward us. I held my breath. Surely he'd pass by! But no, he paused at the end of the row where we sat and looked directly at me as he sang and strummed. I thought he gave me the faintest nod just before turning and making his way back to the stage. When he finished and bowed, the audience gave a collective "Ah!" And then rose to its feet and applauded.

The chevalier held up his hand to quiet everyone. "Mesdames et Messieurs, the next work we will perform is my latest concerto for the violin and orchestra. We shall pause for a few moments to recharge the chandeliers and so that you may stretch your legs and refresh yourselves in the reception room."

Chairs scraped in a raucous chorus as everyone left the theater for its transformation into a concert hall, and so that the servants could lower the chandeliers and replace the guttering candles.

"Whatever transpires after this," I said to Sophie, "I will remain forever grateful to you for bringing me here." Indeed, I felt as if I could close my eyes and not wake up again and my life would have been complete.

Well, almost complete. A vision of Zoltan's face flickered in my mind, and I felt a sudden pang of guilt. The chevalier was very handsome, but very much older. He was certainly an accomplished violinist, though, more so than Zoltan. I also guessed that, if the two were ever to meet in a duel, Zoltan would not come out unscathed.

A duel. What on earth was I thinking? Duels were illegal in Paris, just as they were in Vienna. Arguments of honor were more likely to be settled in a fencing ring with blunted sabers.

We returned to the salon for the second half of the concert after a couple of glasses of wine, and between Sophie's constant chatter and pointing out who was there—including the infamous duc de Chartres, who was a younger, less portly version of his father the duc d'Orléans—

my head was spinning. It wasn't spinning too much to notice, however, that all the men in the orchestra wore full court dress, with their hats and ceremonial swords placed on the benches next to them.

"Why is that?" I asked Sophie as we were settling back into our seats.

"Oh, it's required at any concert open to the public. It's in case the queen shows up unannounced. She's not very likely to come here, though, is she!"

The concerto was everything I expected it to be, and more. The virtuosic passages were so brilliant, I couldn't even imagine Danior being able to play them. At the end I stood and applauded rapturously, mixing my bravos with those of the entire audience.

When the last bit of applause died down, I prepared to exit the concert hall, but Sophie grabbed my arm and pulled me in the opposite direction.

"Don't you want to greet the chevalier?" She asked, knowing full well I would answer yes.

We made our way toward the stage to the door the musicians were filing through, no doubt eager to mop their sweating faces and take off their itchy wigs. We weren't the only ones, of course. Quite a bevy of dazzlingly dressed ladies hid behind their fans as they waited to go and congratulate the maestro before he disappeared into the bowels of the palace.

Seeing the crush, I had second thoughts and held Sophie back.

She struggled against my restraining hand. "We'll miss him! He'll go off to his private apartment, I'm sure," she said, tears in her voice.

But something told me we wouldn't miss him. I watched him pretend to be focused solely on whichever aristocratic lady was in front of him at the moment, but his eyes flicked up now and again as if he was looking for someone, or waiting for someone. I didn't think it was me. After all, our acquaintance was slight enough to be nearly nonexistent. But so long as he wanted to see someone who had yet to arrive, I imagined he wouldn't leave.

We crept along with the crowd until we were only about three rows of admirers away. It was then that the chevalier looked up and saw us. Our eyes met for no more than an instant, but in that instant, I realized that it was, indeed, I he was waiting for. But why? Madame de Genlis perhaps mentioned Sophie's and my visit to her to beg for the coveted badges. And of course, he did see I was there when he went strolling through the audience singing romantic songs and making the ladies swoon with delight. But why would he single me out in that way, other than the fact that he knew I was also a violinist? Did he know anything more about me? Could there be some link between him and the captain I did not know about? The captain had surprised me again and again, and I was beginning to think he had some magical ability to see through walls and into people's minds.

I had little time to ponder the matter, however, because rather than wait for me to come to him, the chevalier politely but insistently pushed through the remaining ladies—clearly not the most aristocratic ones, judging by the simplicity of their gowns and the meager sparkle of their jewels—until he reached me.

He bowed, and when he righted himself, his warm, brown eyes looked down into mine and he said, "I heard you were coming, and I'm glad you have sought me out. We have much to discuss. Please wait for me in the reception room."

I could feel the eyes like poison-tipped darts following Sophie and me as we left the remaining sycophants behind. My heart fluttered about like a captured butterfly. What did we have to discuss? Music, of course, I thought. But his eyes held something more in them, and I began to understand how this man from the islands, son of a slave woman, could exert such power over even the highest-born ladies.

It was no more than a quarter of an hour before he emerged from the chamber behind the stage. In that time, he'd removed his sweat-stained silk jacket and waistcoat and put on a less formal dressing gown. He had also removed the white wig he'd been required to wear for the concert, and his black curls held tight to the contours of his head in a fashion so foreign I had to stop myself from staring.

"I apologize that you had to wait. I regret that you were forced to endure the mob of courtiers and enthusiasts who seek to associate themselves with me only because I am the fashion—not because they are true connoisseurs. In other words, they are nothing like you, Mademoiselle Thérèse."

"Sophie, too, appreciates music deeply, do you not?" I said, sensing my friend's pique at being left out of his flattering attentions.

"*Naturellement*," she said, lifting her chin and flashing a beguiling smile in the chevalier's direction.

"Ah! Do you also play the violin? Or some other instrument perhaps?" He turned to Sophie with genuine interest.

"Alas, no. But that does not mean I do not value music above all the other arts."

I quickly interjected, "I am here solely through Mademoiselle Sophie's good graces. She is the one who knew how much it would mean for me to hear your magnificent performance." I hoped he would understand that, music lover or not, he must include Sophie in the conversation.

"Of course," he said, with a smile that encompassed us both. "Shall we?" He swept his hand toward a door that led out of the public areas, indicating that we were both to follow him. I gave him a grateful look.

We walked some distance through corridors and climbed two sets of stairs until we were at the corner end of the palace on the top floor. I realized we had arrived at the apartment where I must have heard him playing the violin the first time.

His room was not grand, but comfortably furnished, the walls lined with shelves of books and music manuscripts. In the corner stood a pianoforte. I wandered over to it. "It's a Walther," I said.

The chevalier sat on the stool at the keyboard and began to play. Sophie and I listened for a few minutes as he performed for us. Is he an adept on every instrument he touches? I wondered. "That was beautiful." I couldn't find the words to say anything else.

"*Ça vous plait?*" He asked, as if he genuinely cared about my answer.

"Very much."

"It's the theme of the symphony I am composing. But you must be tired. Please sit."

We arranged ourselves on the upholstered chairs. He rang a little bell and a maid appeared. "Tea, I think?" He looked to us both for confirmation. We nodded in unison. "And some cakes, too."

All had been easy and comfortable to that point. But as soon as he started to ask me questions about my musical training, I realized I was wading into dangerous waters.

"My father taught me," I said, hoping to avoid more specificity.

"What method did he use?"

"Leopold Mozart, of course!" I said. I was about to volunteer the information that I was well acquainted with his brilliant son, Amadé, and bit back the comment before it was too late.

"She knows all about the different violins," Sophie said, her opinion of me rising with every additional mark of interest on the part of the chevalier.

"Truly? Who is the maker of your own instrument?"

I sighed. I didn't know who made Danior's violin. Someone in Vienna. It was a fine instrument, but nothing like the violin that he was keeping safe for me while I was away. "My father left me a beautiful Amati, but I had to leave it behind, in—Alsace." I stopped myself just in time.

"Ah! The finest! I know there are those who believe a Stradivari is superior, but I prefer the warmer tone of the Amati. You are fortunate indeed to possess one of the few that exist outside of Italy." He rose and approached an open violin case on a table across the room. He lifted the instrument out of the case, and I recognized it immediately as the one he had played at the concert.

He quickly tuned it, then tightened the horse hairs of his bow. I expected him to play for us, and eagerly settled back for a private concert, when instead he held the instrument out to me.

My expression of confusion made him laugh. "It's all right! I am a teacher as well. I do not expect you to be a virtuoso, but I can see how your eyes yearn to touch this extraordinary wooden box."

I stood and walked over to him and took the offered violin. It felt familiar and yet different in my arms. The contours were the same, the tone of the varnish slightly darker. I stroked the bow across the open strings first, then played a few quick scales. After that, the only thing I could think of was the melody from The Abduction from the Seraglio that I thought I'd heard a fragment of in the chevalier's performance at Madame de Montesson's salon. The sound filled the chamber and looped around me, enveloping me. I closed my eyes and imagined myself back in Danior and Alida's apartment, performing for a private audience.

When I finished, silence. The chevalier must have thought it terrible and was trying to think of something good to say. I looked over to Sophie. Her mouth hung open in surprise. I'm not certain what she expected. I imagine she thought young ladies were not supposed to bare their souls so utterly in front of strangers.

The chevalier spoke first. "Mademoiselle Thérèse. You are not a proficient..."

Oh dear, he's going to criticize me and tell me to give up, I thought.

"...You are an artist."

Tears sprang to my eyes as I handed him back his instrument. He took a lace-edged handkerchief out of his pocket and dabbed a few of their traces off my cheeks before handing it to me to finish the job. I laughed, and it broke the spell.

"I wish I could have you play in my orchestra, but as you see, only men are allowed. It's vexing!" He placed the violin back in his case and paced up and down the room.

I so wanted to say to him, But I can! I do it all the time in Vienna! I simply hide my hair under a wig and wear a man's uniform. But I couldn't utter those words, not if I wanted to protect the secret of my identity.

"At least... Would you be willing to perform with me in a small chamber ensemble? The string quartet is not so much valued here in Paris as it is elsewhere, but I have some fellow musicians who gather here every week to play. I think they would not be unwilling to allow you to join us."

I could hardly speak. "M-Merci!" I said. "Of course, if you think I am good enough to be part of your quartet."

"Do you really have so little idea of your own capabilities? I must find out who your father was and where he studied. The French manner of playing is so much less precise than the Italian, which is Mozart's style."

Although I foresaw some danger in spending more time with this captivating virtuoso—danger that his keen ear would figure out my accent; danger that I would slip and say something about playing in Vienna—I could not turn down the opportunity to make music with the Chevalier de Saint-Georges.

We said our good nights, and Sophie and I climbed into the carriage that would take us through the icy night the short distance back to the Chaussée d'Antin. My head was spinning, and my ears rang with music. This was more than I'd hoped for when I found out the emperor was sending me to Paris! If only I could spend the rest of my time doing nothing but making music in the chevalier's quiet retreat, high above the swirling mass of treachery and gossip that occupied every corner of every elegant dwelling in this city.

Chapter Fifteen

The first couple of days after the concert, I awoke at my normal time—around seven—to a house that was still asleep except for the maids who laid the fires and the cooks and menials who prepared all the meals of the day. I dressed myself in my own clothes and wandered about the rooms Sophie had shown me. I was aware that many more rooms existed in that elegant *hôtel particulier*, including two mirroring suites where Madame de Montesson lived and received her private guests, and where the duc d'Orléans could do the same. I say could, because the terms of his union with Sophie's aunt were that—because of her much lower (but still noble) rank—he could not share a domicile with her. He built his own equally magnificent house nearby, but spent all his days at the Hôtel Montesson, returning to his own house only to sleep.

Sophie had her own suite, as did another distant and much older cousin. Those guest apartments consisted of a bedroom and a dressing room, a reception room, a card room, and a bathing chamber. Sophie's suite alone would have accommodated my entire family easily. I had separate, much more modest accommodations in a large bedroom with a small dressing room attached.

I knew there was a library somewhere, but Sophie had not yet shown it to me. She didn't appear to be much interested in reading. She possessed only a few books, scattered haphazardly around her private sitting room. The latest issue of the fashion gazette was always well thumbed, and tucked away where her aunt couldn't find them were some novels by Choderlos de Laclos. I picked one up one morning, thinking to pass the time in a more productive manner, and found myself blushing uncontrollably by the second chapter. No wonder she hid the books.

While waiting for Sophie to rise at her usual hour of ten, I passed some time in studying the beautifully printed program from the Concert Olympique. I was interested in the names of the pieces that had been performed, and also the list of musicians on the back. But I paid attention as well to the paper, the colors of the ink, and the style of the letters. A printer who could produce such a lovely document would have no trouble churning out the flimsy, mistake-ridden pamphlets handed out in the gardens of the Palais Royale. I suspected the printer would be easier to find than the author, though.

Still, the one could lead to the other, and so I decided that discovering the source of the programs for the Concert Olympique was as good a place to start as any. I had an idea about how I might go about such a thing, but it would require Sophie's cooperation. At the moment, she seemed interested only in pumping me for knowledge about Mademoiselle Bertin and dressing me up in all her last-year's gowns as if I were a life-size doll for her to play with. I tolerated it all, grateful to be out of the Bastille and equally grateful for her efforts to connect me with the chevalier. She also gave me an hour alone every afternoon, while she dressed for the evening, to practice the violin. I had persuaded her that the better I acquitted myself when joining the chevalier's quartet, the more likely it was that we would be invited to other private entertainments at the Palais Royale.

I hadn't yet heard anything from Saint-Georges by the time I woke up on the third early morning on the Chaussée-d'Antin. I had exhausted the limited resources for solitary entertainment in my room and Sophie's suite, and so decided to explore beyond those confines. I went into all the more public rooms—including the music room where the salon I'd attended had taken place, and I managed to find the library as well. I took down a few books and thumbed through the pages, vowing to return at another time. In the gallery, I walked all the way around the portrait busts and other sculptures on pedestals here and there, and peered at the many paintings on the walls. They were portraits of Madame de Montesson's relations and ancestors I assumed.

The large card room, by contrast, was decorated with paintings of ladies and their swains swinging or enjoying picnics in some imagined verdant countryside. Without the illumination of candles, the dreary winter light made most of the pictures look dingy and dull.

I hadn't yet seen Madame's private theater and very much wanted to do so. Apparently she suspended her programs for a few months so as not to compete with the public concerts and the presentations of the *Concert Olympique*, so the theater was dark and deserted until rehearsals began for her Lenten concerts and operas. Since public theaters were closed during Lent, there was less competition, and she could be certain her theater would be full for every performance with aristocrats and nobles desiring any form of entertainment to banish the boredom of long winter nights.

I suppose I could have asked one of the ubiquitous maids to direct me to the theater, but I had a general idea of where it would be and decided to add an element of challenge to the exercise by figuring out on my own how to get there. Since Madame de Montesson loved to put on plays and operas with scenery and machines, the theater would have to have very high ceilings. That meant it most certainly occupied space on the ground floor and below, and extended up through at least the first floor above it. I had in my mind the small but sumptuous theater at the Petit Trianon, which was taller than it was wide or deep.

Down I went, past storage rooms and the kitchens. I almost gave up my search to follow the beguiling scent of baking bread. I hadn't yet had breakfast. I didn't feel right eating before Sophie did, since I wasn't entirely certain of my status in the house. When I continued past the temptation, my stomach growled in protest.

Eventually, I came to a door that I thought must be an entrance to the wings of the theater. Down there I was completely alone, and the light was dim. Although there were windows on one side of the corridor, they were shuttered to keep out the brutal cold. Wishing I had brought a warmer shawl, I grasped the door handle and pressed down to lift the latch on the other side, hoping it wasn't locked.

The latch was stiff, but it lifted with a metallic chunk, and I pulled the door open.

Instead of stepping into the wings of a theater with their bits of scenery and ropes and pulleys, a blast of cold wind hit me and nearly knocked me backwards. I had opened a door to another long corridor, but I was pretty sure this one led not under the house, but underground. To where, I had no idea, and I had not come prepared with a torch or even a candle to light my way.

I struggled to shut the door again. Horrible memories of fleeing through the sewers of Vienna flashed through my mind. Were there similar sewers in Paris? I assumed not, having seen servants emptying chamber pots into gutters that ran through the streets and presumably down to the Seine. I would have to find a way to bring up such an unsavory subject with Sophie, if I could do it without awakening her curiosity too much.

In any case, I wasn't about to venture down into an unknown region without at least some preparation. And, with a sensitive task ahead of me, I would have to make sure to do it in a way that didn't arouse undue curiosity. I had already spent enough time wandering into areas inhabited by servants, and so decided I should return upstairs and see if Sophie had awakened.

Later, after we'd broken our fast and while Sophie was engaged in the serious business of deciding what to wear for the evening's entertainments, I said, "I thought I'd take a look at the theater. I'm curious about it, you know?"

"Why on earth? A theater that's dark, when there are no players, no rush lights, no people dressed in their finest jewels with headdresses they paid a king's ransom for—why on earth would you want to see such a thing?"

It did seem a little tedious the way she put it. Yet I needed to discover whether the passageway I had found was anywhere near the theater. It had occurred to me that it might somehow be connected to it. "Have you ever acted on the stage? Taken part in a play? Given a recital?"

"No, of course not. No lady would do such a thing." She looked away from me when she said it, and I saw a hint of a frown.

"No lady would play the violin, either. Yet I dare to do so."

I smiled at her. At first, she kept her face turned away. But I could see her looking at me out of the corner of her eye in the mirror.

"No one need ever know."

"How silly! What would I do? I don't sing well enough to entertain my aunt's guests."

I heard a wistful note in her voice. How well I understood that feeling of not being good enough, of being dismissed because I was a girl. I had found a way around it, but clearly, Sophie had not. Even if she never did it again, the point was to have dared it. "You don't have to sing well enough to entertain. You simply have to sing well enough to enjoy it. Why not? What else is there to do on such a cold, dreary day?" I knew that would strike a note of sympathy in her. We'd been prevented by the extreme cold from visiting for two days, and already she was restless and out of sorts. "I imagine we might find some costumes somewhere down there, and could perhaps have some fun dressing up."

She looked away and her shoulders sagged. "Playing at such a thing is for children. I am no longer a child."

"How old are you?" I asked.

"Sixteen."

Nearly three years younger than I was, and already so weighed down by what the world expected of her. She had told me when we first met that she'd been sent to Paris to find a suitable husband. A husband! Apparently her mother and her aunt had several candidates in mind. Even at my age, I didn't quite feel ready to take that leap, and I knew someone whose arms I should by all accounts be rushing into. Yet I wasn't, for reasons not entirely clear to me. If I wasn't ready, how could Sophie be? She made a great show of being obsessed with all things superficial, yet I sensed that at the concert she had been moved as well. When we were in the chevalier's apartment afterwards, it wasn't just his dashing presence that had kept her enthralled. I could see it in her silent attention as I played. "Well, whatever anyone else thinks, you are still young. And I am your guest, and I need to be entertained. So, I would deem it an honor if you would escort me to the theater where we can create our own spectacle, solely for our own amusement. I shall bring my violin, and you shall bring your voice!"

❧❧❧

Sophie conducted me down to the theater not through the servants' quarters or past the kitchen, but through a door from the music room that led to an elegant, curved stairway. I guessed that it was the route those who had been invited to supper after the performance would take to enter the private living quarters of the Hôtel Montesson. We entered via the door at the back of the audience into a beautiful theater that rivaled the queen's. Where hers had been decorated in shades of blue, however, Madame de Montesson's was a jewel box of dusty rose and gilt. From high on either side, windows let in filtered daylight, making it possible for us to see to make our way to the stage and the wings.

To my surprise, Sophie seemed well acquainted with the machinery in the wings, and quickly found the great ropes that would open the heavy velvet curtain. "Don't just stand there!" She said, and I rushed over to lend my strength to pull the curtain open.

There would be no rush lights, of course, but that didn't matter. "Do you know where the costumes are stored?" I asked.

"Of course!" Sophie said, and led me behind the stage to a half-dozen dressing rooms. Each of them had chests full of costumes in them, and we soon lost track of time in childish play as we became everything from shepherdesses to oriental potentates.

"Let's go and act out a scene, or play some music!" I said when we'd tired of that activity. I'd left my violin in the wings and was eager to sample the acoustics of the theater.

I tuned my instrument and played a spirited country dance as Sophie skipped around the stage in time to it. When I switched to a romantic ballad, she mimed a love scene so well I had to stop playing when I could no longer suppress my laughter.

"You're a real actress!" I said as she swept an extravagant bow in my direction. "Now, it's time for you to sing."

"Sing?" Sophie said, the light suddenly draining from her eyes.

"Yes! Why not? We are entirely alone here. No one will hear you, and I promise not to be critical."

She went to the edge of the stage and checked to make sure the stalls and the boxes were completely empty, then into each of the wings to examine them as well. When she found no one, she returned to the center of the stage and cleared her throat. "What shall I sing?" She asked.

"What's your favorite song?"

She thought for a moment, then smiled. I lifted my violin to my shoulder, prepared to accompany her, but without warning, she opened her mouth and out came the tender notes of a beautiful ballad.

As I listened, her voice grew stronger. I lowered my violin and stood mesmerized. Sophie could sing. She could really sing. Her soprano voice was clear and the notes perfect. It occurred to me that she must have had some training. Why had she been so reluctant?

After the ballad finished, we played some popular airs from Grétry's latest opera, which she seemed to know quite well, although she'd never said that she'd attended the opera in Paris. I suppose she must have, though, since everyone did, whether they liked opera or not.

When we finished the last one, Sophie said, "Could we try Iphigénie's air?"

This request took me by surprise. "It's very difficult," I said, not sure that I remembered it well enough to play it myself. The image of Herr Gluck, such a wonderful composer, sitting in his office back in Vienna handing me music to copy made me smile.

"You said it doesn't matter. No one's here to listen." Sophie's voice rang out with confidence and echoed in the empty theater.

She was right. We could do whatever we wanted. "All right. Do you need the note?" I wasn't even sure I knew what key it was in.

Before I could lift my violin to my shoulder again, Sophie started singing. And to my amazement, she found precisely the right pitch. I joined in to accompany her as best I could, letting her light, pure voice take charge as it gained strength and took on the contours of deep emotion. This air, more than any of the others we'd attempted, consumed Sophie. Before my eyes, in the dim twilight of a theater illuminated only by whatever afternoon sunlight found its way from the windows high above, this débutante transformed into a character from Greek mythology. As I listened to the words of this air from an opera about Iphigenia and and her brother Orestes, it occurred to me that I'd never asked Sophie whether she had a brother or a sister. The thought of putting myself and Toby in that circumstance, of nearly having to sacrifice him to the gods as Iphigenia must in the opera—it was unthinkable.

Sophie held the last note. When her breath gave out, I put down my violin. We looked at each other, and I could swear I saw the sparkle of a tear in her eyes. I was about to say something, when we were both startled by loud clapping. It came from a single person, standing at the back of the dark audience. Sophie looked horrified.

Before I had a chance to say anything, a figure stepped down the aisle in our direction.

It was the chevalier.

I didn't know whether to be relieved, or confused, or terrified. He cut an imposing figure there, the darkness of his skin blending into the dim depths of the orchestra, rendering him nearly faceless until he smiled. He looked even taller, somehow, and in his waistcoat and shirtsleeves, I could see his muscles and was suddenly aware of the physical power he possessed.

"So, there are two musicians residing in Madame de Montesson's *hôtel particulier*. Why did you say nothing the other night, Mademoiselle Sophie?"

By now, the chevalier had reached us, and I could see him clearly enough to discern the kind expression of his eyes. I let out the breath I'd been holding.

"You mustn't say anything to my aunt! I promised my mother I would not sing." The confident Sophie of a moment before was gone. She sounded genuinely frightened.

I wanted to ask Sophie why her mother would force such a promise from her, why she would deny such a talent, bury it under her conventional role as an heiress looking for a mate who will elevate her rank in society. But I sensed that such confidences would not be appropriate to share with a gentleman within hearing. And why should she trust me with them anyway? I was hiding as much—perhaps even more—than she was. So instead, I changed the subject.

"Where did you come from, Monsieur Le Chevalier? I didn't hear the door open at the back, and we would have seen you come in through the wings." I tried to make my tone light and merely curious, but something told me secrets were involved.

"Ah! You did not know?" He looked from one to the other of us. "When I became music director for the Concert Olympique, and retained my position here as Madame de Montesson's music director, my mistress had an underground tunnel dug to connect the two theaters, so that I could, if required, conduct two performances in a single night."

I couldn't help it. I laughed. The idea of the chevalier in his full court attire dashing through a long underground passage and popping up at the other end without a fiber of his wig disturbed seemed the height of absurdity. "And has this unlikely event occurred?" I asked.

"Thankfully, no," he said, and all three of us laughed.

I wondered. Could this passage he spoke of be the one I'd discovered earlier that morning? It would explain its location, somewhat near the theater. I found it difficult to credit his explanation for the existence of such a passage, though. I was certain it had been dug for another reason altogether, and that he'd come up with his reason on the spur of the moment. Something made me believe the chevalier was acquainted with the real reason for the existence of the underground tunnel, but I held my tongue.

In any case, now that I knew for certain where the passage led, and also knew that someone could travel its length unscathed, I decided right then that I would explore it myself. Late that same night, after everyone had gone to bed—this time with a stout candle to light the way, I would retrace my steps to the door I'd stumbled on and see where it went.

Why did my adventures always seem to lead me into circumstances like this? I really hated the dark and hated being enclosed. I guess my curiosity has always been just enough stronger than my fear to make me brave. And possibly also foolish.

Chapter Sixteen

For the rest of the day, Sophie was very quiet. When I tried to talk to her about music again, to tell her how wonderful I thought it was that she could sing so well, she changed the subject as if she hadn't quite understood what I was talking about. I could only press her so hard, since I really barely knew her and hadn't even known of her aunt's connection to the house of Orléans until four days ago, when she orchestrated my deliverance from the Bastille and explained it to me.

I had so many questions.

When Sophie went to her room to change for the evening's entertainment—a card party—I quickly changed into one of her cast-off dresses and then sat at the little escritoire, took a sheet of the fine paper, trimmed a quill, and started to write down what I had discovered so far. It was dangerous to fix the words to paper, I knew, but things had become so complicated and confusing I could no longer hold it all in my head. The threads didn't just intertwine, they tangled and knotted.

I marked a half-hour's burning on my candle so I wouldn't lose track of the time, and started writing, in tiny script so I would fill no more than a page and could easily destroy my work.

1. The duc de Chartres—who will be duc d'Orléans when his fat, ailing father dies—detests the king and queen.

2. The duc de Chartres also dislikes his stepmother, who is Sophie's aunt, and who is not styled the duchesse d'Orléans because she is of too low a rank

3. Also because of the difference in rank, the duc d'Orléans—who is not so unfriendly to the queen as is his son—may not live in the Palais Royale, ordinarily his privilege as the senior member of the house of Orléans. So he vacated it for his son, gave his wife this

magnificent *hôtel particulier* with its own private theater, and built his own house around the corner.

4. Madame de Genlis used to be the lover of the duc de Chartres, and is now governess of his children and lives in an apartment in the Palais Royale. She acts as mediator between the two estranged Orléans houses—I know not exactly why—and is very kind. Sophie and I would not have been able to attend the Concert Olympique if she hadn't given us her subscription badge.

I lifted the quill to dip it afresh in the ink, and paused. So far nothing I had noted led directly back to Versailles, except for the continuing enmity of the duc de Chartres. But he never went to Versailles, as far as I knew, and certainly wouldn't be invited to pass among the queen's intimates at the Petit Trianon. So who was it who had arrived and given the note alleging the queen's affair to one of the guests?

One thing common to all three residences, though, was the existence of a theater, where there were performances of operas and symphonies and plays. Had all the actors in the play I'd been in at the Petit Trianon been courtiers? Or were there some professional players among them, players who would be hired to perform at the theater in the Palais Royale or here on the Chaussée d'Antin? I recalled that everyone appeared to be acquainted with one another except for me, but the peculiar informality of the Petit Trianon blurred distinctions of rank, so it was hard to know.

There had to be a connection I wasn't yet seeing. I couldn't help thinking it all had something to do with the Chevalier de Saint-Georges. Even if the secret passage hadn't been dug simply for his convenience, he knew where it was, and was clearly familiar enough with it to think nothing of using it. I continued writing.

5. The Chevalier de Saint-Georges is music director of both the private theater of Madame de Montesson and the Concert Olympique—an orchestra disguised as a Masonic lodge in order to avoid the necessity of being under the jurisdiction of the Paris police. Could he have something to do with the pamphlets?

How very convenient, I thought. The Palais Royale was sovereign property, and therefore off-limits to the police. If the pamphleteer sought shelter within its walls, there would be no way to bring him— or her—to justice. At least, not while they were on the premises.

And another puzzle: why had the chevalier come to Madame de Montesson's theater that morning? She had no plans for any performances until Lent, so she said. Sophie and I had both been so surprised that we hadn't thought to ask him.

A drop of ink plopped from the nib of my quill onto the paper. I watched it spread, the threads curling away from it, draining its substance but increasing its reach in a web that kept crawling away until its ends absorbed into the paper. It spread like gossip, becoming more twisted and incomprehensible the farther it got from its source.

I looked up and noticed that my candle had burned down below the mark I had put on it. Time to destroy my notes.

I had just torn the paper in half and risen to take it to the fire in the grate when I heard Sophie's quick steps coming toward the door of my guest chamber. Should I proceed, and provoke her curiosity by being caught in the act of burning what appeared to be a letter when she entered? Or should I simply hide the paper beneath the pile of books on the desk, and hope that no one had reason to discover it before I came back after the card party?

"There you are! I've been waiting for you." Sophie rushed over and took my arm, thankfully not noticing that I'd tucked a piece of paper just out of sight. "What have you been doing? This is no time for writing letters!" Without asking, she placed the top back on the ink bottle and tossed the quill into its stand, took my hands and inspected them for ink stains. "You'll do." She said.

Her eyes were bright with excitement. "What is it?" I asked.

"He's here. My aunt told me."

"Who's here?"

"You'll see. He's a marquis, and very wealthy, and he wants to marry me."

"Have you been carrying on a correspondence?" I was amazed I knew so little about Sophie. Less and less, it seemed.

"Don't be silly! We've never met each other. But to be married—to be free."

She appeared to genuinely believe that marriage would free her, but I had no idea from what. Her life seemed quite idyllic here in Paris, in her aunt's sumptuous household.

"You look especially lovely tonight," I said, noticing that she had taken more care than usual with her appearance. Her cheeks were pink where she had applied rouge and then rubbed it off. I could imagine her sitting before her glass, frowning as her lady's maid powdered her hair and curled it into its current confection, with pearls and ribbons threaded through.

"Thank you," she said, and I knew she meant it. "Thank you, as well, for not trying too hard to draw notice to yourself. I fear you would outshine me if my maid could have the dressing of your hair."

I wasn't certain whether I should take what she said as a compliment or not. I thought I was as elegantly dressed and well-turned-out as I'd ever been, even if my only ornament was the silver cross on a thin silk ribbon that my mother had given me last Christmas. I was not accustomed to fine lace trimming on my sleeves and décolletage, and the crisp, pale-blue silk of my gown whispered expensively as I moved in it.

"Come!" Sophie said, and grabbed hold of my hand to drag me out of the room. I glanced back to see if the paper I'd had barely enough time to hide was sufficiently out of sight, and was chagrined to see just the corner of it poking out from beneath the book I'd pushed it under. Well, it was unlikely anyone other than a chamber maid would enter before I returned, and then she would just turn down the covers on my narrow bed and stoke the fire. She probably couldn't read anyway, I thought.

"You seem distracted," Sophie said, now a little breathless because we'd run through the corridors that led from the wing with the private suites to the interlinked rooms where company gathered. "Are you worried about something?"

The murmur of voices grew as we approached. "No! Of course not." I wasn't worried, or was I? Why was Sophie being so kind to me, someone she had never met before I stumbled into her aunt's salon? Every time I had tried to ask her why she had helped me, why she had gone to such lengths to have me released from the Bastille into her custody, she waved her hands, shooing away the question, and turned the conversation to other topics.

Now, she clutched my hand with her cold, clammy fingers as if letting go would release her into the depths and she would drown. We stopped dead just before we came to the door beyond which we could hear laughter and the indistinct chatter of high and low voices. Sophie turned me toward her and took my face between her two hands, pressing my cheeks so that I could feel the imprint of her gold rings. Her eyes, normally lit with the possibility of laughter, drilled into mine, serious and dark. I caught a glimpse of the sorrow I had detected in them after she sang the air from Iphigénie, but there was something more. Deep inside, just the slightest corner peeking out of wherever she tried to hide it, fear glimmered.

"Promise me, whatever happens, you'll stay by my side."

What could she imagine would happen? "Of course. You're my friend. I won't abandon you."

There it was again. A sparkle of moisture. Then she let go of me and smiled, clearly amused by something, and I saw her withdraw behind the mask she wore most other times. Had she just given me a performance? Or was it a glimpse into something deeper? "You do know how to play Quadrille, don't you?"

She gave me no time to answer, just nodded to the footman to open the door. Chin high, shoulders back, she swept us both into the room where about eight card tables had been set up, only one of them occupied as yet. Clusters of guests stood about with glasses of champagne and wine, clearly more interested in exchanging gossip than winning at cards—at least for now.

Before I had a chance to get a good look around and see if I recognized anyone, Madame de Montesson swooped in and drew Sophie across the room to where a rotund young man stood, his face shiny with perspiration, his left hand tucked behind his back and his body curved into that fashionable position meant to make a man appear elegant and powerful. His eyes grew round when he realized Madame de Montesson was steering Sophie in his direction. Even in his costly evening garb, he was a sparrow to Sophie's swan.

It wasn't simply that my friend was clothed in the height of fashion and draped with precious jewels—so were all the ladies in that room, except for me. Something else made her stand out. Watching her like that from a distance, I realized what it was. Sophie was one of those people who, at her core, possessed an indefinable power of attraction. In that moment, I understood that she had exerted it upon me and I hadn't even noticed. I had thought that the reason I remained in the Hôtel Montesson was entirely my own decision, because in that house, with its connection to the Orléans cadre, I was perfectly situated to undertake the secret investigations I had been sent to Paris to conduct. There was truth in that, but somehow in the midst of it all I had also allowed myself to become Sophie's property. Had I insisted, I could have returned to the house where Madame Chrétien and her ladies plied their trade. But it never even occurred to me to suggest it, let alone insist.

I believed in my heart that I hadn't stayed simply because I enjoyed the luxury of dressing well beyond my means and sleeping nested in soft, clean linen and silk-covered down. I was less willing to admit that the fact that my adoption into this noble family gave me some access to the finest violinist in Europe exerted an irresistible attraction for me. Nonetheless, if Sophie had continued to be no more than that flighty girl I met at a salon less than a fortnight earlier, I would have extricated myself—or contacted the captain so he could extricate me—from her sphere of influence and not looked back.

In fact, the balance of power between Sophie and me was never about my social inferiority. She swept that aside from the moment we met as if it wasn't the most important thing in this rank-obsessed world. She needed something from me, and I had yet to discover what that was. For all her seeming naivety, I was beginning to discover that Sophie acted in a manner calculated to result in the outcome she desired. I stayed because Sophie wanted me to stay. If she had tired of me, or decided I wasn't of use to her, I had no doubt I would find myself politely dismissed and returned to the very modest circumstances whence I'd come.

Watching her then, I understood that Sophie was a creature who had been bred for a role she was on the point of assuming, and she'd been practicing on me. She was eminently capable of becoming this unprepossessing young marquis's Madame de Montesson, her vivacious beauty drawing the cream of society to what would otherwise be a dull and uninspired establishment. Where did her promise to her mother about not singing fit into it all? I had no doubt it did, but it made no sense to me. Wouldn't displaying her talent enhance her value in the market where she was up for sale?

Sophie glanced back at me once on her way across the room, a mixture of hope and humor in her face. Doubtless the marquis had been described to her as somewhat more imposing than he was in actuality. Yet whatever his looks and personality, he could be her means to a very important end: that of having her own elegant home, perhaps with a private concert hall or theater, where she could construct a world that suited her needs for company and stimulation.

"Might I persuade you to join my table?"

The question jolted me out of my contemplative state and I turned to find the duc d'Orléans in all his corpulence standing far too close to me. I don't know why I was surprised to see him there—this was his wife's residence, after all—but I'd put him out of my mind ever since the night of the salon. Sophie had rescued me from him then, and that had been the beginning of our friendship. But tonight, she was occupied with greater concerns, and I feared she would not notice my discomfort. "I'm afraid I don't know the game we are playing tonight."

When his eyes lit with a mischievous sparkle, I instantly regretted my choice of words.

"Perhaps you would allow me to instruct you." He pressed in closer still, and I edged away. But he threaded my arm through his and clutched it tightly to his side so that I would have had to struggle visibly to remove it, and drew me to a table where two other older gentlemen were already seated—by the look of it having had far too much wine to play at cards well.

What was I to do? Could one say no to the duc d'Orléans, a person who was as close to the throne of France as it was possible to be without being a Bourbon?

Then, I remembered what Lucienne had said. It was but one story in her unending stream of meaningless gossip. Mademoiselle Bertin had been besieged by the duke when his first wife was still alive, and had dared disapproval and censure to defy him in the boldest manner. I knew from what Lucienne had said that the duke was not above using force to get what he wanted. But he had been much younger then. I doubted he could outrun me, or overpower me other than by sheer force of weight. Still, I did not like the look in his bloodshot eye. He could undoubtedly command his own household guards to abduct me if he chose, as he had Mademoiselle Bertin. For now, though, all I had to do was suffer him sitting next to me on a delicate gilt chair that could barely hold his weight, and know that his eyes flicked constantly from my face to my décolletage. I wished I had tucked some extra lace there. Instead I had left myself fashionably exposed.

"Now, the first rule when you play cards is to decide your stakes."

Was it my imagination, or did the duke pass his tongue over his lower lip after he said it? I shrank away a little. "I have no coins with me, Monsieur," I said, thinking perhaps that would excuse me from having to play altogether. I glanced around the room, hoping to see Sophie, but she must have withdrawn somewhere more private to talk to the marquis.

"Oh, you needn't worry about that. I will provide you with whatever you need." He looked up at the other players, one of whom yawned and the other leaned his elbow on the table with his chin in his hand and his eyes half closed. "Shall we say an opening bid of ten Louis?"

Ten Louis! I stood up quickly, my shoulder connecting with the duke's chin as he had just leaned toward me to deposit the gold coins in front of me on the table. The chair he'd been sitting on must have been fragile as well as unstable, because when he was knocked backward by my sudden movement, he not only tipped over, but the chair broke apart like so many sticks of kindling. Two footmen ran forward and helped the duke to his feet. I didn't know where to look, and could feel my face burning with embarrassment and shame.

"How is it trouble seems to find you wherever you go?"

I recognized the voice in my ear immediately, and turned toward it. "Captain," I said. "And how is it that you seem to find me wherever I go?"

Chapter Seventeen

I was only a little surprised to see the captain at that card party in the heart of the enemy camp, so to speak. I had begun to understand a little of the workings of his mind. I had made it my aim to stay just ahead of him, but I feared he was too clever to make that possible, that he intended to keep me steadfastly two steps behind.

The captain's presence didn't surprise me. But the events that transpired before my eyes once more twisted my view of the world almost to a complete reversal. The captain set me aside as soon as he first spoke to me and stepped in to help the footmen get the duc d'Orléans on his feet. But the old man staggered as he walked away seeming confused, and I saw Madame de Montesson talking quietly to a servant I had not noticed before. In a short while, that servant and the captain led the duke out of the room, and fortunately that was the last I saw of the lecherous nobleman that evening.

It was not the last I saw of the captain, however. I had wandered away from the card table, leaving the two elderly players to whom I had not been introduced to shuffle the cards and play some game suitable for two, when Sophie returned on the arm of the marquis from wherever they'd withdrawn to. I started to raise my hand to signal to her, hoping she would join me, but something in her made me let my hand drop once more to my side.

Her face lit up in a way I'd never seen before as she looked across the room, not in my direction. I followed her gaze to see who she was looking at.

It was the captain.

He made his way over to her without hurrying, and she did not move toward him. Yet I could tell that she remained aware of him with her entire body. She stood close to the marquis and to the untrained eye appeared to be focusing her attention on him. Despite the fact that his face now ran with perspiration that dripped down the front of his jacket and left damp spots on the velvet, she simpered in his direction, placing her hand lightly on his sleeve, snapping open her fan to titter coquettishly. His pleasure at being the object of her regard was obvious. Yet all the time, Sophie kept a corner of her eye on the captain's progress across the room. Graf Adelbert von Bauer, Rittmeister des Hussars, now an officer in the Swiss Guard, paused and spoke to people, bowed over proffered hands, took a moment to make some inquiry or other into someone's ear, stopped to watch the progress of a hand of Quadrille, and moaned in displeasure when one of the players lost an obscene amount of money. The way he was going, he would arrive at Sophie's side in a few minutes without seeming to have had that object in mind.

Indeed, his leisurely progress began to make me doubt it was his true purpose. Yet drawing the captain to her was certainly Sophie's aim. Her eyes could not lie. Knowing what I did of her, I would guess that Sophie was in love, not with her intended marquis, but with the captain. There could not be a less suitable match. Sophie surely knew that. Was she really already planning her first affair? Where could they have met? How had she formed such an attachment, even if it was very possibly one-sided? They had never been in each other's company all the time I'd been residing in the Hôtel Montesson, that was certain. As to what had transpired before I first met Sophie, and between then and when she sent someone to collect me from the Bastille, I couldn't begin to guess.

Oh, wouldn't it infuriate Mirela! I decided then and there that I would never tell her. Sophie had been too kind to me. I would not subject her to a Gypsy curse, especially since—knowing the captain as I did—I doubted very much he had his eye on a sixteen-year-old daughter of a minor aristocrat as anything other than a temporary, pleasant distraction. It would be enough to justify Mirela, though, and her claws would come out. No doubt she had taken up with Olaf again. And no doubt, she would drop him like a stone into the Danube if it pleased her to dally with the captain upon his return to Vienna.

And then, it occurred to me. This had all happened before. A different place, a different time, a different mystery, but the captain's involvement had followed the same pattern then as it appeared to be following now. He only told me what he thought I needed to know at any given moment, when in fact, he was possessed of knowledge that would not only help me, but would contribute to my safety. It was infuriating. Had he been acquainted with Sophie all along and arranged the entire episode with her, from my first moment in her aunt's salon, through my participation in the play at the Petit Trianon, through my discovery of the slanderous note, through the Lettre de cachet that sent me to the Bastille, through its revocation, and now through my current residence at the Hôtel Montesson? But how could that be? I did not initially come to the Chaussée d'Antin because of Sophie. It was the chevalier who had invited me.

The chevalier. His fame was not only as a violinist. Everyone I met acknowledged him to be the finest swordsman in Paris, probably in all of France. The captain, too, was a champion fencer. Could they have met at the fencing club? I had no doubt that the captain would rise to any challenge of his mastery of the épée.

While I sat at a table with two ladies and a gentleman who staked only sous, my attention was not on the play of the cards. I let my mind wander back to everything that had led up to that moment, and at least some of it became clear. The captain knew I would agree to come to Paris. He knew I would be incapable of resisting the allure of a new musical world to explore while I did whatever else I was supposed to do. He knew the Chevalier de Saint-Georges was an intimate of the house of Orléans, and that I would no doubt encounter him and be drawn into his circle.

Forcing me to work in Mademoiselle Bertin's atelier and disdaining the idea that I would bring my violin to Paris when my task had nothing to do with performing—it was all to throw me off, to confuse me, to put me in a frame of mind where I didn't know enough to countermand his instructions—and where if I were ever suspected, I could with truth claim ignorance that might protect my life.

And now, I knew for certain that Sophie was not what she seemed either. I spent the rest of the evening trying to reconcile my new insight with what was still to come.

ೇ◉ঙ

I watched Sophie from a discreet distance say goodnight to the marquis de Bonesprit. She curtsied to him, hiding behind her fan and somehow manufacturing a blush. He took her hand and pulled her gently up to stand in front of him, and she pretended to stumble a little—just enough so that he had to take hold of her upper arm and draw her closer. Or did she step toward him without any encouragement? I was too far away to make out the expression in his eyes, but his smile beamed uncontrollably. He glanced left and right, and when he saw that no one who mattered was watching, he leaned forward to kiss Sophie. She turned her face away at the last moment so that his kiss landed awkwardly on her cheek. Then she rounded her lips in a shocked oh! pretending she had not orchestrated and rehearsed the entire scene for days—perhaps even weeks. Leaving her hand in his, she fluttered her fan nervously before her face. As he stepped toward the door, she let her arm extend as if she was reluctant to release him. When she finally had to let go, he backed out through the door, his fingers to his lips, and she held his gaze until he could no longer see her.

At that point, she snapped her fan closed and dropped her hand to her side, letting her shoulders relax and ungluing the smile from her face. I predicted a betrothal announcement within the week.

Sophie turned to walk in my direction toward the private wing of the house, but did not see me right away. She cast her eyes down to the floor as if keeping them raised would be an effort beyond her capacity at that moment. The captain had left sometime earlier, I didn't see exactly when. The marquis was the last guest to depart. Now long past midnight, even with her late sleeping habit it must have been exhausting for Sophie to have played that role so assiduously for hours.

I stepped out of my semi-sheltered observation post, an alcove that should have housed a statue but that was currently empty. Sophie stopped, startled for a moment. She recovered herself quickly and smiled, trying to resurrect the vivacity that had been on display the entire evening. I held up my hand. "There is no need for you to pretend with me," I said. "I think I can guess it all."

First, she simply stared at me. Then she frowned. After a few seconds, she hitched up one corner of her mouth and one eyebrow and said, "The captain warned me you were smart. It was something of a wager between us."

I gestured toward our rooms. We walked side by side in tense silence, and I could feel her trying to come up with something to say to me. I was tired too, but nothing would make me go to bed if Sophie were willing to talk that night. I feared I might find a completely different girl upon waking the next morning and have to start peeling away the layers of deception all over again.

She dismissed her maid. I helped her unlace and unpin her elaborate gown and remove the stuffed roll of fabric that held it away from her hips and she did the same for me. In our night shifts, our hair braided for sleep, we huddled under the covers of her large bed and talked for an hour, until the candles in the sconces began to gutter. I was right about everything I'd been able to guess just by observation. She and the captain were indeed having a flirtation, as she called it, and she seemed to think they would continue it beyond the day of her marriage.

"I knew it was out of the question from the first moment. My family would never sanction a match with a mere captain of the Swiss Guard, no matter his distant family ties." She sighed.

And that's a very good thing, I thought, but did not say. "But is that wise? To plan on dallying with the captain so soon after your marriage?"

"Oh, it's all quite innocent now." A pale blush, like the beginning of sunrise on a cloudy day, crept up from her neck. "I would have to produce an heir before I could have a true liaison."

"How did the captain persuade you to help me? When did you know I would find a way to hear the chevalier?" I was very curious to discover the extent of her knowledge about what I was doing in Paris.

"Bertrand—the captain," she smiled and looked down at her hand. "The captain said he had a distant cousin who had come to Paris to continue her violin studies, and would I be able to introduce her to the chevalier."

Bertrand, I thought. So she doesn't know everything. "Yes, but, I came to the salon before I knew you."

Sophie laughed. "I guessed who you were the instant I saw you, partly from Bertrand's description. And you were clearly so enraptured by the music, which is highly unusual for any of the young ladies in my social circle, that I knew I couldn't be mistaken."

"But... I don't understand why you couldn't just tell me."

"Bertrand said you were a little stubborn—pigheaded was actually the word he used—and were determined to make the connection yourself, on the strength of your own talent."

Pigheaded! Well, I supposed such familiarity served to make our status as relations a little more believable.

Sophie yawned. Had she told me everything? Did she really not know that both the captain and I were in Paris on the service of the emperor of Austria, who wished to protect his sister Marie Antoinette from the slanders and lies that were stirring up sentiment against her? Could she be clever enough to play the kind of double game the captain was adept at?

Her eyelids drooped. I started to ease myself out from under the covers so I could creep back to my own chamber. Sophie reached out her hand, and in a sleepy voice said, "Stay. It's so cold." Then she rolled on her side away from me, and I burrowed into her lavish covers and closed my eyes.

Chapter Eighteen

A much-more-relaxed Sophie and I spent a quiet time together the next day. Even if we had wanted to go out somewhere, we could not have done it. The mild mid-November weather had given way to an increasingly fierce winter. What had started the night before as a light snow became heavy and constant, and soon the streets were too deeply covered for horses to navigate safely. We heard the curses of carriage drivers who had attempted it anyway and found their wheels completely stuck. They would have to unhitch the horses, leave the carriages where they were, and walk the poor beasts back to the stables.

It may have been inconvenient for most people, but I was thrilled. Such weather reminded me of Vienna in the winter, of sleigh rides and running through the Augarten making paths with our sturdily booted feet and playing fox and geese. I wondered if it was snowing there too, and whether Greta would take Anna out to play. I knew my mother would not. Her spirits were still delicate four years after Papa died. I had thought perhaps she'd marry again—she came close to it—and that it would give her a new purpose. As it was, all she had to do was gossip with her few friends, fret over Toby at Herr Goldschmidt's atelier, and be reminded of Papa every day by Anna. Born a couple of weeks after Papa's murder, Anna looked more and more like him as time went on. She had his smile, his sparkling eyes. And she had inherited his musical ability, her sweet little voice singing perfectly in tune, and she'd already started to pick out melodies on the pianoforte before I left for Paris. When I returned, I vowed I would start teaching her to play properly and read the notes on the page. Like me when I was her age, she would doubtless learn to read music before she learned to read words.

The thought of dashing out into the snow with Anna gave me a fierce desire to walk to the gardens of the Palais Royale through the thick, lacy flakes. It must be beautiful all covered in pristine white. But the only shoes in my possession were satin slippers suitable for card parties and concerts. In the week since arriving from the Bastille, I had gone everywhere in a carriage and didn't notice my lack of sturdy footwear. Whatever had happened to my stout, Austrian boots was, for the moment, shrouded in mystery. My simple brown skirt, bodice, and muslin fichu languished on a hook in the armoire in my guest chamber like a poor relation being fed out of sight in the kitchen, but my boots—clearly, they were too déclassé even for that.

As I thought about my boots, I remembered something with a start. Something very important, something I'd completely forgotten. I don't know why it hadn't come to mind until after our three-o'clock dinner. We had all gone to our rooms to rest before what promised to be a mildly entertaining evening listening to an actor from the Comédie Française recite a soliloquy from The Marriage of Figaro. The play by Beaumarchais had originally been banned by the censors but was now wildly popular in Paris. I doubted many guests would be hearty enough to brave the weather, but the ones who lived close by could come in sedan chairs, forcing their servants to trudge through snow for the sake of their own amusement.

Thinking of the theater brought to mind the play at the Petit Trianon, which inevitably brought to mind my brief imprisonment in the Bastille, and Sophie rescuing me and—the indecipherable threads of connection among everyone in these Orleanist houses, which I had started to figure out on a piece of the elegant writing paper so conveniently provided in this guest chamber.

I froze. I guessed the unexpected appearance of the captain must have distracted me from the other business, and my heart started to pound and the blood in my veins turned to ice as I remembered. I rushed to the escritoire.

No scrap of paper poked out from beneath the books on the desk. I could feel the heat rising in my face. Had the books been moved? Were they the same books that were there the day before? I hadn't made a point of noticing, the only one I could recall was a book of verse by Jacques Delille, which was still on top of the pile. I lifted the three books, and exhaled in relief when I saw a sheet of creamy white linen paper still beneath them. My relief didn't last long, though. I had forgotten for the moment that I'd torn the sheet in half first. When I picked up the paper to take it to the grate and destroy it, I discovered it was but half of what I'd written, not the entire document. Had the chambermaid spied the corner that poked out and pulled it, not wanting to disarrange the books, possibly after that throwing it in the grate? I knelt down and peered at the ashes beneath the blazing fire. It was impossible to tell. In any case, last night's ashes would have been cleared away by now. But would a servant dare to dispose of such a thing anyway? Would she not assume it was something the occupant of the room wished to keep?

Or perhaps she would assume it had been left there by someone else, and should be taken to the mistress of the house to reunite with its author.

Merde. It was no use trying to figure it out. The point was that half of what I'd written was no longer in my possession. I scrutinized the scrap in my hand. Would someone who had the other half be able to understand what I was up to? What a fool I was! I could have made up an excuse for Sophie and burned the entire thing last night. I could have said I'd been writing a poem, or a song, and it was so terrible I simply had to destroy it.

My error made one thing clear to me. If I were going to explore the tunnel, it would have to be that very night, after the house was asleep. Without knowing who might have taken the paper or when, I had no way of knowing if my real project—of finding the pamphleteers and the printer and bringing them to justice—had been deduced by whoever possessed the other half of the paper.

After all, it would be a simple thing for Sophie to declare my visit at an end and send me back to Madame Chrétien's. Or for her aunt to do so, for that matter. With no entrée to Versailles any more and no certainty of being able to enter the Palais Royale in the future, once I left the Hôtel Montesson, all would be lost, and I would probably have to return to Vienna having not accomplished anything. But wasn't that what I wanted? To be home in time for Christmas?

Not if it meant admitting defeat. The emperor himself had given me this task. I did not want to let him down, even if what I discovered only confirmed his suspicions. Even if I found eventually that the pamphlets were not full of lies and exaggerations, but revealed secrets about the queen's true behavior at court.

I paced back and forth in front of the fireplace, planning how I would manage my adventure that evening, when I heard the whisper of paper against the floor. I looked over to the closed door of my chamber. Someone had slid a note underneath it. I ran to the door and threw it open, scanning the corridor. Empty. Whoever had delivered the note had vanished.

Once I'd closed the door again, I picked up the letter. The red wax seal was blank. I cracked it and unfolded the stiff paper, and read.

Mademoiselle,
It would be far better for your health if you would keep your nose out of other people's business. Events will unfold anyway, and I would advise you to leave Paris before you find it is no longer possible.
—A Friend

Well. That set aside any doubts that the missing half of the paper upon which I had made my notes had disappeared through some innocent mishap. I re-read the letter and looked at it closely. The quality of the paper ruled out its having been penned by a servant. The handwriting, too, suggested education and means. I did not recognize it. It bore no similarity to Sophie's round and expansive hand. The way the "S" was written made me doubt it could have been written by the captain, who would have no reason to warn me off anyway. It was a very French "S."

What the author of the letter didn't realize was that, by warning me away, he or she had achieved the very opposite outcome. Now I was even more determined to get to the bottom of the slanders against the queen.

I would have to get through another social evening. This time, I would not return with Sophie to her room, though. Perhaps I would claim a headache and retire early to make my preparations. I hoped I could retrace my steps to the door I'd found.

That, at least, would be to discover something. If illegal pamphlets could be smuggled out of the Palais Royale through a tunnel that led to a house like many others occupied by nobles in the city, it would explain why they had been so difficult to trace.

It was not difficult to persuade Sophie that I was tired. She looked grateful that she, too, would have an excuse to go to sleep. I waited until the house quieted, until after the distant sounds of doors closing and buckets clanking as chambermaids carried spent ashes out of the heating stoves and fireplaces in bed chambers, emptied them into ash cans in the courtyard, and then climbed up to the attics to sleep for the few hours they were allotted. I did not fear discovery by the overworked staff.

I changed out of my finery into the plain clothes I had worn in prison. Anyone who saw me from a distance would assume I was simply a servant, sent on a late-night errand to fulfill a whim. No one would question, either, that I took the woolen blanket off my bed and folded it so it was no larger than a shawl, and draped it over my shoulders. The corridors of the house were cold enough that I could see my breath in clouds of vapor. Without knowing precisely how long the tunnel would be, I made sure I had a stout candle that would burn slowly. I prayed it would last long enough for me to go through the tunnel and back again.

I descended down two flights of stairs to the ground level as I had the day I went in search of the theater. With no light filtering through the windows, everything looked different, and I was afraid I would not remember the way. But I spotted a few familiar details—a door to the courtyard; an alcove with a broom in it—and I continued.

At last I reached the door to the tunnel. I recognized it right away. It was narrower than the other doors that led out to the courtyard, and it had a distinctive latch on it. What I hadn't noticed before was that near the top was a bolt that could be thrown across from inside the house, preventing anyone from coming through. That was unsettling. What if I entered and followed the tunnel, and then by the time I came back, someone had bolted it for the night, thinking no one would need to use it?

I glanced around to make sure I was entirely alone, then reached up to try the bolt, to see how easy it was to engage.

The screech of rusted metal was so piercing it sent a rat running across the corridor a few feet away from me. I nudged the bolt back to where it started. Well, there was my answer. No one bothered to bolt this door. The gates from the road into the courtyard would be chained closed at night, and the porter would rouse at the slightest suggestion of someone trying to enter, so the doors that gave onto the courtyard would not necessarily have to be locked. Yet, as far as I knew, they all were. I heard the housekeeper go around to them one by one late at night, her ring of keys jangling. She locked and tested each door for security.

So, perhaps others knew that this door did not give onto the courtyard, and that it was to remain open. For what?

I would have to pray that no one would decide that tonight would be an exception to that practice. I took a deep breath and eased the door open, keeping my candle out of the draft so it would not be extinguished, and stepped down the first stair. Of course, to avoid detection, I would have to close the door behind me. The thought of doing so brought back other times when I had been locked into small spaces, unable to get out again and fearing for my life, and I felt an icy finger of dread trace a path down my spine. But there was nothing else to do, not if I wanted to get to the bottom of the mystery surrounding the slanders against the queen. I closed the door, then continued down ten steps to the beginning of the subterranean tunnel. I prayed that the chevalier had not lied to me about the tunnel's path. What reason would he have had to do so? Still, in such circumstances, it's easy to assign hidden motives to everyone.

The candle only cast its illumination a short way in front of me, so my progress was slow. Thankfully, although cold, the tunnel was well constructed and lined with stones that kept out water—at least, at that time of year. I heard the expected scrabble of mice and probably rats fleeing at the approach of my light, but I had encountered much worse in my time and it didn't bother me.

It was hard to tell how far I'd come. Judging by the amount my candle had burned down, I'd been below the ground for about ten minutes when I saw to my surprise that another tunnel branched off from the one I was following. I believed I'd been going north, although the tunnel could have curved imperceptibly with nothing to act as orientation. But if I was going north, the other tunnel led to the east from there.

What was to the east? More similar neighborhoods filled with aristocrats and wealthy merchants. Beyond that, though, was the Marais, with its warren of streets too narrow for carriages. I had heard it called the *Cour des Miracles,* where beggars who roamed the street hobbling on canes or with their eyes apparently blind would return at dark—and their daylight infirmities miraculously disappeared.

Beyond that, the Saint Antoine district, full of hovels where laborers lived. The Bastille loomed over it all, casting its ominous shadow and giving rise to those absurd rumors of torture and death.

At that point, I faced a choice: continue toward what I assumed would be the Palais Royale, or take a turn and see where the other tunnel led.

I did not have time to decide, however. Ahead of me in the main tunnel, I could see the growing glimmer of approaching candlelight, and hear a low murmur of men's voices, made strange by the complete lack of echo, as if the walls swallowed up the sounds as soon as they were uttered. I extinguished the flame of my own candle and stepped into the side tunnel, where I hoped the profound darkness would hide me.

Taking soundless breaths and willing my heart to slow its pounding, I waited. The light grew, and I soon picked apart the voices of two different men.

"I fear the queen's spies are getting closer to us," said one of the voices, which I did not recognize.

"I could have predicted that. You know how foolish I believe this entire enterprise to be."

My God, I thought. Could it be? I recognized the chevalier's voice, and gasped before I could stop myself.

"Did you hear that?" The other man said, now close enough to the entrance to the side tunnel that the space immediately in front of me in the main tunnel was brightly lit.

I shrank back, slowly. How far would a candle's glow be able to pierce the deep darkness? I could feel an icy breeze at my back, and noticed that the tunnel I was in began to angle downward to what I believed was the south. I could perhaps ease myself beyond the curve and not be visible.

"Just a rat, I imagine," the chevalier said.

"Still, I should take a quick look. Our friends at the Louvre would not appreciate being discovered in the midst of their enterprise."

To my horror, the other gentleman stepped directly into my view at the end of the tunnel. His face was fully illuminated by the candle, and there was no mistaking who I faced, who had placed himself between me and the safe return to my bedchamber at the Hôtel Montesson. It was the duc de Chartres himself, whom I had only seen once before, from a distance at the Concert Olympique.

I pressed my back against the tunnel wall and turned my face away before inching around the curve, hoping it was enough of one that the glow of the candle would pass me by and the duke would not see me lurking there. My heart leapt up into my throat as I heard the scrape of boots stepping in my direction. Two steps. Three. The flickering light of a candle being teased by a gentle breeze illuminated the outline of the passage just beyond me, but I was still in shadow.

He stopped. "No one's there. But we have not solved the problem of Roland. He has been making demands, threatening to reveal all."

Roland, I thought. A name I was somehow familiar with, but could not remember exactly why. I could feel my shoulders sagging with the release of tension as the candlelight faded and I knew the duke had returned to the main tunnel to join the chevalier once again.

The two men continued their progress in the direction of the Hôtel Montesson, and I could only catch a few more words before their conversation was out of my range to hear and had been swallowed up once again by the absorbing stones of the tunnel. The last thing I heard was very distinct, however. "There are ways to ensure he does not tell tales to anyone."

I recognized the fluid, warm voice of the chevalier, and perceived its veiled threat. I shivered.

Chapter Nineteen

I was safe from immediate discovery. But the chevalier and the duke had continued toward the Hôtel Montesson, for what purpose exactly, I could not know. That meant there was every possibility that when I returned, I would meet them coming back, or that they would hear me when I opened the door to reenter Madame de Montesson's vast residence.

But why was the duke going there at this late hour? Wasn't he Madame de Montesson's sworn enemy? Didn't he blame her for his father's banishment from court and diminished rank? Yet his father's diminishment had led to his elevation. Surely that was to the good for him. It made no sense that he be so against the lady who couldn't even claim the title of duchess and was prohibited by law from having any of her own progeny supersede him.

These were questions I knew I couldn't answer at that moment. Far more important was figuring out how to get out of the tunnel without being discovered. And how to do it in complete darkness. I had extinguished my candle to avoid detection. I thought perhaps my eyes would become accustomed to the absence of light once the final glow of the chevalier's candle had faded. But that was not the case. With not even the faintest bit of light coming from anywhere, I was completely blind. I stretched my arms out to feel the walls of the tunnel, not caring what I would encounter there. Anything was better than this sensation of simply not existing, of having vanished utterly from the world I knew.

I felt as if I was rehearsing for my own death.

As soon as that thought entered my mind, a fresh breeze tickled the back of my neck from farther down the tunnel where I had sought to hide. I knew it was from that direction, because I had not turned away from facing the junction with the other tunnel, perhaps in hope that I would return there and be able to go back to the house and find my warm bed.

The breeze was cold and unpleasant, but it told me something important. That way, the opposite way from where I faced, was an exit. An opening. Otherwise, I wouldn't have been able to feel a breath of cold air from it. I had no way of knowing how large it was or where it would lead, but I was small and had squeezed through plenty of tight places before. It would take me outside somewhere. That was all that mattered. After that, I'd have to decide what to do from there, but I would have escaped discovery and freed myself from the tunnel.

I turned, clutching the candle and my blanket around my shoulders with one hand and keeping the tips of my fingers of the other hand in contact with the wall of the tunnel, and stepped forward. It was slow going. I didn't know if I'd find stairs, or if the tunnel would turn again suddenly and I would collide with a wall. I inched one foot out, then put my weight on it before stretching the other foot forward.

Some fifty or more paces on, I perceived a lightening, a lessening of the darkness. The air grew colder as well, strengthening my sense that ahead lay an exit to outdoors. I still couldn't make out the wall, but light seeped in from somewhere in front of me. I took a long slow breath and forced myself not to quicken my pace, since I had no idea what I was heading toward, whether I would come out in the middle of a busy thoroughfare, inside some kind of building, or in a dark alley where thieves might hide—although on a night such as that one, I doubted many people were abroad.

Another twenty paces and I could see well enough to take my hand from the wall and step forward with more confidence. I spied an ill-fitting door, with an inch of light around the top and one side and gaps between the hinges on the other. I rushed forward and grasped the handle, desperate to run through and find myself outside the tunnel at last.

But I forced myself to wait and listen. I knew well enough that it would be better to have some sense of what was beyond the door before passing through it. I noticed that the air, though cold, was not as icy as I would expect if the door led directly to the streets of Paris, where snow had been swirling only an hour at most before, blown into drifts by a merciless wind from the north. I put my ear close to the gap.

Nothing. I waited a few more seconds, then pressed the latch down and heard it click on the other side. I pulled the door toward me, stepped through and jumped, letting out a little shriek.

I thought I'd seen a man. But it was only the portrait of one, wearing some kind of uniform. And he wasn't alone. A single oil lamp hung from the far wall, illuminating what looked at first like a store room. But not just any store room. Paintings of all sorts leaned up against every wall, some facing out, some with their wooden-strutted backs on display. Those that faced out were mostly portraits, but I saw some landscapes and at least one not-very-well-executed history painting. Perhaps a sketch for a grander work, I thought.

The room was very large and divided by stout pillars, suggesting that the floor above contained many rooms. The stone floors and walls were topped by a low ceiling of wooden planks and beams. I knew where I was. I was in the basement of the Louvre palace. Probably beneath one of the wings that had never been finished, thus the freezing cold. That explained the storing of paintings and sculptures, doubtless the cast-off works by some of the many members of the Académie Royale who had lodgings and studios up above. But why would a tunnel connecting Madame de Montesson's *hôtel particulier* and the Palais Royale give onto a tunnel that turned south and ended up here?

I had been very careful not to make any noise after my initial little exclamation of surprise. That turned out to be a good thing, because after only a few moments, I heard something coming from a room beyond the one I was in. I couldn't figure out what it was at first. There was a sound as of clunking, heavy metal being shifted into place, and then a grinding, like a crank being turned. I crept in the direction of a door on the opposite side from where I stood. It, too, was ill fitting, as if little care had been taken in the construction of rooms the public would be unlikely to enter. I approached the door, stepping softly, and put my eye to the crack around it.

At first, all I saw was the back of a man's brown homespun jacket. I held my breath, and in a moment, he stepped away. Beyond him was another man turning what looked like a ship's wheel and feeding sheets of paper into a machine.

A printing press. Not like any I had ever seen before. The ones I was familiar with could print sheets only one at a time and those had to be removed by hand. This one had a roller mechanism that made the entire process considerably faster. What could they be printing in the middle of the night?

"Let's see what the bitch is up to now," the man whose back had originally been to me said. He took one of the printed sheets off the finished stack and waved it in the air to dry the ink. "More incest! And drinking the blood of poor people. Oh dear. However will she survive this."

"I don't like it. Not a bit."

"You like the money though, I wager. So keep quiet and do your job."

Of course, I knew then what I'd stumbled upon. They were printing pamphlets full of lies and slanders about the queen. But why here in property belonging to the crown? Why not in the Palais Royale, where the crown and the police would have no right to enter?

It was clear too, from what I heard, the men in that room were not themselves the authors of the pamphlets. I kept listening.

"Soon as you've printed a thousand, I'll take them through to the palace, along with the gazettes."

He said through, I thought. The only way through was the way I had come. I listened yet more closely.

"Just this lot then."

I watched as about twenty more sheets of paper spewed out of the press and the two men gathered them up into piles and tied them with string before sandwiching them between two other bundles of paper. Then, to my horror, the man who hadn't been operating the press turned and strode directly toward the door I was peering through. I dashed as quickly as I could to hide behind a large painting leaning against the wall.

The man flung the door open and hurried across the room to the tunnel entrance I had only recently passed through, on his way taking the oil lamp that was hanging on the wall. I'd left the tunnel door open behind me, I realized. He stopped when he reached it and pulled it open and closed, tested the latch a few times, then called back to the other room. "They should fix this damn door! The least wind blows it right open."

The man who had operated the press simply grunted, then closed the door to the printing room. I heard him shoot the bolt across. The other man entered the tunnel and closed the door behind him, taking the only light.

Now what? I couldn't go back through the tunnel, which now appeared as busy as a thoroughfare. Fortunately, up high, just above ground level, were a series of oblong windows. Several of them had snow piled up on them, but a couple let in just enough light that it wasn't pitch black down there. I could barely make out a door on another wall, quite far down past several pillars. I hoped it might lead to stairs up to the next floor. Then what? I pictured myself wandering around lost inside this unfinished palace for days before anyone found me, but it was go or remain trapped in the cellar.

To my great relief, the door indeed opened to a staircase, which led up to another door. I passed through that one easily enough and found myself in a long corridor. At the far end was another door, larger than the interior doors I had passed and noticeably stouter. I crept down the length of the corridor until I reached it. To my relief, it wasn't locked. I opened it, and was greeted by a blast of snowy wind.

Never have I been so happy to be cold in my entire life. I was outside. At last. Out on the Rue du Louvre, by the look of it.

I knew of only one place where I could be certain of admittance at this time of night. I put the blanket over my head and clutched it tight under my chin, then ran as fast as I could through the snow to Madame Chrétien's house on the Rue d'Argout.

Chapter Twenty

I arrived at the house at the same time as a sleigh that had pulled up and expelled a tumbling mass of drunken officers. As they stumbled through the snow, calling and laughing into the roaring wind and then pounding on the unmarked door of Madame Chrétien's house of pleasure, I inserted myself among them. The concierge stood in the vestibule with his hand out and each of them dropped a few coins into it as they passed.

"*Et toi, Mamzelle,*" he said, grabbing hold of my arm.

Of course, I had nothing to offer him. I took the blanket off my head hoping he would recognize me and let me go, but his wiry fingers dug into my arm and he kept his other hand out in front of my face.

"She's with me..." One of the officers threw his arm around my shoulder and squeezed me to him, tossing another couple of coins in the concierge's palm.

"Thank you sir, but—" Before I could finish, he covered my mouth with his and slobbered his sickening, wine-laced saliva over my face. I pushed him away and wiped his spittle off with my sleeve.

"That's no way to treat..." He staggered back and one of his friends caught him just before he fell.

"Gentlemen! Upstairs!"

Never have I been so glad to hear Madame Chrétien's commanding voice. Once we stood on the landing—"stood" being an imprecise term—she swept her gaze over the group and her eyes lit on me. I tried to indicate with a look that I did not belong among these drunken louts. She raised one eyebrow and flicked her head slightly in the direction of the parlor door. Before anyone could stop me, I dashed to it and through, closing the door behind me and leaning against it, my heart racing and my breath coming in short gasps. I was vaguely aware of Madame herding the men elsewhere and assuring them that they would be well cared for.

Only then did I realize that my legs were shaking and could hardly support my weight, and I was so chilled through my teeth chattered. I moved toward the blazing fire in the grate and put out my hands, white with cold. I sank rather than sat in the nearest chair and closed my eyes, feeling the flickering warmth gradually seep into me.

I must have dozed a little, because I awoke to someone patting my face.

"Thérèse! Thérèse! Come. Let's take you up to bed."

I recognized Odette's voice. I had no idea how long I'd been slumped in the chair, but my back ached and my feet felt as if they belonged to someone else. Somehow she managed to get me up the three flights of stairs to our attic room, and I hardly remembered lying down.

I awoke the next morning tucked into extra blankets and wearing only my chemise. Odette sat in a chair next to me with a bowl of hot chocolate in her hands. "Here, drink this."

It was forbidden for any of the girls to consume food or drink in the bedrooms because of the mice, so at first I shook my head.

"It's all right. Madame sent me up with it. Once you're dressed, you're to come down to the parlor. I think she's sent for the captain."

The captain. What would I tell him? I had important information, to be sure, but I hadn't followed his instructions. Would he be glad, or angry? And why did I care anyway?

After I drained the hot, sweet chocolate from the bowl I was wide awake. I dressed quickly. Odette, on the other hand, undressed and slid her own exhausted limbs beneath the covers on her bed. "Thank you," I said, and pulled the blankets up for her as she closed her eyes and nestled into her pillow, then tiptoed out of the room and closed the door softly behind me.

I heard the captain's and Madame's voices arguing as soon as I reached the first floor.

"You should have sent her back!"

"I am not so cruel as to do such a thing. You should have seen the state of her. The Virgin knows what they did to harm her, or how long she'd been out in this deathly cold and snowy weather!"

I knocked firmly on the door. No sense going in with my tail between my legs like a naughty puppy. The two of them stopped talking and Madame called, "*Viens!*"

The captain, as I might have predicted, had a face like thunder. He leaned one arm on the mantelpiece, his hand balled into a fist that he pressed against his forehead. The corners of his mouth turned down and his nostrils flared. Madame stood in the middle of the room, straight as a pillar, with her chin high and eyes flashing.

Just as the captain opened his mouth to begin haranguing me for what I did, I spoke. "Perhaps you would like to know what I discovered last night."

He clamped his mouth shut and gestured toward a chair. I looked at Madame, whose house this was and who should have been the one to invite us to sit. She lowered herself sedately into her customary chaise and gave her most gracious smile. "Please, sit."

I took a seat and waited for the captain to do the same.

Madame rang the little bell that summoned Agathe. "Tea, I think," she said to the maid. "And some cakes."

I flashed a look of gratitude in her direction. The chocolate had been hot and delicious, but I was still ravenous after my adventures of the night before. I could feel the captain's agitation, his masculine impatience to take control of the situation, but here, in this house, women held the power. Whatever bargain they had all struck with virtue, they wielded the access to pleasure with finesse and self-knowledge. It had taken me aback at first to witness the confidence and assurance of these women of the night, but I came to respect them, after seeing their kindness and humanity to each other and to me. No one was there other than by choice, whatever life circumstances had driven them to making that choice. It saddened me to think, though, that this life could be preferable to anything that awaited them elsewhere, that they had been so unsafe as to desire controlled servitude to men's appetites over whatever they had fled from at home or on the streets.

While I well understood that Madame would become rich through their hard work, she also protected them. Madame in particular knew how to preserve the appearance of submission while keeping an iron grip on everything that transpired under her roof. No one entered there without her permission, and the slightest suggestion of violence or bad behavior saw a man unceremoniously booted out. I suspected that the captain, for all his seeming disregard for my comfort, had chosen this safe house for me carefully.

Taking my cue from Madame, I related in calm, unhurried terms what had transpired the night before. I admitted to losing half of my handwritten note and felt the captain stiffen at that, but I saw no benefit in hiding the facts. They gave my resulting actions the urgency they deserved, after all.

"Did you actually see one of the pamphlets?" The captain asked.

"No, but I heard the men talking about them."

"Why didn't you steal one?"

I glared open-mouthed at him. "You do realize I was in the next room, and hiding? How would I ever have managed such a thing!"

He looked down at his fingernails and made a great show of picking some imagined thread out from underneath one of them. "Oh, I don't know. You seem remarkably capable of doing other things that seem humanly impossible."

It struck me with force that he didn't believe me. Not believe me? How could he! And what a weathercock he was! "You may believe what you choose. But I could lead you through the tunnels to the basement of the Louvre, if you wish. I would give you the benefit of a candle for the entire exploration, however. I wouldn't expect anyone to have to duplicate my own harrowing experience." I stopped talking and took my time to finish my tea and eat one of the delicious cakes. The conversation was in the captain's hands now.

"You must return to the Hôtel Montesson," he said finally. "I shall arrange it." He stood, as if that was the end of the conversation and I would hear nothing more about what I was to say to Sophie about my absence.

"I dare say that will create some difficulties," I said, cross.

"Difficulties your actions caused, I might add."

"And that resulted in the first definite information about the origin of the pamphlets, I might also add."

"Enough!" Madame Chrétien rose. "Captain von Bauer, you will make sure Thérèse's absence is explained. Say she was called away to attend upon a friend who had suddenly become ill, or something. Thérèse, you will do as the captain says, so long as you feel it is safe for you to do so."

And so, at about one o'clock in the afternoon, I found myself being ushered into the morning parlor at the Hôtel Montesson. Sophie looked up, relief flooding her eyes, only to be replaced almost instantly by vexation. She pressed her lips into a line and sniffed, making a great show of pouring out a cup of tea and pushing it across the dainty table in my direction. "I suppose you'll tell me where you've been."

"I am so sorry I didn't leave word. The summons came very late at night that a friend—one of the girls I worked with at Mademoiselle Bertin's—was very ill. I was commanded to attend upon her immediately, and her fever did not break until near dawn, so I stayed away until now."

"Fever! You bring fever into this house?" She hoisted herself half out of her seat and reached for the bell to ring for a servant.

I rushed over and took her hand. "I have been assured by a mutual friend that there is no risk of contagion." I held her gaze until I was certain she believed me.

She relaxed and sat down again, a slight smile nudging her cheeks. "What is his name?"

Although I had intended—with the captain's blessing—to imply that I had crept away on a romantic assignation, for some reason her question caught me by surprise. The name Zoltan almost escaped my lips before I could come up with a suitably French alternative. "Alfonse," I whispered, then put my finger to my lips. In answer, she made a gesture as if she were pinning her lips together, and we both smiled. "Let's have some cakes!"

Chapter Twenty-One

To my surprise, when I returned to my room to change for dinner, I found a letter propped up against the candlestick on the escritoire. A beautiful hand had written *À Mademoiselle Thérèse* on one side. I picked it up, enjoying the weight of the heavy paper, its smooth, eggshell finish. Someone had taken care to fold it so perfectly and seal it with bright red wax that it seemed a shame to open it. I waited, carrying the letter around my small room at first, tapping it against the palm of my hand, and finally decided that I should change out of the plain skirt and bodice I had worn the previous evening for my adventures in the tunnel and into the silk *robe a l'anglais* the maid had laid out on my bed for me. Such a beautiful letter deserved to be read when properly dressed, I reasoned.

I rang the bell for the maid, who came in and helped lace and pin me into the bum roll and petticoats, and held the dress so I could step into it and she could tighten the laces underneath the loose fabric that hung from my shoulders like a train. The gown was a lovely shade of gray with little pink rosebuds embroidered on it. The lace at my décolletage and on the elbow-length sleeves was very fine—not as fine as the Valenciennes for the queen, though. I guessed this had been a favorite gown of Sophie's when it was in fashion the previous season. I wondered why she hadn't had it remade for herself in the more current style.

Once the maid had finished pinning up my hair, dusting it with powder, then shaking the powdering cloak out over the bare floor and sweeping up after it, I dismissed her. Now, the letter. It drew me toward my desk, like a light in a high-up window. I put it to my nose first, inhaling the scent of dried ink and perhaps a hint of something musky, then slid the paper knife under the seal and unfolded it.

Chère Mademoiselle,

We have some unfinished business, I think. You expressed an interest in benefiting from my meager talents, and I invited you to come and play chamber music with me and my fellow musicians. It would give me great pleasure if you would attend me this evening in the Palais Royale, in the small music room, to spend an hour under my instruction and then join in some companionable music making. I have the latest string quartet by Franz Haydn, and have longed to read through it with other like-minded music lovers.

Avec amitié,

Joseph Bologne, Chevalier de Saint-Georges

I had been yearning for such an invitation ever since I first heard the chevalier's playing through the window in the Palais Royale. And one of my godfather's string quartets! A happy coincidence, or did he know something about me I'd hoped to hide? Plus, after everything I'd overheard the night before, could I trust him? He had quite clearly mentioned the illegal pamphlets in conversation with the duke as they passed from the Palais Royale to the Hôtel Montesson. The way they spoke, like equals despite the gulf between their ranks, meant the chevalier was evidently not simply a valued dependent of the duc de Chartres. He must in some way be involved in the conspiracy to disseminate obscene lies that inflamed public opinion against the queen. But why?

I suppose I ought to have been frightened to go alone to the heart of the enemy camp. But I didn't know enough then to realize just how frightened. And so I penned a quick response accepting the chevalier's invitation and gave it to a maid to deliver. I also decided it could do no harm to tell Sophie where I was going. In fact, it occurred to me that it would provide a measure of safety.

Sophie was quite happy for me to leave her after dinner, as the marquis was coming over for an intimate card party. "Since you don't enjoy cards, I think we can get along without you." She winked. That was the moment I realized she thought I was, in actuality, going out to an assignation with the fictitious Alfonse. I decided it wouldn't hurt to play along.

"I don't know how late I'll be. I presume the concierge will let me in?"

Sophie insisted I take a carriage the quarter of a mile between the two residences. Since I wore a borrowed pair of her slippers, I didn't argue. Although much of the snow had been cleared away, it had been trampled to mud and dung by the horses already.

To my relief, I was expected. The footman led me to an elegant music room, which, in any other domicile, would not be called small. The high ceiling was painted with a heavenly host of cherubs playing everything from lyres to harpsichords. The walls were decorated with cartouches of ladies and gentlemen supposedly playing music, but clearly with other activities in mind. I was still examining them when the door at the opposite end of the room opened to admit the Chevalier de Saint-Georges.

I'm not sure I realized before exactly how tall he was. I judged that he must be a few inches taller than the captain. And yet, there wasn't a suggestion of awkwardness about him. He walked with the grace of a dancing master. Of course. He would have learned the elegant poses and movements of fencing, his sense of timing no doubt contributing to his complete mastery of that art as well. He would be very difficult to get away from, I thought, as he approached me and bowed. His long legs would easily outpace me. I curtsied and put out my hand. He did not kiss it, but took it and led me over to the clavier.

Lying on its closed lid were two violins. My own was in the case I had laid on a chair upon entering the room. "I should—"

"I thought we'd use two of my instruments. You admired my Amati, and it would please me to hear you play it again."

"What about you?" I asked, not intending to refuse his offer. I couldn't hide my delight, in any case.

"I have a Stradivari that is nearly as fine."

I hardly remember, now, exactly how we passed that first hour. I lost myself in practice, and he showed me some bowings and techniques that were unfamiliar to me. We also played a duet for two violins that he had composed. I, of course, was second fiddle, but he'd included enough technical challenges in that part to make it interesting, and it was a lovely piece.

When we finished, applause echoed in the nearly empty room, and it made me jump. I looked up and saw that two men—one carrying a viola, the other a cello—had joined us, I knew not when.

The chevalier made the introductions, then said, "If you will excuse me for a short while. I have another brief engagement, but I will return in a quarter of an hour."

He left without further explanation. The musicians, I discovered, played in the Concert Olympique, each of them the leaders of their sections. Their names were Alfonse Martel and Pierre Ordogne. I couldn't help stifling a laugh when Alfonse introduced himself. He had a kind face and lively blue eyes, but the lines radiating out from their corners suggested that he must have been at least fifty years old. I wondered if Sophie would think this was my invented Alfonse, and that I had sneaked away to meet him for a lover's tryst.

We were still talking when the chevalier returned, again with no explanation. He gave us his A and we tuned to him. I sat next to him, of course. The string quartet, although new to the chevalier, was familiar to me, and I therefore acquitted myself quite well. The last time I'd played it had been in Danior and Alida's apartment.

It was near eleven by the time we finished. The time had flown, and I didn't feel at all tired. I was filled with music and elated, my feet barely touching the ground as I returned the Amati to its case. The other two musicians left first. The chevalier took his time gathering up the music, and I helped him, sensing that he wanted me to stay behind for a few minutes.

"Well, I should be getting back to Sophie," I said, hoping he would ring for a servant to bring me my cloak and make sure the carriage had been pulled up to the door.

"Before you go, I want you to know something. Something very important."

He came close to me and took my hand, sandwiching it between his two so that I felt warm and in no hurry to remove it. He had perspired a little as we played, the room having been kept warm through the four heating stoves, and the faintest smell of his body tinged the scent of cologne he wore. "Yes?" I said, when he didn't continue speaking.

"You may hear things about me—things that are not true. I wish you to understand what a difficult position I am in here. I have status other Black people could only dream of, but it comes at a price." His eyes searched mine. His were a beautiful shade of warm, greenish brown, and I felt the pull of attraction to him as I looked up into his face. No wonder, I thought, so many husbands were jealous of this extraordinary man.

"We are not so different," I said. It seemed odd, but it was true. "As a woman, people expect certain things of me and don't like it when I push away from those expectations."

He nodded. "I think perhaps we have other similarities. Ones you have no doubt been instructed not to mention."

I froze. Did he know I was a spy? "Oh, you mean the music, of course!"

He nodded, but I could tell he saw through me.

"I just ask you, Mademoiselle Thérèse, not to judge me before you are in full possession of all the facts."

He was being very mysterious. "Of course," I said, lowering my eyes from his at last. Aside from not being able to bear their intensity for much longer, my neck was stiff from looking up.

That's when I saw it. A spot the size of a fingernail, and another drop a little further from it, on the lace cuff of his left wrist—the side of the cuff that would have been hidden from me while he was playing.

Blood. I gasped and tried to pull my hand free of his, but he held it tight.

"Remember, Thérèse. Nothing is as it seems." He took his left hand away and bent over mine, planting a soft, tender kiss on its back.

The door opened behind us. A footman held my cloak. I rushed to him, grabbing my violin case on the way, and didn't look back.

❧

I slept badly that night, worse than I had for a long time. The luxurious bed linens I'd become accustomed to twisted around my body as I thrashed, first cold as my legs and arms stuck out at odd angles and then too hot when I finally succeeded in burying myself beneath all the blankets. The evening's card party had been long over by the time I returned from the Palais Royale and Sophie was already abed. I wished I could have talked to her about trifles for a while before trying to close my eyes. I would have been grateful for gossip about her insipid marquis and her dreams of marrying so she could have illicit affairs. Such subjects would have helped to dispel the confusion of thoughts that occupied my mind with nothing to cushion me from what I had last seen when taking my leave of the chevalier. And she might have appreciated hearing about the music making, too—if she would allow herself to show that part of her I glimpsed in the theater a few days earlier. I had thought of sending for a glass of brandy, or at least some cocoa, to see if I could trick my body into sleepiness. But I didn't have the heart to rouse a servant from her exhausted sleep, which would all too soon end anyway.

And so, my mind reeled with everything I had heard and seen that evening. I had spent hours in the company of the Chevalier de Saint-Georges, sharing the kind of intimacy that only came from performing music together. A warm glow washed over me as I relived the evening, hearing the notes we each released from our instruments mingle and meld together. I felt as if I had risen far beyond what I thought I was capable of as we played. But I knew it was an illusion, that the proximity of the chevalier's greatness bestowed the false luster of greatness upon me. He was brilliant in the sense that he shone, and his light could not help but touch those around him. Back here, in this quiet house where only the creaking of timbers broke the stillness, I was just myself. No matter how much I wanted to be better than I was, it would take a great deal more than a single evening of chamber music to elevate me even to the level of someone like Danior.

And yet, with that brilliance, or despite it perhaps, the chevalier appeared such a gentle soul. His playing had fire, of course, but also tenderness that hinted at depths of emotion. I suppose I realized he must have had a difficult life before he reached the heights he now occupied, and I admit to being curious. How was it that the son of a French landowner and a slave from the island of Guadeloupe could attain such privilege, could be so accepted in the rank-obsessed society of Paris? Had he been teased and taunted? Bullied and tormented? The color of his skin surely would have put a great burden on him to be better than everyone else, yet he had managed—aside from the one skirmish over his directorship of the opera. Whatever remarkable qualities he possessed, whatever the exact circumstances of his childhood and young life, the need to overcome his disadvantages had pushed him to become the best violinist in Paris, the handsomest man and the most sought-after lover—and the deadliest swordsman.

The deadliest swordsman. I had seen the drops of blood on his lace cuffs. I could not say where they came from or when they had been acquired, but I knew enough about him to imagine that he was too fastidious to allow a stain to remain on his clothing any longer than absolutely necessary. Had the spots been there at the beginning of the evening? I forced my thoughts back, tried to recall the details of his dress. But I hadn't been looking. I hadn't been noticing. At least, not his cuffs. His eyes and his smile had me in thrall, and once we started playing, nothing else in the world existed. I could not have seen the blood until he took my hands in his and kept them there. Did he mean me to see them? Was he sending me a message? Nothing is as it seems, he said at the end.

A flash of memory jolted me out of my doze and I sat up, throwing the covers aside. He'd left the music room. When the others arrived, before we started playing the Haydn string quartet, the chevalier had excused himself. He would be gone for a quarter of an hour, he said. Some previous appointment. Had it been only a quarter of an hour? I did not possess a watch, and I didn't recall seeing a clock in the music room. There wouldn't be one, I thought, lest its regular chiming interfere with the enjoyment of music.

Where had he gone? He didn't appear in the least bit ruffled upon his return. He certainly had not been outside in the cold. Would he have had time to pass through the tunnel that separated the Palais Royale from the Hôtel Montesson? And if so, why? What was there?

It didn't fit at all. The chevalier had taken his place calmly in the first violin chair upon his return and led us perfectly through the four movements of the quartet. If he had inflicted harm on some other person in that time and could come back and immerse himself so fully in the beautiful music, then he was the most cold-blooded, unfeeling of men. I could not believe it of him. He was not such a man, I felt certain.

But what other explanation was there?

I forced myself to go back to bed and pressed my eyes closed until I could see stars underneath my eyelids. There was nothing I could do about it that night. I would try to find out more in the morning. But how? Something told me this was not a matter I should talk to the captain about. At least, not yet, not until I had a measure of certainty one way or the other. I so hoped it would be the other.

Chapter Twenty-Two

I still hadn't decided what I should do about the chevalier, whether I should mention anything at all to anyone about what I'd seen, when a footman entered the breakfast room with a card on a silver salver and presented it to me. I had only a moment to register Sophie's curious expression before I picked up the card and saw whose it was.

"The captain is here," I said, looking to Sophie for what to say next. I didn't feel I could invite him in myself.

"Why would he ask for you?" Sophie said.

Why indeed, I thought. "Perhaps for the sake of..." I flicked my eyes toward the footman, hoping Sophie would fill in the missing word, discretion.

"Ask the captain to join us in my boudoir," Sophie said to the footman, taking the situation over without a thought, clearly leaping to that understanding I'd intended. Once the footman had bowed out of the room, Sophie reached across the table and grabbed my wrist, her eyes dancing with mischief. "You're to stay with me, some distance away from us so you can't hear what we're saying. You understand?"

Of course I understood. She wanted a chaperon, but not a witness. So I nodded and followed her to her large bedchamber. She carefully arranged herself on her divan, spreading her dressing gown out provocatively, holding a hand mirror up as though she was about to start dressing. "You sit over there," she said, pointing to one of the chairs by the window a long way from the fire in the grate. My shawl wasn't warm enough to shield me from the icy weather only a pane of glass away, and I was shivering uncontrollably by the time I heard the approach of the captain's crisp, booted footsteps.

I hadn't seen Captain von Bauer since the morning after my adventures in the tunnels, when he had scolded me about not finding out more. I had no idea why he would appear at such an unaccustomed time and ask for me.

He didn't knock, but burst through the door and swept his eyes around the room. He passed over Sophie, whose nascent smile disappeared as soon as she realized he wasn't looking at her, and his gaze alit on me. He marched straight over and perched on the chair on the other side of the window. "I came to make sure you were all right," he said.

I looked back and forth from the captain's concerned expression to Sophie's look of gathering fury. How would I ever make this right? I thought, deciding that a calm demeanor would be best. "As you see, I am in perfect health."

He lowered his voice. "You haven't heard, then?"

"Heard what?" Sophie said, making no effort to hide her vexation. I had only heard that tone from her once before, when the chevalier had surprised us in the theater and heard her sing—something she apparently wasn't permitted to do, for a reason I had yet to discover. She rose and walked over to the two of us, forcing the captain to relinquish his chair to her.

I could tell he didn't want to explain himself in front of Sophie, but how could he not? "Whatever it is, I am Mademoiselle Delalande's guest, and can have no secrets from her in her own home."

"Very well." The captain paced back and forth in front of us. "There has been a murder."

Sophie emitted a tiny gasp. The silence that followed was broken only by the ticking of the clock on the escritoire and the whistle of the wind.

"What could such a thing have to do with Thérèse?" Sophie said eventually, her voice hardly more than a whisper. She reached out to take my hand, her affectionate nature asserting itself over any jealous feelings. Or perhaps she was simply relieved that the captain had not singled me out for flirtation.

"I believe...it has nothing to do with Mademoiselle Thérèse. But it has to do with someone she knows from Mademoiselle Bertin's workshop."

I rose and clutched my throat. "Is it Ondine? Lucienne? Are they all right?" I pictured an angry marquise breaking into the workshop and stabbing one of them to get her hands on the queen's Valenciennes lace.

"Yes, yes, they are well, at least in body. But Mademoiselle Ondine—it was her beau who was killed."

I sank back into my chair. My relief that the victim was not one of my friends was short lived. Ondine had said little about her beau Roland, other than that he was a printer who would ask for her hand in marriage as soon as he had made enough money. She was so proud of him.

A printer. Named Roland. I gasped. "When did it happen? Tell me everything! Poor Ondine. I must go to her!"

"An artist found him by his printing press in the basement of the Louvre. He'd been stabbed through the heart with a long blade. Possibly an épée."

My stomach knotted and my mouth went dry. The chevalier. The blood. "When?" My lips formed the word but I barely had the breath to make it sound.

"Sometime last night is all the police can determine. No one heard anything, which means it must have been after the artists had left for home or gone to bed in their apartments."

I knew, then, that I would have to tell the captain about what I'd seen. But first, I must visit Ondine. And then, the chevalier. "I'll dress and go to Mademoiselle Bertin's."

"I'm coming with you!" Sophie said, and took hold of the captain's arm and pushed him out of her room.

Once he'd gone, she turned to me and said, "A murder! How exciting!"

I wanted to slap her. Instead I said nothing, but went back to my room to dress for a visit to a grieving friend.

As I expected, Ondine was inconsolable.

"Why? He was such a good man. I don't understand! He was just doing his job, printing the gazette. What happened? Why?" She sniffed and sobbed between every other word.

I knelt down next to her where she sat at her workbench, wringing her sodden handkerchief and no longer trying to use it to mop the tears that fell in an unending stream down her cheeks. Lucienne had cleared the work away so Ondine's weeping wouldn't spoil the delicate trimmings, and stood next to her friend, holding a cup of tea, which Ondine ignored.

"Hush, Ondine. The police will find out who killed him." I shuddered to think of it even as I said the words. What if it was the chevalier? What if he had left our pleasant evening of music and raced through the tunnels to the basement of the Louvre to plunge his deadly épée into the printer's heart?

But it couldn't be. There would have been more of a clue. He would have been out of breath, or agitated in some way. No one could commit murder and, minutes later, play first violin in a Haydn string quartet half a mile away.

I knew I wouldn't find the answer there, but right then Ondine needed comfort more than answers. "Drink your tea. I'm sure Mademoiselle Bertin would let you go home if you need to." I looked to Lucienne for affirmation, not actually certain that—even in such extreme circumstances—that would be the case.

Lucienne shrugged. "Mademoiselle Bertin has gone to Versailles, and I do not expect her to return before the end of the day."

"And you see, Lucienne will not tell her you left the workroom, will you?"

Lucienne looked sad for her friend, but she also cast a critical eye around the room, no doubt assessing whether she could get enough of the work done herself to keep Ondine's absence a secret.

"Don't touch that!" Lucienne said, and I turned to see Sophie with a length of embroidered silk wrapped around her head and draped over her shoulders.

"Please excuse my friend," I said. "She is no doubt delighted by all she sees here and forgets that she is in the presence of grief."

"Yes, I'm sorry, I didn't mean..." Sophie's face went pink. She unwrapped the silk and handed it to Lucienne. "At least you can work surrounded by beauty. It must be a great comfort."

At that, Ondine redoubled her crying.

I knelt down beside her. "Ondine, I vow to you that I will do all in my power to help discover who committed this terrible deed."

"You? What can you possibly do? You are not a policeman. You aren't even Parisian!"

Of course, she didn't know how deeply involved in all this I was, so I smiled and stood. "Well, I will give what assistance I can. We must leave now. I have to pay a call on a friend."

Ondine appeared calmer when we left, and I suspected she would end up staying and working. Perhaps in her circumstances I would do the same. The apartment she shared with other girls who worked in shops around Paris would be empty and probably cold. At least in the workshop she would stay warm and could drink as much tisane as she pleased.

"Where are we going?" Sophie asked.

We'd walked to the Rue St. Honoré, judging it to be faster than calling for the carriage and probably safer, as the cobbles were still slick from the recent snow. The temperature had not risen above freezing, and people on the street said this was the coldest winter they could ever remember. My heart sank at the idea that such a winter would make travel from Paris to Vienna impossible, and I would likely not be home for Christmas as I had hoped.

But this was a small concern compared to the question of who had murdered the printer in the basement of the Louvre. How odd, I thought, were the threads of connection among the small number of people I'd met in Paris in the last month. That Ondine's beau could have been involved in printing the very pamphlets whose authors I had been tasked with discovering, and that the chevalier would have knowledge of the tunnels that would lead to where such illegal activity was taking place.

"Shall we go down to the river by the Louvre? I have heard that people are skating there," Sophie said, interrupting my thoughts.

We had bundled ourselves well against the cold, with bonnets and scarves and fur muffs, and to my surprise, Sophie owned shoes that were much sturdier than the silk evening slippers we normally wore, so walking would not be too difficult. And it might give me some time to think, as well. It also occurred to me that I could take the opportunity of walking past the Louvre to make some observations of the palace itself, perhaps spy the door I had exited from the night I had gone through the tunnels. I wished I could find some excuse to enter again and see for myself the scene of this murder. I'd have to do it without Sophie, though, and I couldn't see how to accomplish such a thing.

As we set off for the Quai du Louvre, it became clear that we weren't the only people bent on going outside despite the weather. Something about the crystalline cold, and the fact that having frozen over, the Seine had lost its power to poison the air, made many people who might otherwise avoid its banks flood there out of curiosity, if nothing else.

And, as Sophie had intimated, there was indeed a group of young people out on the ice near the bank, squealing with delight as they slid around on the surface. Young ladies and gentlemen clutched each other tighter than necessary with the excuse of keeping themselves upright. Most of the skaters didn't have blades attached to their shoes, but that didn't seem to matter.

"How delightful!" Sophie clapped her hands like a little girl. "Let's go and join them."

"I don't think it's safe," I said. I didn't believe it had been cold enough for long enough to thicken the ice so that it could support so many people.

"Oh nonsense! See how everyone is skating out there with no danger? *Viens!*"

She grabbed my hand and pulled me down the steps to the river's edge. Before I could stop her, she was out on the ice. Almost immediately, her feet went out from under her and she fell in a heap on her backside. I smiled when I saw that, within seconds, a young officer raced to her rescue and helped her stand, then took that opportunity to escort her around the perimeter of skaters with one arm around her waist.

"Sophie!" I called. But she didn't hear me over the laughter and conversation.

I had no desire to go out on the ice in borrowed shoes that pinched my feet. Yet I was Sophie's chaperon, apparently. I looked around in consternation for a place to sit, and was about to give up and fetch Sophie to go home, when I heard someone call my name.

"Mademoiselle Thérèse! Mademoiselle Thérèse! I am come!"

I looked for the source of the voice, and there was the marquis, Sophie's soon-to-be betrothed, huffing and puffing down the stone steps.

"I went to the Hôtel Montesson, and they said Sophie had walked out but they didn't know where, and I thought she must have come here to join in the fun." He was out of breath, his corpulent figure not equal to so much exercise.

"Sophie is out on the ice, as you see," I said. "I think she'd be grateful if you would go and rescue her."

He caught my meaning immediately and grinned, taking off on his inappropriately shod feet to join the revelers. I watched him teeter out from the bank, arms spread wide to balance himself, trying in vain to reach Sophie—who was by now flying around in a circle in the arms of an officer who clearly knew how to skate. I could barely suppress my laughter.

But I had more important things to do than watch Sophie navigate between such dissimilar partners. I had not been hired as a chaperon, and she could hardly come to harm out here surrounded by so many people. So I decided to go back into the Louvre and find the printing press in the basement again and look around for myself. I would tell Sophie later that I had grown cold and, since I could leave her in the capable hands of the marquis, I had returned to the Hôtel Montesson to await her there.

Chapter Twenty-Three

After walking back and forth along the Rue du Louvre and trying every door I saw, I could not find the one that had led me out into the cold the night I stumbled on the room where the scurrilous pamphlets were being printed. But knowing that room and the printing press was in the basement of the Louvre, I decided I could explore from inside on such a cold day, find some other doorway that would lead me below ground. I headed to what appeared to be a public entrance, where both young men and ladies walked in carrying portfolios and palettes under their arms—doubtless bound for drawing or painting lessons with one of the many artists whose studios were within. No one paid any attention to me. They were all busy chattering away about art, about the latest scandals to do with different painters, which of them had been snubbed by the Académie and which had been awarded lucrative royal appointments.

"Can you imagine it!" one young woman whispered to her friend so that everyone else in the corridor could hear her, "That scheming, ambitious Madame Le Brun has been named portraitist to the queen!"

"I'm shocked," her friend whispered back, "after her picture of Marie Antoinette in a chemise dress. Do you know, they made her take it down from the salon last August and replace it with one of the queen in a different gown. How embarrassing! What can the queen have been thinking?"

"Well, you do know she's very thick with Mademoiselle Bertin, who persuaded Marie Antoinette to wear such a gown in the first place."

The second woman—neither of them much more than girls, I perceived—said, "I hear the modiste's star is waning. I think the king is tired of paying her outrageous accounts."

I'd stopped where I was to listen, and was about to continue on my way when they'd passed on to what must have been their drawing teacher's studio, when I turned and found myself face-to-face with the Chevalier de Saint-Georges. I staggered back a little and he put out his hand to steady me.

"Mademoiselle Thérèse! How delightful to see you. But what brings you to this part of the Louvre on a day when there are no exhibitions?"

"The cold!" I said, thinking fast. I examined his garments, which seemed quite unsuitable for day. He was dressed in full court regalia, with his tricorn tucked beneath his arm, his épée at his side, his medals and honors pinned to his breast, and the Amati grasped lightly by the neck.

He must have guessed at my confusion, because he said, "I am here to have my portrait painted by Joseph Vien. I would have postponed it to a warmer day, but he is much in demand."

"Who wants this portrait of you?" I asked, because that was really the only reason anyone went through the tedium of sitting to be sketched and painted. And then I realized it could as easily have been some lady, a lover of his, and I blushed.

The chevalier smiled. "You assume I do not want it for myself?" He shook his head. "No matter. It is to hang in the salon at the Loge Olympique. An honor that I do not deserve."

So, the duc de Chartres would pay for it, I assumed.

I did not think I could continue my original project, now that I had encountered the chevalier and given him such a feeble excuse for being there. "Sophie is skating with her marquis. I am planning to go home, now that I have warmed myself a little."

"Home?" He asked as though he well understood that the Hôtel Montesson was not my home, that I was as out of place there as a sparrow in a lark's nest. "Come, stay a little longer, talk to me while the master works. Then I would be delighted if you would come back to my apartment with me so we may continue our conversations about music, perhaps play together a little."

I couldn't help glancing quickly at the lace ruff that spilled out of his left sleeve. Of course, it was quite clean. No spots of blood this time. "All right," I said. "I don't think I'm expected back before supper."

Later, I would regret having been so specific about the time. But just then, whatever he was hiding, whatever was going on, I could not resist the prospect of once again making music with this beguiling man.

We were in the artist's studio for an hour. In that time, Monsieur Vien made sketches only, I assumed so he could discuss with his sitter what pose would suit. The chevalier quite dwarfed the diminutive Vien, who darted around moving an arm here, angling the violin so, encouraging the chevalier to look more serious, happier, more thoughtful, playful, and so on. Every once in a while, the chevalier would look up and make a face at me when the artist wasn't looking, and I had a hard time keeping my countenance.

When it came time to leave, Monsieur Vien approached me and took hold of my chin, angling my face this way and that. "If you would ever consent to model for the painters here, I think you could make quite a handsome living," he said.

My cheeks must have given away my embarrassment, because the chevalier interjected, "Mademoiselle Thérèse is not an urchin. She is the guest of Madame de Montesson and the duc d'Orléans."

"I meant no offense," Vien said quickly. "Only to point out that your aspect has more dignity than most of the models in Paris, and would be suitable in history paintings or allegories."

Not having much knowledge of such things, I chose to take his words as complimentary, and left with the chevalier. "Where is your cloak?" I asked him as we passed back down the corridor by which we had approached the studio.

"Oh, I don't have one with me."

I stopped. "And the violin! The cold will ruin it."

"Do not be uneasy, Mademoiselle Thérèse. We needn't pass out of doors to return to the Palais Royale from here, as you well know."

By now, the chevalier had my upper arm in a firm grip. It was a grip that would betoken no more than friendship to anyone glancing in our direction, but it held a great deal more meaning than that to me. If I had been determined, I probably could have broken free and run away, as he would not want to drop the violin, but I was afraid that might convey more information to him than he already had. As far as he knew for certain, I had no reason to fear him. And I had seen him emerge from the tunnel to come to the theater in the Hôtel Montesson, after all, so perhaps he only referred to my general knowledge of tunnels. I prayed that was the case even as I tried to suppress the need to swallow nervously.

Once I had control of myself, I smiled. "I suppose there are more tunnels below ground than people know about." He returned my smile, but did not say anything.

We walked through many corridors, twisting and turning until I had no sure idea which direction we were going, when at last we passed through a door that led down a flight of stairs. "Where are we going?" I thought to ask, not wanting to give away that I might have any idea. "Isn't this the way to the basement?"

"A tunnel, by definition, is below ground," he said, continuing to propel me in front of him.

We reached the lower level and soon were in a large room where the carcasses of discarded artworks were stored. In the middle of the room sat the large printing press I had seen through the cracked door two nights before. I couldn't help gasping.

"Yes, Mademoiselle Thérèse, this is the scene of a heinous murder."

I whirled around and looked full in his face. He did not appear angry, or frightening. Instead, he looked sad. I furrowed my brow and cocked my head on the side.

"I did everything I could to prevent it, but I was too late," he said.

"You... prevent..." My mind was whirling.

"What I don't know is what you were doing in the tunnels the night before last."

I had turned away, fascinated by the strange atmosphere in this room where illegal doings had the perverse habit of occurring, and turned to look back at him, mouth agape. He stood blocking the door that would lead me back out and up the stairs. "You don't think I..."

What could he think? I came out of nowhere, suddenly an intimate in a house opposed to the queen. And I had previously been working with those who were her most ardent supporters. What's more, the murder victim was the fiancé of someone I had worked with for a number of weeks. But how did he know that?

"You are grossly mistaken!" I yelled. "How can you think—I would have no cause to—I am quite on the other side—"

"I am willing to give you the benefit of the doubt, Mademoiselle Thérèse, but I will not release you from my custody until I am quite satisfied as to who you are and what you are doing here. After you."

He gestured toward the door that would lead through the other storeroom to the tunnel entrance. What else could I do but obey? I could not call for help, I could not run anywhere that he would not apprehend me. And part of me, too, was immensely curious. If the chevalier was not working for the Orléans faction against the queen, what was he doing?

In any case, I refused to believe that anyone who played the violin so beautifully would willingly harm another violinist.

Chapter Twenty-Four

Ever the gentleman, the chevalier first rang for tea and cakes after we entered his apartment. Then he proceeded to remove his ceremonial garments, starting by unpinning his orders and medals, then unbuckling his épée, taking off his hat and wig, and finally removing his brocade coat, so that he was only in his shirtsleeves. Without his wig, the tight curls in his nearly black hair cupped his ears and trailed on the back of his collar.

If anything, he was handsomer without his regalia, and I couldn't stop staring at him as he moved around the apartment. I watched his delicate, muscular hands as they picked up a score that lay on top of the pianoforte and slid it neatly into one of the drawers in what I now saw was a cabinet full of manuscripts and printed music. I had quite forgotten how I'd come to be there, and jumped when the servant entered with the tray of refreshments. This servant—a young black boy in elegant livery—bowed deeply after depositing the tray on a small table near the fire. Rather than ignoring him, as most people who employed such servants would, the chevalier said, "Thank you, Pierre," and tossed the boy a coin he teased out of his watch pocket with two fingers. The boy caught the coin, and his face lit up with a broad smile before he disappeared out the door.

I poured out the tea and lifted my bowl to my lips with two hands, afraid that using only one would reveal that I was trembling.

"If you are innocent of any wrongdoing, there is no need for you to be afraid of me."

My deception hadn't worked. "You will forgive me for appearing anxious," I said. "Even the most innocent young woman would be fearful in this situation. I am alone with someone I hardly know who is a master swordsman, and who could easily overpower me if he wished."

He nodded. "Forgive me. I look to my own heart when I judge whether someone else ought to fear me. I know that I would not willingly do you harm."

We sipped our tea in silence for a few moments. My mind worked furiously to figure out what I should say to him, how much of my purpose in being there I should reveal.

But it was the chevalier who broke the silence. "I have guessed that you are not only not Parisian, but that you are not French at all. Someone has sent you here, for what purpose I am not entirely certain."

I tried not to react. I realized it would be pointless to lie to him, that there would be no benefit in doing so. But I would not give up my information easily. "How did you guess?"

"I, too, am an immigrant. A foreigner. Despite my careful tutoring by the best masters, I will never entirely shed that slight trace of accent that reveals my upbringing in the islands. While most people do not hear it, those of us with the keen ears of a musician can perceive such things. So it remains for you to tell me first where you are, in fact, from, and what is your true station."

I considered making up a story, giving myself a more interesting origin. It would merely be embroidering on the truth, just as Lucienne and Ondine embroidered plain scraps of fabric to make them appear more costly. An innocent deception. But what was the point?

I replaced my teacup on the tray and sat up straight. "I am from Vienna. A common Austrian." I remembered in that moment the captain teaching me that if caught, a spy was never to answer a question with more information than required.

"Whoever chose you to come and insinuate yourself into French society and the court chose wisely. I would like you to tell me who exactly that was."

Again, what to say? The emperor himself gave me my commission. But it had been on the recommendation of the captain, who was also under cover of an adopted identity of sorts. I remained silent.

"Mademoiselle Sauvé—which I know is not your real name—it is in your interest to answer me truthfully."

"Why should I? Other than because you have me entirely in your power at the moment. What do I gain by giving you any more information about myself without knowing why you are asking me for it? For all I know, you yourself could be the murderer." A door had opened in my mind. I understood that it was indeed unlikely that he would hurt me. I had friends who would be alarmed if I did not reappear in sound body within a reasonable amount of time, and such violence would undermine his position in society. This gave me the freedom to refuse his demands for information and invoke my friends if need be.

"A fair point. You may believe the only power I possess is that of harming you. However, that is not so. I know things that could interfere with the happiness and prosperity of your friend, Sophie Delalande. She, too, is not who she would like everyone to believe her to be."

"Sophie? You must be mad!"

He shrugged. "I know her family, from the provinces. Although they can claim a distant connection with Madame de Montesson, Sophie herself has, shall we say, a stain. Were a noble such as the marquis to hear of it, he would not marry her. You see, she is the natural daughter of an aristocrat who had an affair with a creole opera singer."

An opera singer! Of course. Now it made sense. Her voice. If what the chevalier said was true, it would not only account for her reluctance to sing, but it would go a long way toward explaining her desperate need to secure an alliance with the marquis.

"Here is the truth of the matter," he continued. "I am not a murderer, whatever you choose to believe. I gain nothing through the death of the unfortunate Roland. In fact, my position here is made more precarious through this occurrence."

With everything he told me, I became more and more certain that it had to be the duc de Chartres and his allies who—whether or not they actually wrote the scurrilous pamphlets certainly facilitated their dissemination. How clever to use the printing press that produced the voluminous fashion gazette, so that no one would wonder at its operating late into the night. "But… Who would have wanted him dead?" I didn't mention to the chevalier that I'd heard him and the duke discussing Roland's dissatisfaction in the tunnel that first night, and understood his implied threat.

He spread his hands, palms up, and smiled. "Who knows? But for the moment, that is not to the point. We were discussing you and your situation. I am determined to discover what you are doing here and why. Shall I guess and see how close I come to the truth, since you have been so lacking in candor?"

"All right," I said, now curious.

"Let me see… First, I believe that you are not in sympathy with the Orléans faction, that rather, you have been sent here to gather information about those who want to discredit the queen. The queen is Austrian, after all. I don't know whether it was luck or design that landed you in the Montesson orbit."

Was it so obvious? What had I done to lead him to perceive my exact instructions?

"I see by your expression that I am correct, and that you are now berating yourself for having allowed me to guess at your position with such accuracy." He smiled. "Do not be alarmed. I have no intention of interfering with your purpose. I feel sorry for Marie Antoinette, and do not believe she is responsible for any of the despicable acts the pamphleteers accuse her of."

"Then what are you doing here, accepting the generosity of a man who would see the Bourbon dynasty destroyed?"

He took his time crossing one leg over the other and flicking a bit of imagined dust off his knee. "I care nothing about gossip and pamphlets. I care only about music and art. I exercise my bow for whoever provides the handsomest remuneration and evinces the most appreciation for my talents. Right now, it is the duc de Chartres. If the king were to offer me a better position—but he is no music lover. And the queen has her favorites. In point of fact, I know that she bears me great animosity simply because I depend upon the duc de Chartres for my livelihood, and perhaps because of the color of my skin. She knows—because her own spies tell her—that this safe, autonomous space in the heart of her realm hosts those who want to topple the monarchy, or at least change its character for good. The ideas that escape into the atmosphere of this building, in the Masonic rooms especially, could be interpreted as high treason and send many men—and women—to the gallows."

"What ideas are those?" I had heard of such things in whispers here and there. In fact, Emperor Joseph himself was said to embrace many of the reforms espoused by the *philosophes*. But I wanted to know more.

"The idea that the nobility should pay its share of taxes rather than be exempt from them because of their birth. That the poor deserve the ability to earn a wage that raises them above the level of near starvation. That positions in the government should be awarded based on merit and capacity to govern rather than on connections and the ability to pay."

Such thoughts did not seem unreasonable to me, and I said as much. "And I also believe the queen herself cares deeply about the poor."

At this, the chevalier opened his mouth wide and laughed. "It matters little what the queen cares about. She has no power at all, except to set fashion and produce heirs—something she has failed to do as of yet. But I cannot blame you for your naïveté. Nor for your royalist sentiments. You and I and all the musicians and composers in the world depend upon the good graces of this unjust system in order to achieve our highest purpose."

I thought about this for a moment. "But, if the public were allowed to purchase tickets and to support musical and artistic endeavors, would that not be a suitable replacement for the system of patronage that now exists?"

He shook his head and poured me another cup of tea. "The public, even if the concerns of everyone were able to rise above mere survival, would never support the kind of expense involved in, say, producing an opera, or a ballet, or even many plays. Therefore, we all must exercise our talents as best we can within this very unequal world. We must accept the opportunities we are given, compete for the coveted positions, and suffer those with more money than they can count to distribute it to their pet musicians and painters and actors and dancers." By the end of his speech, a deep furrow had appeared between his eyes, and his normally cheerful, serene face had fallen into a state of gloom.

"And what about swordsmen? Who is willing to pay for you to exercise that talent?" I asked, feeling that beneath all his apparently heartfelt words, he was purposely misleading me.

"My sword is at the service of honor and truth alone. I do not resort to its aid for any personal reasons, nor do I accept payment for its use. I am not a sell-sword. I have many times been insulted and subjected to calumnies of the most insidious sort. It is not easy to look like me. Yet I have not allowed my vanity to tempt me to respond in a manner that would undoubtedly result in the death of the other person."

His gloom had been replaced by steely hardness. Something burned deep in his eyes. I shivered. I would not want to provoke the wrath of such a man who had so much buried passion.

He breathed deeply through flared nostrils and smiled. "I think you understand more than you pretend," he said. "We are more alike than not, despite our apparent differences."

With those words, my mind was suddenly opened to the tableau of the chevalier's life. He might not have to disguise himself to be allowed to perform, but, like me, he had to be better than everyone else in order to achieve anything at all. He had to distinguish himself above all others to be seen as the artist he was, not some curiosity of exotic birth and beguiling looks. Despite being an example of how the lowly and disadvantaged could rise to a pinnacle of achievement, he was forced to support the very fabric of a society that would grind him beneath its heel if it could. "So you are willing to allow these libels against the queen to continue, as long as you remain safely in your protected musician's tower."

The chevalier stood and ambled over to the window. He gazed at it as though he could see outside, but the sun had set and all was dark.

It seemed to me he was stalling, trying to think of an answer to my accusation of self-interest on his part.

When at last he turned to speak to me again, all trace of emotion had left his face. "I do not mean to condescend. But I have seen a great deal more of life than you. I have heard secrets I may never reveal, and have been present at conversations that would turn your blood to ice. I assert once more that I had nothing to do with the murder of the printer. What would it have served me, after all? And I think you will find that this murder—far from bringing the operation to light—will drive everyone involved further underground and out of sight. And that will be dangerous for us all."

He put out his hand to me. I stood and went to him, wondering what he would do. He tucked it under his arm and strolled with me toward the door of his apartment. "Now you must return to the Hôtel Montesson or you will be missed."

I was relieved, and yet sad to be parting from this extraordinary man, who had spoken to me like an equal. An equal, when he was in all ways superior to me and almost everyone I had ever known.

Chapter Twenty-Five

I was nonetheless a little relieved that the chevalier was true to his word and escorted me to the entrance of the Palais Royale that led out toward the Chaussée d'Antin, ensuring that my walk back to the Hôtel Montesson would be as short as possible in the cold weather. I turned after I stepped through the door and curtsied to him. "Thank you, Monsieur. I hope our acquaintance may continue."

He gave me a deep, courtly bow in return, and said, "I, for my part, hope you will come and play chamber music with me and my fine musicians again sometime soon." Then he looked up at the sky, no longer clear, but overcast with heavy, wintry clouds. "A change in the weather is coming. There will be no more skating this month, I wager."

His words reminded me that I longed to be able to return to Vienna in time to pass some of the winter festivities with my family and friends. But as I huddled against the bitter wind, I thought he meant more than his words had said. A change was in the air, certainly. What he had told me, the deep currents swirling in the political world of France, was both thrilling and terrifying. It seemed that ideas outstripped reality now, but such ideas—that would help the poor and diminish the power of the nobility—would face fierce resistance by those who did not desire change. If such change occurred, would it be for the better? All I knew was that, one way or another, I would not be in Paris to discover it for myself.

The walk back to the Hôtel Montesson was just long enough for me to be disturbed anew by unanswered questions. The chevalier claimed to have had nothing to do with the printer's death. But what about the spot of blood I'd seen on his cuff the very night of the murder? If he was not responsible, did he have some contact with whoever was? And if so, why keep it a secret?

He'd certainly made sure I could not run to the authorities myself. If I did, he might well raise the possibility that I was somehow involved in the affair. Being confined to the Bastille once was enough to satisfy any curiosity I might have about that fortress. Therefore I would have to continue to act in the shadows, to try to expose the perpetrator through indirect means.

And that meant that I must somehow get a message to the captain that I must see him, that I had information to convey to him that directly concerned the matter of the murder. How could I do such a thing without arousing suspicion?

A footman greeted me at the door and took my cloak and muff from me. "Has Mademoiselle Sophie returned yet?" I asked.

"Mademoiselle Delalande is not at home. Madame de Montesson was under the impression that she had gone out with you, Mademoiselle."

I couldn't tell whether he was concerned or just curious, so I said, "We met the marquis de Bonesprit, who escorted Mademoiselle Sophie on the ice. I'm sure they'll be back presently."

I hoped that was enough to satisfy his need for information, and hastened to my room. Sophie wasn't there, which gave me an opportunity to quickly write a note to the captain and, once I'd dressed for the evening, to find a servant to deliver it to him at Madame's right away. In it I referred as obliquely as possible to the need to meet with him. I didn't want to commit too much of what the chevalier said to me to so permanent a medium as a letter. Such things could fall into the wrong hands and create havoc—as I knew all too well. I decided it was safest to imply that the matter I wished to discuss with the captain was of a personal nature.

I finished my note and started to dress for supper. I soon realized that I would have to ring for a maid to help lace and pin me into my pearl satin gown—one of the castoffs Sophie insisted she no longer wore and that she claimed looked better on me than on her anyway. I had taken hold of the bell pull, not certain it would achieve the desired result because I had never needed to use it before, when my bedroom door flew open and Sophie burst into the room.

"What a delight! I wish the Seine would freeze over all year round!"

I was quite surprised at her high spirits. I didn't think the awkward marquis possessed the qualities necessary to entertain her so effectively. "So, you had a lovely time with Bonesprit?" I asked, doing my best to suppress my surprise.

"What? Oh, he fell down a few minutes after you left and hurt his wrist. His footman carried him off the ice. You should have seen it!"

"Who were you with, then?" I asked, now feeling very guilty for having left her alone.

"Oh, everyone was there! I must have known half a dozen people at least." Her cheeks, already pink from the cold air, deepened to scarlet. I guessed that Captain von Bauer had arrived and escorted her around the ice, and was about to say as much when she spotted the letter I'd propped on the writing desk. Even from across the room it was possible to read the direction to the captain.

"Now that you're here, could you help me with my gown before you go and change?" I asked, hoping to distract her.

But she appeared not to hear me. Instead, she marched over to the desk and picked up the note. "Why would you be writing to the captain? What can you possibly have to say to him?"

Before I could stop her she broke the seal and scanned the words I'd written to conceal my real purpose. I saw her read it through from beginning to end at least three times. When she finally looked up at me, her large brown eyes filled with tears that soon spilled out over her lashes and streaked her face. "How could you!" She said. "I thought we were friends!"

She threw the letter down and ran from the room before I could stop her. I still wasn't securely fastened into my gown, but I hurried after her, my stays and bum roll clearly visible from the back, I had no doubt. She slammed the door of her room just before I reached it. I heard her sobs through the panels. When they subsided into sniffs and gentle weeping I tapped on her door.

"Go away!" She called out, but I could tell her heart wasn't in it.

I tried the handle, and the latch lifted. She hadn't stopped to throw the bolt across. "Sophie, we need to talk. I should have told you before, I know, but I didn't want to hurt you." It occurred to me that I could extricate the captain from Sophie's needy infatuation at the same time as I ensured that her betrothal to the marquis would be unmarred by scandal, if I was careful about it. "I have known the captain for a long time, from before I came to Paris. He is very charming, and takes it as a challenge to capture the hearts of the most beautiful women, whether he cedes his own to them or not."

"So, he must think I'm beautiful?"

She sounded like a little girl. How was it that she could feel so vulnerable, so unsure of herself? She was related to one of the foremost families in France. She was educated, charming, and full of vivacity, whatever the secrets of her birth. "What is it Sophie? What's troubling you? I wager it is not the captain's heartlessness alone."

I took her hand and pulled her over to sit on the edge of her bed. She didn't resist. When I put my arm around her shoulder and pulled her to me, she leaned against me and curled her feet up onto the bed, taking my other hand and playing with my fingers.

"Your hands are so strong, but delicate. It's because of the violin, isn't it?"

"Yes. But let's not talk about me. What are you not telling me Sophie? I am your friend. I swear to you anything you say to me will go no further than my ears. You know I'm capable of keeping secrets."

She heaved a deep, shuddering sigh and pressed her handkerchief to her eyes. "If you only knew how I've longed to tell you everything. I know you're much cleverer and prettier than I am, but I felt a connection with you the first time we met. I saw you, so out of place and awkward, looking on the outside how I felt on the inside."

"You? Out of place?"

"The reason my mother sent me to Paris to make a match was not just because she wants me to marry well. In fact, she isn't my mother at all. She can't wait to be rid of me, and would have married me off to the butcher's son if my father had allowed it."

"Was your father a widower when he married your mother? Your stepmother, rather?"

"No. My father has only been married once. It is my stepmother's family that has the connections to Madame de Montesson. It is for my her sake that I am welcomed here, that I am introduced as a relative rather than a bumpkin from the provinces. I would not be so welcome if anyone outside of my father and stepmother knew that I am my father's child by an opera singer of mixed race, who died giving birth to me."

I didn't let on that it was a little too late for her to keep it a complete secret, and that I already knew these things thanks to the chevalier. "Does your stepmother have any of her own children?"

"No. That is what makes her so very angry. She is forced to pin all her hopes on me, a child she never wanted, but who her husband had sworn to raise as his own." Sophie sat up straight and turned me toward her. "No one else knows! You mustn't breathe a word. It would ruin everything. That's why my mother—stepmother—made me promise not to sing. Apparently, my father's affair with my real mother before he married was well known, but not the fact that she bore his child. My stepmother passes me off as her own. If I don't marry well, it will bring shame on the family, and her efforts will be for naught."

I decided it wasn't the time to point out that her infatuation with the captain could well have undermined this goal, as well as potentially lead to a repetition of her real mother's mistakes. "How old were you when you first knew that your father's wife was not your mother?"

"She didn't tell me until I was old enough to keep quiet about it, and until I swore I would never tell my father that I knew. He dotes on me, you see, and would keep me from harm if at all possible."

Her words brought to mind the image of my own father, dead these four years. I often wondered what he would think of my double life, of the danger I had faced. "Would your father condone your flirtation with the captain?" I asked.

She shook her head slowly. "No. I've been a bit foolish, haven't I. And now you know all my secrets. Was it unwise of me to tell you?"

Unwise? Sophie was not the most prudent of young women, but she had unwittingly chosen the one person to whom she could confide anything and it would go no further. "No. You can trust me completely."

"Swear. Swear it on the captain's life!" She stood and put her hand over her heart.

I did the same. "I swear it."

"Of course, I know your secret too." She wandered toward her garderobe and opened its doors, running her fingers over the opulent silks and velvets before choosing a dark blue gown in the newest style, a robe a la polonaise with its outer skirt gathered up in artful flounces that revealed the contrasting petticoat beneath.

"What secret?" I asked, suddenly alarmed that she might know that I was in fact sent to spy on the family she belonged to.

"About the captain, of course!"

I tried my hardest to blush. How useful that she should accept without question that my interest in the captain was merely amorous! "What can I say?"

I unlaced her from her day dress and carefully removed all the pins, then held the evening skirt open for her to step into and helped her put on the bodice and conceal all the fastening ribbons, before pinning the bodice securely to the skirt. "I have an idea," she said. "You want to see the captain, I understand, and you do not want your feelings known. So be it."

She turned me around and began lacing me into my own gown and pinning the panel that hid the laces across the back. "Tomorrow, the chevalier de Saint-Georges will perform at my aunt's salon again. I shall invite the captain to come as well, and cover for you both when you steal away for a tryst. And tomorrow, the marquis de Bonesprit will also attend, and I have reason to believe he will propose to me."

"How exciting!" It was the perfect scheme for my purposes. I had a momentary pang of disappointment that I would probably not hear the chevalier play, but for the moment, I had more important concerns. I hoped that together, with the chevalier occupied and out of the way, the captain and I would be able to discover who had killed the printer in order to assure his silence. But how could I be certain Captain von Bauer would come at Sophie's invitation?

"I want to look my best for the captain," I said. "And I wager you want to appear at your finest for the sake of the marquis." I took her hands in mine. "Why don't we go to the atelier of Mademoiselle Bertin in the morning and have our gowns trimmed for the occasion? Some new lace and ribbon would freshen us both up, I think."

"But Mademoiselle Bertin is booked months in advance!" Sophie said.

I touched the side of my nose. "You forget that I have a connection. I can take you around to the workshop behind the store and get my friends, Lucienne and Ondine, to do us a favor in exchange for a little extra money." I had no idea if they would agree, but it was at least an excuse to go there. I would leave a note to be delivered to the emperor himself in the event that events went horribly wrong. Ondine would agree, I was certain, if I assured her that doing so would help in the investigation of her fiancé's murder.

As Sophie and I went arm-in-arm to the dining room for supper, I hoped that my actions the next day would not precipitate any retribution that would cause my friend harm. Knowing her as I now did, I felt it my duty to protect her. She should not suffer for her father's transgressions. She deserved—as much as anyone did—happiness and fulfillment. And once she was safely married to the marquis, I hoped she would allow herself to sing, and attract others who cared deeply about music to her glittering social circle.

Chapter Twenty-Six

All had gone according to plan in the morning. Although at first resistant to the idea, Lucienne and Ondine had soon changed their tune at the sight of the gold coins in Sophie's purse, and we left with our gowns suitably enhanced. I also parted from Ondine with the assurance that she would give the note I wrote to the emperor into Mademoiselle Bertin's hands if I failed to achieve my object and ended up in prison—or worse.

And when the guests arrived for the salon, I was relieved to see the captain among them. Sophie and I had agreed that he would disappear as soon as the chevalier arrived, and that I would join him after the performance began, slipping out from the back of the audience at a moment when I was sure the chevalier would not notice.

"You shall meet in the library—no one ever goes there," Sophie had said. So I wrote a new note to the captain containing those instructions, and adding a little more of the kind of language Sophie would expect to find in a message arranging an illicit lovers' meeting. In fact, she had recovered completely from her disappointment about the captain and thrown herself so wholeheartedly into facilitating this supposed tryst that I wondered if she had really ever had her eye on him. I had a feeling that expressing her misgivings and sharing her secrets with another had lessened the burden for her. I also perceived that she relished the idea of being the one to pass a secret note to a dashing young officer. I hoped she would not draw attention to herself when she did it.

The chevalier arrived with a flourish, as was his style. All around the room, ladies' eyes glowed and cheeks reddened. Fans were snapped open and fluttered suggestively, and I watched as the subtle dance of flirtation commenced. I was relieved that the captain's normally beguiling presence was overshadowed by that of the chevalier, who could not fail to attract notice wherever he appeared, and did everything in his power to magnify through means of dress and bearing his ability to charm. Even the gentlemen—perhaps falling back on their sense of innate superiority and therefore not feeling threatened—bowed to his magnetic appeal.

As to me—my hands had started to sweat before any of the guests arrived, and I'd had to get a new handkerchief when the first one I gripped had nearly soaked through. I wondered, too, if I was the only female employing my fan for its true purpose.

I saw Sophie approach the captain and give him her hand to kiss while she curtsied, fluttering her eyelids at him and smiling, her head cocked to the side. Anyone who saw her leave a tiny, folded note in his hand would think it was a love note from her. I hoped the captain did not think such a thing and dismiss the note as nothing more than a young girl's fancy. When Sophie stood next to him and opened her fan, leaning toward him to say something quietly into his ear, I prayed that she, too, saw that possibility and was disabusing him of the notion.

I took my position at the back of the chairs set up for the performance and glanced to where the captain had been standing. He was gone. My heartbeat slowed a little, and I was able to applaud enthusiastically when Madame de Montesson introduced the chevalier. As was his practice in such gatherings, the chevalier also spoke, casting his eyes around the room until they settled on mine. *What is he doing?* I thought.

"Distinguished guests. For my first piece, I would like to do something a little different this afternoon. I know you came to hear me play, but I have since made the acquaintance of a young lady who it would give me great pleasure to perform with for your enjoyment."

He raised his hand and gestured toward me. Not exactly pointing, but indicating me clearly enough that all eyes turned in my direction. *No!* I thought. *This would ruin everything. How could I get away now to tell the captain what I knew? Had the chevalier guessed that, too?*

The guests cleared a path, and the chevalier walked back to me and took my arm, pulling me up to the front. "I have no instrument here," I whispered, trying not to move my lips, hoping he would hear over the surprised applause of the guests.

"Trust me," he said, and handed me his Amati. A servant approached him holding out the Stradivari he had played the evening we were together. On the music stand was the same duet from that night, I was relieved to see. At least I had some acquaintance with the music.

"Fancy a lady playing the violin," one of the guests said loudly enough for me to hear.

The chevalier caught my eye, raised his instrument to his shoulder as I did too, lifted his bow and nodded his head to start us off.

At first, I was terrified. My sweaty fingers made the strings squeak a little, and I shot a nervous glance at the chevalier. He smiled so warmly in my direction, and was so clearly caught up in the music, that I felt my heartbeat slow as I gradually was able to focus on the score in front of us.

As I played, the room disappeared. Only music surrounded me. The vibration of the beautiful fiddle resonated through my body, and I recalled the music well enough to close my eyes during the tender parts, letting my ear alone match my playing to that of the best violinist in Paris, perhaps in the world. When I held the final note and the chevalier played a cadenza over it, eventually coming to rest in unison with mine, an overwhelming sense of peace washed over me. Nothing mattered outside of myself. The world was not my concern. I listened as we synchronized our notes dying away, finally lifting our bows off at the same moment, and lowering our instruments from our shoulders.

The invited guests erupted into rapturous applause. The chevalier and I took bow after bow. I looked up into the smiling faces and saw Sophie at the back, standing next to her marquis, who had a delighted look on his face. I gave her an almost imperceptible nod. Then my eyes traveled around the room. Part of me wished the captain had been there to witness this, to hear that playing the violin was not simply some pleasurable pastime for me, but a true artistic expression. But of course, he wasn't there.

I extended my hand to the chevalier, who planted a kiss on it and held it up to a renewed accolade from the audience.

When at last he let me go and reclaimed his beloved Amati, I threaded my way quickly through the chairs, catching bits of phrases, "How lovely!" "Such talent!" "Who would have thought it possible!" I didn't know whether to laugh or cry. But at least now I had an excuse to leave: I had perspired quite through my gown in several places, and no one would wonder at my desire to change my clothes.

As soon as the footman closed the door behind me, I ran to the library and burst through the door.

The room was empty. Where had the captain gone? I had had no opportunity to tell him what I knew, or to make any suggestion concerning where he should go and what he should do.

He did know about the tunnels, though. I had described them to him in detail when I last saw him at Madame Chrétien's establishment.

Without a thought as to my own comfort, I ran out and down the stairs to the lower floor, heading toward the theater and the entrance to the tunnels. My one hope was that the chevalier would be occupied for some time yet, and that I might be able to reach his apartment and search it for something—anything—that would either prove he was telling the truth about his involvement in the murder, or not. I hoped that the captain had had a similar idea, and that I would catch up to him and convey the information he so desperately needed to know.

I lit the candle that had been left inside the door and hurried as fast as I could without accidentally dousing it to the door that led into the Palais Royale. I paused there and listened, in case someone was on the other side. When I heard nothing, I lifted the latch and pushed the door open, taking care to pinch my candle out and leave it where I could find it if need be to go back.

I quickly got my bearings and tried to recall the exact direction the chevalier had led me when he'd forced me to go with him from the Louvre, and soon discovered the staircases that led up to the third floor and his capacious apartment.

By the time I reached the top, I was gasping for breath. My heart pounded so hard in my chest I thought it would break my ribs, and my pulse was so loud in my ears I was sure it was the sound of footsteps coming after me. After a few moments, I had recovered enough to continue. I quickly prepared an excuse as to why I would be in the chevalier's apartment if someone happened upon me. I would say he'd forgotten an important piece of music he meant to perform for the salon at the Hôtel Montesson and sent me to retrieve it for him.

Armed with my plan, I opened the door and entered.

I had hoped to discover the captain inside. Excuse or not for my own presence, it would be comforting not to be entirely alone in my clandestine endeavor. But I had work to do, and no idea of how much time I would have. So I got to it right away, opening drawers and rifling through papers; taking books off the shelves and shaking them upside down to see if any documents were hidden there; lifting ornaments and rugs to inspect what was beneath them.

At last, I found a stack of letters with broken ducal seals hidden at the back of a drawer in the chevalier's desk. I started looking through them and soon realized that they contained enough evidence to incriminate the house of Orléans in a far-reaching scheme to sow discord and foment rebellion by spreading lies and slanders against not just Marie Antoinette, but the king and all his family.

I was so engrossed in my endeavor that I failed to hear the door of the apartment open. When it closed with a bang, I whirled around and found myself face to face with the man I recognized as the duc de Chartres, the incriminating letters spilling out of my hands.

Chapter Twenty-Seven

For a moment we simply stared at each other. I cleared my throat and opened my mouth to say something, not certain what would come out. But I was stopped by the duke himself.

"Come to collect your love letters?" He said, a mischievous smile spreading across his face.

So, he didn't know what the chevalier had in his possession, clearly. I decided the safest thing would be to play along.

"I...I asked him to return them, but he wouldn't. And now..."

I played the coquette and blushed, putting my hands full of letters behind my back as if I didn't want him to see them. The duke pushed the door closed behind him, then reached into his waistcoat pocket and withdrew a gold snuffbox. Without taking his eyes off me, he flipped it open with one hand and took a generous pinch, inhaling the fine tobacco first in one nostril then the other. In a sequence of movements that were so habitual I doubted he had to think about them, he put the snuffbox away, drew out his lace-edged handkerchief, and gave a sneeze that was so loud it made me jump. I felt like a mouse being toyed with by a cat that wasn't actually hungry, only enjoying the chase.

Once he'd tucked his handkerchief away again, the duke started towards me, rubbing his hands. "I thought there was something more than music between you and my brilliant chevalier. Madame de Genlis has told me of your visits with him."

I didn't correct him to say that it had only been one visit, I simply backed away from him, trying to look beyond him for a way out. "I should just take my letters and leave. All will be well."

"Leave? Without allowing me to become acquainted with what my dusky protégé has discovered about your many charms?"

He continued forward until I had nowhere else to go. The duc de Chartres was not a small man. In addition to being quite tall, he was of a girth that would make him difficult to circumvent in a small space. My back was soon pressed up against a bookcase, and I could feel the edges of the shelves and the spines of some of the books. "Please, Your Grace, I implore you. Just let me go."

He ignored my plea and reached his arm around my waist to pull me to him. I started to struggle against him as his face lowered to mine. I turned my head this way and that to avoid his slobbering kisses.

"No! Take your hands off me!"

"Oh, come now, we both know you are not a virtuous woman," he said, putting his moist lips on my ear.

At that moment the door of the apartment flew open again and I heard rapid footsteps crossing the room toward us. "Let that girl go, you blackguard!"

To my great surprise, it was the captain. He reached out, but did not touch the duke, unwilling to provoke the calling of guards and perhaps precipitate his being put in shackles for assaulting royalty.

Nonetheless, at the captain's commanding tone, the duke took his hands off me and turned to face him. "It is my own business how I choose to behave with ladies of the night. I've seen her coming and going from a bawdy house. Be gone!" The duke's voice boomed.

Then the captain did something so wholly unexpected, I froze. He reached into his waistcoat, drew out one of his elegant white gloves, and threw it on the floor in front of the duke. "I challenge you, Your Grace, for slandering the character of a young woman whom I know to be virtuous."

The duke laughed. "Are you so certain of that? I caught her in here trying to steal back her love letters to Saint-Georges."

I widened my eyes to the captain and gave my head the tiniest shake.

"If that is indeed the case, they are innocent letters. Those of a girl infatuated with a man of many talents. I demand that you answer my challenge."

The duke drew himself up to his full height. "Very well. If you insist. But as you may know, because your rank is so decidedly inferior to my own, I am not permitted to engage in a duel with you. I urge you to withdraw your challenge. If not, I may name someone to meet you in my place."

The captain gave a short nod of acquiescence.

"So be it. You will meet the chevalier de Saint-Georges on the field in the Bois de Boulogne tomorrow morning at dawn. Since we, as the challenged, have the right to name weapons, let it be sabers."

At that, the duke strode out past the captain, not turning back to look at me.

As soon as the door closed behind him I cried, "What in God's name do you think you're doing? What could a duel achieve?"

The captain stepped forward and took hold of my arms, steadying me on my feet. "Are you quite well? Did he hurt you?"

I shook my head. He was looking at me so strangely. "I-I need to show you what I found," I said, stooping to pick up the letters now scattered over the floor. "Then we can go back to discussing how to stop this folly of a duel." The captain knelt down to help me, and our hands brushed each other's occasionally. The contact made me shiver, not in an entirely unpleasant way.

"These could send the duke and all his family to the Bastille, if ever they could be apprehended outside of the palace," the captain said after scanning a few of them.

"Only if those messages can be proven to have originated with the duke himself."

The captain and I were both so preoccupied with our task that we failed to hear someone enter the room. We looked toward the source of the voice at the same time. Just inside the door, still wearing his performance attire with his violin in hand, stood the chevalier de Saint-Georges.

"Which I think you'll find is more difficult than you anticipate," he continued, stepping forward, hand outstretched for the letters.

I gathered the rest of them up and took those that the captain had collected and held them out to him.

The captain faced the chevalier, crossed his arms over his chest, and planted his feet wide apart. "Nonetheless, I think the emperor of Austria would be interested in discovering what calumnies one of the highest nobles in the land was spreading about his beloved sister," he said.

"So, that is what this is about. I wasn't certain." The chevalier placed his violin gently in the open case lying on a table before loosening the hairs of his bow. "Do you have any idea what mischief you would cause by poking that beast? The duke has many powerful friends, here and abroad. There are regiments in the guards who are ready at his request to rise up in open rebellion."

I thought, based on what the chevalier had told me before, he was playing for time, exaggerating for effect. But I stayed silent. The atmosphere in the room was heavy with unspoken threats and my head was beginning to ache.

After a few moments during which only the clock ticking broke the stillness, the captain breathed out a long sigh, lowered his arms, and spoke. "I understand that we are to meet on the field in very few hours to solve the matter of this lady's honor." He looked toward me again. I could not read the expression on his face. Deep in his eyes I thought I perceived sorrow, or the memory of sorrow, and it stabbed me through. Would he lose his life tomorrow because of me?

The chevalier shook his head. "Whatever persuaded you to such an act of folly!" He flopped into a chair and drew his handkerchief out of a pocket inside his waistcoat, using it to mop away the delicate sheen of perspiration that had collected on his brow during his recent performance. "You know what the outcome is likely to be. Of course, it will be hushed up. Dueling is still illegal." He tossed the handkerchief on the floor and massaged the pad of his left thumb with his right. A deep furrow between his brows altered his normally placid, friendly face almost beyond recognition. I realized then how constantly the chevalier must have to suppress his emotions, remain calm, so that his strength and natural bearing would not frighten people he had no intention of harming.

The captain said, "I had a very good reason for the challenge. I, like you, would prefer matters not to end in this manner. But I cannot let insults directed at Mademoiselle Thérèse go unanswered. She does not deserve them. Indeed, she deserves our admiration and thanks."

Admiration. In what way did the captain admire me? I had been about to leap in and stop this verbal parrying, but I swallowed back my protest.

"Captain von Bauer, I know you to be an excellent swordsman. Nearly as accomplished as myself. It would grieve me more than I can say to put an end to your brilliant career."

The chevalier's words reminded me of the very real potential outcome of a duel and at last I spoke. "No. This will not happen. Not because of me."

Both of their grim faces turned to me. Yet they looked over me, through me, as if they'd already started on the downhill slide that would end the next morning at dawn. I placed myself between them. "Stop it, both of you! It's ridiculous!" I turned to the captain. "You must leave Paris. We must both leave Paris. Tonight." I took hold of his arms and shook them, but he stood as straight as a pillar and did not look at me.

"A gentleman does not rescind his word," the captain said, his voice icy. "And we still have not resolved the matter of the murder of Roland the printer."

The chevalier stood as well and straightened his waistcoat. "Very well. As you will have it. Let us shake hands, at least. I respect anyone who bears affection for this talented violinist whom I have come to regard as my friend."

I wanted to cry, to scream, to tear out my hair—anything to prevent this foolish, unnecessary action! But the captain had taken my hand and was pulling me toward the door. I resisted, but I was no match for him.

He talked over his shoulder to the chevalier. "We may as well discuss the precise terms of the duel, since we find ourselves together. We can be civil. My quarrel is not with you."

We had reached the door and he forced me to step outside of it. I tried to go back inside, but now he had hold of my shoulders and made me face him. "You must leave this to us. Trust me. Are you well enough to find your own way back to the Hôtel Montesson?"

Trust him! What reason had he ever given me to be able to do that? "Yes, but—"

Before I could utter another word, the captain wrapped his arms around me and kissed me as no one had ever kissed me before—rough but tender, full of passion and regret and sadness. This kiss wasn't like the one at Madame Chrétien's. Then, he'd been toying with me, trying to knock me off balance, as was his habit. This was altogether different. Something cracked inside me as the kiss continued, letting a confusion of emotion flood through my body. I wanted him and I hated him. I was angry and distraught and desperate. I lost the battle with myself, letting go of the image of Zoltan that threatened to remind me I was not this person, I was not like Mirela or Sophie or any of the captain's other conquests. I reached my arms up around his neck and clung to him, returning his kiss with passion—for what? Not for him, surely. We were enemies of sorts. He tormented me and teased me, toyed with me and ruined my plans. But what if this was the last time I would ever see him?

When the captain finally let go of me, tears stood in my eyes and had started to spill down my cheeks. He took hold of my chin and tipped it upward, then traced the outline of my face with his finger. "Remember, little Theresa, that it was I who defended your honor. I who have always believed that you are capable of remarkable things." He stepped away, clicked his heels together, and bowed.

Chapter Twenty-Eight

I arrived back in my room at the Hôtel Montesson in a terrible state of confusion and fear. I quickly tore off my fine gown and put on the modest clothes I'd worn while I was working at the Atelier Bertin, then paced back and forth across the floor, biting the side of my thumb, wracking my brain for a way to prevent the duel but not able to think of anything.

Just as I had decided I must seek out the captain again whatever the cost to my peace of mind, somewhere away from the chevalier, who seemed to provoke that masculine rigidity that so often led to tragedy, and try to persuade him not to go through with this ridiculous affair, I heard the approach of Sophie's satin-slippered feet. Within an instant—as was her custom—she burst in without knocking.

"You must surely have guessed." Her eyes were full of that unique combination of innocence and mischief that made her such an entertaining friend.

It required a Herculean effort to wrench my thoughts back from the captain and the chevalier to remember that I had seen Sophie at the salon with the marquis de Bonesprit, and it seemed apparent that he had made the offer of marriage. "My sincerest felicitations," I said, plastering a smile on my face and taking her hands before kissing her on both cheeks. "I see that you have become betrothed to your marquis, as you wished, and as I predicted. I hope you will be happy."

She shrugged and laughed. "I will be as happy as anyone with an immense fortune and a title can be. Which I wager is the height of happiness, or so I've been told ever since I was a child."

If my mind were not occupied with other matters, I might have taken the time to point out to her that although they undoubtedly make up for a great many evils, money and position do not guarantee happiness. Instead, I simply smiled.

Her smile faded as she took in my expression and my garb. "You are not yourself, Theresa, and why are you wearing such clothing?" Then all at once her face brightened again and she formed her mouth into an astonished Oh. "You're going to elope! Tonight! It must be! Tell me that was the result of your private meeting with the captain, and I shall be delighted for you."

I wished in that moment that I could pretend what Sophie assumed. It would be so much better than the real cause of my demeanor and my actions. I shook my head. "I truly wish it were." I was still so *bouleversée* by all that had happened in the past hour, I believe I would have agreed to marry the captain if that could have forestalled his challenge and saved him. "You find me in a state of indecision, confusion, and distress."

Despite her tendency toward the superficial, Sophie had a good heart. She took my hand and led me to the chairs by the fire and made me sit. "What is it?" She said. "You know you can trust me."

As quickly as I could, and without the details of why or where or how, I told her that the captain and the chevalier would meet in a duel at dawn the next morning unless I could figure out a way to stop them.

After she recovered her composure, she said, "You? Why would you be able to stop them?"

"Because..." I hesitated. "Because the duel is about me."

Her mystified expression was soon replaced with what I could only describe as glee. "How romantic! Tell me more. I need to know everything." She leaned forward with her elbows on her knees and her chin in her hands.

"I would, except if I am to have any hope of exerting my influence to prevent something that will take the life of one or the other gentleman, I must go." My tone was stern. I rose and walked to the armoire, where I took out my warmest cloak and muff. "Please don't tell anyone where I've gone or what I am doing. It's terribly important."

Sophie's face had become serious. "I see now that you must do what you can. Go. I shan't sleep a wink tonight until I know the outcome, so please find me the moment you return," She said, practically pushing me out the door.

I ran through the streets of Paris, noticing that where there had been ice yesterday there were now small puddles, and that the horses moved at a brisker pace as they pulled the carriages through the torch-lit darkness. I didn't know for certain where I might find the captain, but I started by heading to the brothel. If he was not there, Madame Chrétien might know where I would find him, and I could at the same time try to enlist her help in preventing this insane duel.

I flew in the door past the concierge and strode directly into the parlor, expecting to find Madame Chrétien alone at this hour, gathering herself before the onslaught of drunken customers later in the evening. But she was not alone. Sitting calmly by the fire opposite her, one leg crossed over the other, was the captain. He picked up a glass of wine that sat on the table by his elbow and sipped it.

My eyes flitted from one to the other of them before they rested on Madame Chrétien's serene face. I raced to her and knelt down at her feet, taking her hand in both of mine. "Please, Madame, join me in persuading the captain against this dangerous folly! I am not offended. I need no one to take my part. I am a humble Viennese girl of no consequence. Duels should not be fought over such as me." By the time I finished my speech, tears dampened my cheeks again.

Madame took my chin in her free hand and looked into my eyes. "Sit, Thérèse. The captain needs to talk to you. I shall be in my boudoir. Ring if you need anything."

She stood, relinquishing her chair to me. I took off my cloak and muff and dropped them on the floor. The captain sat staring into the fire, infuriatingly calm in the face of this impending disaster. "Well? What is it you have to say? I hope it is that you have decided not to meet the chevalier at dawn."

"The murder of Roland is solved."

Just like that. Without explanation or preamble. He let the words hang in the air between us, until I finally asked, "Who was it? Was it the chevalier? Because I saw some blood. I didn't want to believe it was him, but—"

"It wasn't the chevalier, you may rest easy in that knowledge."

I was growing angrier and angrier. "Then who? You must tell me!"

"Are you certain you wish to know?" He said. "Once known, such a thing cannot be unknown."

Why was he being so mysterious? Why would he not simply say the words and end my misery? "Yes, I wish to know. You must by now understand me well enough to believe that digging out the truth of a matter is vital to me, and that I am capable of reconciling myself to whatever that truth might be." Even if it involved the destruction of my self-control.

"Very well. I shall tell you." He looked directly into my eyes. His were expressionless. Cold, almost. "It was I. I alone killed Roland in the basement of the Louvre."

I opened and closed my mouth to speak. His answer was so unexpected I felt the world turn on its head yet again. I didn't know what to say. I, who was almost always capable of filling a silence with a witty remark, had no words at my command. My mind and heart flooded with thoughts and sensations. I had trusted this man. Although I believed I did not wish it, I had allowed myself only an hour before to be kissed by him, and to return his kiss. And yet, now I discover he was a murderer. How could he be? I stared at him, my eyes asking for more information.

"I used the same type of sword as the chevalier would have, to cast suspicion upon him. Apparently I succeeded!" He chuckled softly.

"But...why? I don't believe you. I don't believe you're capable of such a thing." I found myself, despite what I'd assured him, wishing I did not know his secret. And then in the next moment, going back to not trusting him. He'd lied about so much else. But what reason would he have to take the blame?

"It was the only way to ensure that those operations would cease, that the duc de Chartres would have to regroup and take his campaign underground somewhere else. That would take time, and by then, the queen might well have produced an heir, and the populace would be appeased, rendering the falsehoods spread abroad less potent."

I decided that was not the moment to point out that the populace was angry about much more than the queen's inability to provide her husband with an heir. "So, you say you did it for the emperor's sake. At least, that is your excuse. If so, why must you fight this duel? Why can you not just flee?"

"And assure that I would be hounded by the duke's assassins for the rest of my life? For they will surely figure it all out. He is not a man to forgive and forget."

The captain appeared serene. Unperturbed. He was facing what he must know was certain death, and yet, "What if you best the chevalier?" I said. This was a devastating thought too, however. The idea of such a fine musician being cut down at the height of his abilities didn't bear thinking about. I had grown fond of him, too.

"Ah, I can see, Theresa, that you don't desire such an outcome. I assure you, I am as fine a swordsman as can be found in any other place. But the chevalier's prowess is legendary." He turned his gaze back toward the fire for a while. "Now that you know this one important fact, I would like to explain myself to you more fully. As someone who has willingly participated in this scheme, you deserve an account of the events that resulted in such an outcome. I imagine you have long been wondering what led me to suggest the emperor send you on what has become such a perilous mission."

I nodded, my mind too full of conflicting thoughts to speak.

"You no doubt think I hold your musical abilities in low esteem. But you couldn't be more wrong. It was part of what drew my attention to just how extraordinary you are. That you were able two years ago to solve a complicated plot with so many threads, and do it in a manner that showed your compassion for those different from yourself, surprised me. Your powers of observation and of reasoning are acute—more so than that of most men, I wager, and a rare thing indeed in a woman."

I was about to protest that he perhaps underestimated the abilities of most women, but decided to allow him to continue unimpeded.

"I knew from the start that a man would not be able to insert himself into the enclaves where gossip so often originates. I also counted on your musical ear to help you learn to speak French without your Viennese accent. With the exception of the chevalier's acute hearing, you succeeded admirably.

"Also of import in my decision was your beauty. Paris values nothing so much as a pretty face and an elegant bearing. I knew you would be welcomed in company of many different ranks. Since there was no way of knowing before whether the slanders originated from inside or outside the queen's intimate circle, I needed to know you could move from one to the other with ease."

I forced myself not to dwell on the fact that he had called me a beauty. Although his recent actions seemed to reinforce the fact that he thought I was pretty, how could I know what he said was really true? How could I be beautiful when I did not primp and fuss the way other women did? That was unimportant right now. What mattered now was persuading the captain not to go through with the duel. In addition to my feeling that the slight to me had been nowhere near damning enough to provoke such violence, I had another idea, and I wanted time to see if I was right. "I have some money saved from working for Mademoiselle Bertin. I could go right now and purchase seats for both of us on the midnight coach to Vienna. It's the sensible thing to do, don't you see? There is no need, simply no need, for you to lose your life because of me."

"It touches me, Theresa, truly, that you care enough to be so distressed over this circumstance. I assure you, I am at peace with my decision. I am a captain who has lived by my sword. And, as the motto goes, I am fully prepared to die by the sword."

I looked down at my hands, twisting my handkerchief, unable to rest quietly in my lap. He would not change his mind. There was nothing I could do. I stood. "I see my pleas will not shake your resolve. Therefore I must part from you." I didn't say, but I was also eager to follow my intuition and see if I could find something to support my own ideas about who had murdered Roland. I just couldn't shake the feeling that it wasn't the captain. Such a thing was not like the man I had come to know, infuriating, confusing, and complicated though he undoutedly was.

The captain stood as well and came closer to me to take my hand and bend over it to press it to his lips, keeping them there a long time. I found myself staring at the top of his head noticing that he was not wearing a wig, and that his soft, dark-brown hair curled over the top of his ear, just as I remembered my brother Toby's doing when he was a toddler. I placed my hand on his head and let my fingers separate the strands. As he righted himself, I let my hand slide down to his shoulder, allowed him again to pass his arm around my waist and draw me to him. What was it that made me forget about everyone else in the world when he looked at me that certain way? I was not in love with him. That I knew. But I was drawn to him, as a fly is drawn to honey, or a river to the sea. At that moment, I felt his pull. Before I was fully aware of it, the distance between us had closed once again, and we were pressed against each other. I buried my face in his shoulder, breathing in the scent of him—the faint mustiness of his wool uniform; the tang of dried sweat; the slightest hint of wine on his breath. His warm lips on the top of my head, his hands cupping my face and turning it up to meet his.

And we kissed. Again. I abandoned myself to that kiss, abandoned myself to this man whose involvement in my life was so full of conflicts and deceit. But he had defended me, very likely at the cost of his life. I would carry that generous act in my heart for the rest of my days. And perhaps I would be able to do something to vindicate him before I left Paris for good.

Chapter Twenty-Nine

I left Madame Chrétien's and ran back to the Hôtel Montesson. I didn't go in the usual way, but entered by a door used by servants and delivery men, hoping no one would know I was there. I knew Sophie was anxiously waiting for me to come and tell her whether I'd managed to dissuade the captain from dueling with the chevalier, but after failing to deter him from that course of action, I had another object in mind. Sophie would have to wait.

Something about the way the captain said it, the way he seemed to be forming the idea as he spoke the words, made me believe he wasn't actually Roland's murderer. I realized even then that my perception had possibly been sharpened by wishing it to be so, by wishing that a man who had kissed me with such passion was not, in fact, capable of murder. But despite all I knew of the captain's propensity for keeping secrets, his reason for committing such an act, while plausible, was not convincing. I knew him as an adept liar. He was entirely capable of lying about his guilt as well. The question was why? And how to prove it?

The only answer was for me to solve the mystery on my own. And I had a good idea about where to start.

I had already decided that as it was evening, the doors of the Louvre would probably be locked for the night, so I would have to get there through the tunnels I had come to know so well. I fetched a candle from the kitchen, where dozens of servants bustled around cleaning up after the feast that had been served to the salon guests. They were much too busy with their own concerns to pay me any heed. I lit the candle from the sconce on the wall and scurried away.

This time, with adequate light and knowing where I was going, it took only a few minutes to reach the door that led into the basement of the Louvre. I paused there and listened, but at that hour, there was little danger anyone would be wandering around in a storeroom, so I let myself in. After a quick look around, I headed to the printing room where Roland had been murdered, and prayed that no one would enter and find me there. It seemed unlikely, but I hadn't gotten far enough in my hastily concocted plan to figure out how I would explain my own presence.

I paused for a moment after I passed through the door, and let my eyes rest on the canvas sheet covering the black iron mass of the printing press. Although I had only seen him through a narrow slit, I could still picture Roland turning the wheel, a resigned look on his face. It struck me that I had been one of the last people to see him alive.

I shook my head to clear it, then quickly lit two sconces to illuminate the room and make my search easier. I didn't know exactly what I expected to find. When the chevalier and I had passed through the other day, all was tidy and organized. But now, the room was a mess. Empty crates had been tipped on their sides and their contents spilled over the floor—paper, blocks of ink, a few pencils. The racks I had spied neatly stacked with lead type had been pushed over, and all around were separate letters of the alphabet and punctuation marks, reversed so they would print in the right direction. Someone had been here recently, searching for something. Was I too late? Had another person come in to look for some piece of evidence, either to convict—or possibly protect—the murderer?

I had a terrible feeling my search would be for naught, but I had to try. Starting in one corner, I scanned the floor for anything that could have been dropped in a scuffle—a button, perhaps. Or a coin—something that might have been on the person of the murderer. I was very thorough. I picked up everything, rifled through the spilled type, searched the corners of the crates, but my search turned up nothing that didn't have every reason to be there.

There was only one place left to examine. I didn't know why I hadn't started there, considering the likelihood that Roland had been murdered as he worked. I took a deep breath, marched to the center of the room, and pulled the heavy cover off the printing press.

A cloud of dust made my eyes water and threatened to make me sneeze. Apparently no one had used the press since the murder. I pinched my nose, and once I was certain I wouldn't sneeze, I held my candle close to the machinery. The first thing I saw made me catch my breath. A dried puddle of blood on one side of the press had not yet been cleaned away. To do what I needed to do I would not be able to avoid it, so I crossed myself quickly and knelt on the ground, reaching into every crevice I could find. I even risked damaging my fingers by inserting them between moving parts. This was too important to worry about that now.

Just as I was about to give up and decide that—even if the captain was not guilty—I would find nothing here to vindicate him, I felt something behind one of the legs of the press, something that wasn't attached to it or to the floor beneath it. The object was wedged into a place my fingers could barely reach, but I strained to fit them as far in as possible so I could tease whatever it was out. It had rounded corners, making it more difficult to grasp.

Gradually, the object budged, and I was able to pull it little by little until I could actually see a portion of it. My candle caught the gleam of gold. It wasn't a button, though. It was thicker and more substantial than that.

A minute later, I had it. I stared down into the palm of my hand at a gold snuffbox. It was heavy, so of superior quality and quite valuable. Etched on the top was a coat of arms that I knew all too well.

The snuffbox was exactly the same as the one I'd seen in the hands of the duc de Chartres. It could only have gotten to that place if it had fallen out of his own pocket. Had it been he who acted on the threat he made in the tunnel, to do something to prevent Roland from quitting the printing enterprise? It seemed the only possible explanation. And yet, it contradicted everything the captain had told me.

I didn't bother to throw the cover back over the printing press. I had been there long enough already, and worried that at any moment, someone might enter and discover me. Besides, my candle was burning down, and I didn't know if it would last to take me back through the tunnels to the Hôtel Montesson.

Haste was more important than stealth, so rather than creep away, I ran as fast as I could, slamming doors behind me. I had to get back to the rue d'Argout before the captain went out to meet the chevalier on the dueling ground.

For once, everything went as I'd hoped. No one stopped me as I passed through the servants' level of the Hôtel Montesson, and I soon found myself hurrying through the dark streets toward Madame Chrétien's establishment. Breathless by the time I arrived, I pounded on the door, and when the concierge opened it I pushed past him, hearing his curses fade behind me as I ran up the stairs to Madame's apartment.

I burst through the door of the parlor, hoping to find the captain still seated there, but instead I found Madame Chrétien with a different gentleman.

"Is this the young lady?" The man asked, preparing to stand up and come toward me, a broad smile on his face.

Madame pushed him back into his seat and said, "No! No, this is not your companion for the evening. This is a maid whom I sent on an urgent errand and asked to find me immediately upon her return. If you will please wait here."

Madame Chrétien walked with unhurried steps to the door, placing her hand on the small of my back and pushing me out in front of her. As soon as the door closed behind her, she whispered, "What in the name of the Virgin are you doing here!"

"I-I found something," I said. "Where is the captain?"

She let out an exasperated sigh. "The captain is not here. I don't know where he's gone, but I expect he is preparing for the trials to come. I suggest you go back to the Hôtel Montesson as he bade you do earlier. As you see, my business must continue as if nothing is happening if we are to deflect any suspicion about the duel."

My expression must have communicated my distress, because she took my face between her hands and said, "There is nothing more you or anyone can do. These matters are not for us women to solve."

"But… I have discovered something. Something important."

Madame Chrétien smiled. "I admire your perseverance. But I don't know where the captain is. Please return to the Hôtel Montesson."

Clearly, she would not help me. I looked down and curtsied quickly, said "Merci" and ran back down the stairs and out into the street.

The still-cold wind acted like a slap in my face and brought me to a halt. There was no point rushing back to the Hôtel Montesson. The captain wouldn't be there anyway, and I needed time to think before I had to face Sophie. I clutched the snuffbox in my hand, turning it over and over, thinking about everything that had happened in the past few days. I had in my possession an object that could exonerate the captain and lead to the arrest of a murderer. But I didn't know what to do with it. As far as I knew, the authorities hadn't yet accused the captain of murder, if they ever would. And their jurisdiction didn't extend to the Palais Royale, so even if I could prove the duc de Chartres had killed Roland, what use would it be?

The duc de Chartres was protected from the consequences of his actions by laws and customs designed to shield the wealthy and privileged from the realities of life—laws that held the poor to account for the slightest infraction. Anger heated my blood. Ondine had been robbed of her chance at happiness because her beloved didn't have the choice not to break the law for someone else. Had the captain, too, been an instrument of such unfairness? I discovered that he hadn't killed Roland himself, but had the actions he'd been a party to resulted in that outcome? Was this the system that Emperor Joseph and Marie Antoinette were so determined to preserve and protect?

Despair mingled with outrage, and I wasn't sure whether I wanted to scream or simply weep. But I had to take control of myself and go tell Sophie what I could of my adventures that evening, and reassure her as best I could that somehow, the duel would be stopped.

I had spent more time walking that night than I thought, and by the time I reached the Chaussée d'Antin it was already near dawn. The servants were stirring in preparation for another day of running an absurdly large household and catering to every whim of its occupants. I didn't have the heart to disturb the concierge to let me in, knowing that news would travel through the ranks and I would no doubt be presented with a cup of cocoa and a bed turned down so I could crawl into it for much-delayed sleep.

Instead of going to my own room, though, I went to Sophie's. She had asked me to tell her right away what had happened, no matter the hour. Assuming she'd be asleep and would not hear me scratching at her door, I opened it and walked in, as she had so often done to me.

The covers on her bed were disheveled as though she'd been thrashing around in her sleep, doubtless disturbed by dreams of violence. I sat on the edge of the bed and started pulling them back, wondering where in all this chaos Sophie lay.

I quickly discovered that her bed was empty. She'd cleverly arranged the covers so that from a casual glance it would appear that she was buried in them and sound asleep. I raced to Sophie's armoire, opening it to see which of her many garments was missing. Her warm cloak was gone, as was her muff. Had she gone to see the marquis? I doubted it. However glad she was to be betrothed, they clearly did not share the kind of passion that led to midnight trysts.

I scanned her room—the mess that was her dressing table, with pots of lotion overturned and brushes set down askew, waiting to be set to rights by her maid; the pristine writing desk, which she rarely used; the table next to her bed, where the same volume of a romance had sat since the first day I entered the place.

That's when I saw the note. She'd tucked it under the book. I raced over and pulled it out. She hadn't bothered to seal it, so I unfolded it and read:

I can't bear it. I know the captain is yours, but I loved him once. I have gone to the Bois just in case your pleas fall upon deaf ears. Perhaps I will be able to stay his hand.

  S.

Oh no! I thought. What would Sophie do? And yet, her hasty action somehow absolved me from my promise to the captain that I would stay away, and I put my cloak back on and looked for a servant who could find me a carriage immediately to convey me to the Bois de Bologne. It was a huge parkland, I knew, with wild forests for hunting game. But surely it would not be so difficult to find the place where men were likely to meet to cross swords in a duel.

Apparently Sophie had commandeered the marquise's carriage, and all that was left was a cart used by the servants for errands. But the reluctant footman arranged for the horse to be harnessed and the gig brought around, with a groom to take me where I wanted to go. The young man looked as though he'd been dragged out of bed, but something in my demeanor must have conveyed the urgency of my errand, and he cracked the whip over the horse's ears and we were soon flying through the streets of Paris, out past the Tuileries to the farmland beyond, and to the suburb of Passy and then the Bois.

"Where now, Mamzelle?" He said as we reached the easternmost entrance of the park. I didn't want to tell him about the duel—the fewer people who knew about such an illegal activity, the better—so I simply asked him to take me wherever it was that Mademoiselle Sophie might have gone, and be quick about it.

I was surprised to discover that he appeared to know exactly where that might be, and after only a little doubling back on roads, I spied the Montesson carriage through the trees. Soon I was seated next to Sophie in the elegant brougham and the cart was headed back to the Chaussée d'Antin.

"Why are you here?" I cried, after hugging Sophie, who had clearly been weeping.

"How could I not try to save him, if you did not manage it? I know where they will be. We must walk there and hide if we are to see them."

I couldn't help peering at her shoes. "Are you certain you can manage it?" Then I noticed that she still wore the elegant clothes she had worn the night before. "You never went to bed, did you?"

"I waited and waited for you to come back with news that the duel had been stopped, and when you didn't, well, what was I to think?"

There was nothing for it now but to go along with her. I, too, still held out hope that, when the two honorable men met on the dueling ground, they would settle their differences without drawing swords. I wanted to show the snuffbox to the captain, to make sure he knew that I knew he wasn't a murderer. And yet, what would that accomplish? Perhaps it would be best if I never showed him the evidence I had found.

All this swirled in an unending loop through my head as I followed Sophie through the woods to a place that gave us a view over an open space. Two carriages waited some distance apart from one another, too far away for us to make out the coats of arms on their doors. Sophie grabbed my gloved hand and squeezed it hard as we watched two men descend from one of carriages and three from the other. I easily made out the captain's uniform and recognized his way of walking, that easy confidence combined with grace. The chevalier was unmistakable from a distance, too, because of the color of his skin and his stature. If the occasion hadn't been so terrible, I would have welcomed the opportunity to see this legendary swordsman in action. Right then, however, I wished I had never met him.

The men who must have been their seconds—I didn't know who they were—conferred for a while as the captain and the chevalier shed their coats and rolled up their shirtsleeves. Even from that distance I could see their words billowing out in steamy puffs into the cold. "I wish we could hear them," I said.

"Should we make our presence known?" Sophie asked.

"No. It would be a distraction. If they are bent on this course, seeing us might disrupt their preparations." I imagined too vividly the captain losing concentration and leaving himself open for the chevalier's fatal blow.

"Who is the third man?"

I saw that he carried a valise, and I said, "I believe that is the doctor. At this point, all we can hope is that somehow the chevalier misses his mark and only manages to wound the captain." I heard myself and the assumption my words contained. I wished with all my heart that were not the likely outcome. But Sophie did not contradict me, only let a single tear escape her eye and roll down her cheek.

By the actions of the seconds, who each accompanied one of the men out to the field a rapier's distance away from each other, I realized that nothing had been resolved, and the duel would take place as planned. Sophie and I put our arms around each other, squeezing, only partly for warmth, as we watched.

The doctor stood between the two men slightly to the side, raised his hand up high holding a white kerchief, and dropped it. At that, they took their positions, swords raised, other arm acting as balance, and their dance of death began.

We were too far away to hear anything. We could only see the two men approach each other, parry, slice, and back away like toy soldiers that had been wound up to go through carefully choreographed motions. The entire scene had an unreal air, as though we were watching a drama performed within a vast theater, where at its conclusion, the hidden audience would applaud and cheer at how well the men had acted their parts and both would walk away unharmed.

I felt as if time was suspended, as if the hands of a clock would not move while the duel took place. I had no sense of how much of it passed—it could have been an hour or a minute—before the chevalier caught the captain at a disadvantage and thrust his sword, piercing near his heart. I gasped as I watched a tiny spot of blood on the captain's waistcoat grow and spread over it, until he fell to his knees and clutched at it with his left hand, his saber still in his right hand.

The doctor raced forward and Saint-Georges threw his épée down and ran to the captain, supporting his head and using his own kerchief to stanch the bleeding.

I couldn't bear it. This was the last thing I ever expected or wanted to happen when I agreed to come to Paris on the emperor's errand. Yet my eyes were dry, as if the excess of emotion I'd felt in the last two days had drained my supply of tears and I would never be able to cry again. "Come, Sophie. We must go."

Sophie had remained uncharacteristically quiet, only shuddering occasionally, perhaps with the cold, perhaps from emotion. I led my much-subdued friend back to the carriage. We said not a word all the way back to the Hôtel Montesson.

Chapter Thirty

Still in shock, uncertain as to whether the emperor would consider that I had accomplished my mission and give me the promised reward or whether he would think I had failed and send me away in disgrace, I prepared to leave the Hôtel Montesson.

"You could stay." Sophie stretched out on the bed that had been mine for the past couple of weeks and watched as I instructed the maid what to pack in the valise Sophie gave me. I was aware that I needed to leave room for the few items of my own clothing that remained at the brothel. The thought of going there, where I had last seen the captain alive, threatened to bring on the tears that, contrary to my previous belief, had not dried up, and had only managed to stop after a night's sleep and a morning walk.

"Not that one," I instructed, as the maid took the silk robe a l'anglaise off its hook.

"Don't be absurd!" Sophie said. "You must have to attend balls and salons in Alsace."

So many times I had been on the verge of explaining everything to Sophie. I wanted to tell her that I wasn't stopping in Alsace, but continuing to Vienna, where I had a mother and a brother and sister and friends, and a life as a violinist and teacher. I decided, in the end, that such knowledge might prove inconvenient to her in the future, and kept my secret. "You forget that I am not of your class. My sort are not expected to dress so elegantly, but to attend teas and soirées wearing muslin trimmed with ribbons."

She frowned. "Very well. But you must tell me where to write to you, so that I may send you a parcel with my last-year's gowns in it. Don't protest! You're quite pretty enough to attract a higher class of suitor. Your education and talent are useful as well, and would make you a suitable wife for an aristocrat, or at least a wealthy merchant."

I smiled. Sophie, in having made a brilliant match, was eager to see everyone else around her settled. I couldn't tell her that there was every possibility I would marry a Hungarian baron, but that life on his country estates would still not demand I wear such finery. "I don't know yet where you will find me, since I will be hiring myself out as a governess. In the meantime, you can send me letters through Ondine, at Mademoiselle Bertin's workshop. I will receive them eventually." I didn't dare give Sophie the address of Madame Chrétien's house.

I had had to lie, too, about the manner in which the duel had come about, inventing a scene worthy of a romance novel like Dangerous Liaisons. It worked, as I knew it would. Sophie was a romantic at heart.

"Well, that's all, I think," I said. "I should be on my way."

I had purchased a ticket on the midnight coach to Vienna. This coach traveled through Alsace, so Sophie did not question the choice.

"But you don't leave for hours!"

I was afraid Sophie would start crying again, so I sat by her on the bed and took her hand. "I told you, I have a few other stops to make before I can depart. Besides, it's better to be quick about goodbyes."

She brightened. "Of course, you'll come for my wedding, in the spring!"

I nodded. "I wouldn't miss it!" I didn't tell her that it might not be possible for me to come if my part in the whole matter was ever discovered. No point in mentioning it now.

Sophie wanted to order the carriage for me, but I told her my valise was not heavy, and that I was only going to the workshop of Mademoiselle Bertin to say my goodbyes to my friends there—a short walk from the Hôtel Montesson. At the door, she embraced me and kissed me as if I was her sister. And I admit to feeling sad to go. I would have loved to see Sophie blossom in her own establishment, where she could admit to all her talents, and be secure enough to gather artists, musicians, and philosophers around her. And where her wealth and position would wipe out any stain about her scandalous ancestry.

My farewells to Ondine and Lucienne were not as emotional as they were to Sophie. Although I believe they had become fond of me, they were more practical and less fanciful than my aristocratic friend. They also knew that Mademoiselle Bertin bore me no great affection, and that their own fates were closely tied to currying favor with her.

"I'm surprised you don't think yourself too fine for us now," Lucienne said when I told her I was returning to Alsace. "First you go to Versailles, then you are invited to stay at one of the grandest *hôtels particuliers* in Paris. I'm sure I don't know what to think."

I didn't tell her about my detour to the Bastille. She probably wouldn't believe it anyway. "But, as you see, I am unchanged. Just as plain as ever." I twirled around in my muslin day dress.

I turned to Ondine, whose eyes had lost their sparkle since her fiancé's murder, and who could wonder at that? I could not, in all conscience, enthusiastically tell her that I was certain the police would soon solve the mystery. I had toyed with the idea of giving her the snuffbox—which was no doubt very valuable—but I soon realized that having it in her possession could cause her more trouble than it would solve. "I'm very sorry for your loss. I wish I could be of more comfort to you." I didn't say but I thought that she was young, and pretty, and I hoped would soon have another suitor to take her mind off her tragic loss. I asked her if she would deliver any correspondence that arrived for me into Mademoiselle Bertin's hands, as she would know where I was. I had never told my friends that I was rooming in a brothel, but Mademoiselle Bertin had that information from the captain, and I hoped was not too prejudiced against me to do me the courtesy of sending on any letters.

"I shall miss you both, if not the work itself," I said. Lucienne merely nodded to me, but Ondine rushed over and embraced me just before I opened the door and left.

My final stop before going to the Hôtel de Ville to await the coach was my former lodgings with Madame Chrétien. My steps slowed as I approached. I went over so many scenes from the past two months in my mind. I was still confused and troubled by the captain's actions toward me at the end, and my inability to prevent his death.

And I was so very sad that he would not be there, that I would never again sharpen my wits sparring with him, becoming infuriated when he did something to upset my equilibrium and turned my ideas on their heads. Whenever I was in the captain's presence I was constantly aware of danger, of unpredictability. It was disconcerting, but exciting. He challenged me. He challenged my mind and my ability to solve problems. I had spent comparatively little time with him in the past two years, and yet he was as vivid to me as someone I might have known all my life.

I wondered how many of my feelings about him were colored by the fact that he wasn't there anymore, and that I knew I wouldn't see him ever again.

The concierge let me in without a word and I went directly to the room I shared with Odette. It was early evening, before the hour when customers came to the whorehouse for their nightly trysts. I found Odette lounging, half-dressed, on her bed.

"Thérèse!" She leapt up and ran to me, engulfing me in a tight embrace. "I am so sorry. I heard about the captain, about the duel. It is sad, but so exciting! I don't know when the last duel was fought in the Bois. The penalties for dueling are severe. The chevalier and the captain must have had friends in very high places to hush it up so completely."

"You must promise not to say a word about it! You know that." I could only guess that Madame Chrétien had told her, since all participants were sworn to secrecy.

"Of course. In my work, it's very important to be able to keep secrets." She tipped her chin up and looked down her nose. I laughed, and so did she.

After Odette finished helping me squash my remaining clothes into my valise and I had reclaimed Danior's violin from beneath the bed, I took my leave of her and went down to the parlor to say farewell and to thank Madame Chrétien. I would never have expected myself to admire and be fond of a woman who ran a house of pleasure, but I had come to realize what care she took of the girls she employed, and how refined she herself was. She was an educated woman who, if she were a man, might have made a career as a diplomat or an attorney. If she had been in a higher class and wealthier, she might have become a saloniste, like the marquise de Montesson. I supposed that she made the best of her abilities, and was a smart enough businesswoman to find a profitable niche.

The weather had turned much milder, and I took my time strolling around the streets of Paris before making my way to the Hôtel de Ville where the pubic coach deposited and took on passengers. My thoughts turned to the chevalier and his role in the entire affair. The chevalier. Why was it that—although he killed my friend—I was sorry I could not take my leave of him? I suppose it was because I didn't blame him, not really. He was forced to act by the duc de Chartres. Yet another casualty of a system where the power was concentrated in the hands of those with wealth and a certain pedigree. If he had refused, he would probably have lost his position. Yet to take a life, just for the sake of maintaining one's post as music director, still seemed cruel and thoughtless.

Without thinking, I found myself passing the entrance of the Palais Royale, at the exact spot where I first heard the chevalier playing on my way home from work at Mademoiselle Bertin's. I stood for a moment and looked up at the window I now knew was in his apartment on the third floor. I closed my eyes and imagined the music I'd heard then, how beautiful it was, how it made me long for home.

No music sailed out on the evening breeze that day, though. I looked up one more time, smiled, and started to walk away. But a sound as of wood scraping made me stop and look again. A man's arm, clothed in fine linen, the hand of a darker hue than one who normally wore such elegant attire, opened that very window. A moment later, a face appeared. A face I would recognize forever. I thought he was too far away to see me, yet I nodded nonetheless. Perhaps I imagined it, but the slight movement of his head might have been a nod in return—or not.

I quickened my pace toward the coach stop. What did I think of that remarkable gentleman? My thoughts were too muddled to arrange in a way that made sense. In any case, I would have plenty of time to ponder the matter on my three-week journey back to Vienna.

Christmas would be past, but if the weather held, I'd arrive before the new year.

I focused my thoughts on the future, looking forward to seeing my mother, Toby, and Anna; Danior and Alida; and Zoltan. My feelings were less clear concerning Zoltan, but I hoped he would still be in Vienna when I arrived, to remind me of who he was to me and to break the spell of the captain's attentions—which in any case would never be repeated.

❧

"What's to do! What's to do!" My mother paced up and down, alternately throwing her hands in the air and wringing them in front of her.

"Hello, *Mutter*," I said. She stopped her pacing and clung to me. I could feel her tears soaking into my fichu.

I had arrived home, exhausted, after two and a half weeks of jolting over badly rutted roads and sleeping in barely habitable inns. More than once I wished myself back in the luxury of the Hôtel Montesson. Even the Bastille would have been preferable, as far as comfort was concerned. All I wanted to do was bathe, have supper, and go to sleep. But as soon as my mother let me out of her fierce embrace, she began to babble something about the emperor, and a summons.

Greta brought me a bowl of soup without being asked, and I flashed her a grateful smile before sitting at the table and tasting it. How good it was to be home! Our apartment was not large, but the main room with its long table, mismatched upholstered chairs, and heating stove that actually worked wrapped around me and comforted me. The worn wooden floors covered in old Persian carpets, the whitewashed plaster walls and ceiling broken up by rustic beams, the built-in shelves displaying everything from books to toys to porcelain knick-knacks—these were evidence of lives lived in modest comfort, and I treasured them. Our windows looked out on a side street that was busy enough to provide entertainment, but quiet enough not to disturb our sleep. I don't know why exactly, but the sound of carriages on Vienna's streets was different from those that clogged the streets of Paris. Somehow softer, more leisurely. As I drank the hot soup and listened to the familiar cadence of my mother's German fretting, the knot that had been in the back of my neck almost since the moment I left Vienna months ago eased, and I felt a surge of serenity flow through me. I didn't attend to what my mother was saying until I'd consumed every drop of soup and eaten a large hunk of freshly baked bread.

When I was ready at last to look at her and listen to her, she simply continued as if I must already know everything she'd previously said. "The message was most urgent. It said you were to attend the emperor at the Hofburg as soon as you arrived in Vienna. I can't imagine what it could be. You've been so mysterious, and not a single letter while you were away! But you are home again, and in one piece, *Gott sei dank*! And you must attend the emperor!"

I caught hold of my mother's hand as she paced by and pulled her into a chair next to me at the table. "I can hardly think he means me to call at this late hour," I said. "It's nearly curfew! And he's well aware that I've been away from my family for months."

She threw her hands up and stood, starting once again to pace up and down before fetching a folded letter that sat on the mantel. "Here. You judge for yourself whether or not you must go tonight."

I was highly skeptical that the urgency was as dire as my mother claimed, and prepared to continue smoothing her feathers. However, after I'd scanned the lines for myself, I saw that the instructions were clear: I was to come to the Hofburg as soon as I could after receiving the letter. It said I would be admitted at any hour of the day or night. Why such urgency? Thoughts raced through my mind as I put on my cloak and hat again.

"You see! I was right!" My mother stood in the middle of the room, her arms folded over her chest, chin raised.

"Yes. You were right," I said, and rushed over to kiss her on both cheeks before I left.

The emperor is angry, I thought. The captain and I had been unable to completely stop the spread of lies about the queen, although at least we discovered their source. What other reason would have caused him to issue such a command?

"When will you return?" My mother called down the stairs.

"I can't answer that, I'm afraid," I said. My first instinct had been to snap at her and say how on earth do you expect me to be able to say? But then I realized she simply wanted to ensure that I would come back, after I'd been away for such a long time. I might have asked the same thing if I'd been in her shoes.

I honestly had no idea what to expect upon arriving at the Hofburg. The main gates were closed, and I had to apply to the sentry with my name and show him the letter I'd received before he would open them for me. I headed toward the small door on the ground level I'd gone through the time the emperor assigned me my task, assuming he would be in his small study.

"Mademoiselle Schurman!"

The voice came from somewhere above my head. I stepped back to the middle of the courtyard so I could see the first floor.

To my surprise, it was a footman in royal livery standing atop the formal steps that led into the grand entrance from the courtyard. With one hand he raised an oil lamp high and with the other he held the door open.

I climbed the steps, not hurrying, assuming that at the end of my walk I would find disappointment and censure. Wordlessly, I followed my guide through the chain of magnificent rooms, full of ornate gilded decoration and furnishings that looked too precious to use. Unlike Versailles, though, they were empty of courtiers vying for positions at court.

At last, we arrived at what appeared to be an empty ballroom. The footman bowed and said, "*Warten-Sie, bitte,*" and then disappeared through a door that blended seamlessly with the paneling.

I faced the wall with the door and watched, not sure what to expect exactly. The vast room was unheated and I kept my cloak on. Standing still, I soon felt chilled and wrapped the cloak around me more tightly.

I jumped when I heard something behind me, and turned to see the emperor striding in through another hidden door, followed by a group of people I didn't take the time to recognize. I sank into the deepest curtsy I could muster and looked down at the floor, noticing the intricate parquetry.

I rose after a decent amount of time and when I heard more people entering the room. I had started counting them and got up to fifteen when two footmen entered carrying a tall writing table. One other followed with several sheets of paper tucked under his arm and a quill and an inkwell in his hands. A fourth footman carried a sand shaker and a blotter. Together they set the table up in the middle of the floor, placed the accoutrements on it, and all the people who had come in ranged themselves in a semicircle around it, while the emperor took his place standing directly behind it. Without a word, he began writing on one sheet of paper, and then signed his name with a flourish. He blotted it, sprinkled sand over it, then shook the sand off and laid the paper aside before taking another sheet and repeating the same operation.

I tried to read the expressions of everyone there. Was I about to be committed to prison for some unknown heinous crime? I had so mistaken the emperor's purpose the last time I had been called to the Hofburg that I didn't know what to think. Now he was looking up and a little over my right shoulder. I couldn't turn. One doesn't turn one's back on the emperor. I had no time to understand what was happening until I felt the gentle pressure of a hand resting on my shoulder.

"Theresa."

That voice. How can it be? I thought. I'd witnessed his fall. I could see the blood from where I had stood, watched as they carried his lifeless body away. I didn't dare turn around and have the illusion destroyed, the illusion that somehow, my eyes had deceived me on that fateful day, and the captain still lived.

I looked to the emperor for answers. He lifted his hand, indicating that I should turn. And so I did. "Captain." My voice squeaked on the word. Was it really the captain? Or did he have a brother, perhaps?

"It is I, Theresa. I owe you an explanation."

A million feelings fought for supremacy in my mind and heart. Eventually, one of them overwhelmed all the others. I stood tall, and with all my might, slapped the captain hard in the face. I saw my red hand print as I pushed past him and ran out of the room.

Chapter Thirty-One

I ran all the way home, heedless of the cold and the egregious breach of etiquette I had just committed.

When I burst through the door, I was surprised to see Greta laying out our best china and crystal goblets, and my mother selecting a fine vintage for our dinner. They looked up in surprise.

"Why, Theresa, we didn't expect you for an hour at least. Danior and Alida have not yet arrived."

That was when I saw my brother Toby sitting in a chair with Anna on his lap, having just suspended their clapping game.

"Enough!" I cried. "Why was I the very last to know? Why this pointless subterfuge? Why, I ask you, why make me suffer in this way?"

By now tears streamed down my cheeks. Everyone in the apartment stared at me, eyes wide, mouths open. My mother approached me and put her hand on my forehead, testing to see if I had a fever. "Perhaps you should go to bed," she said.

"I am not ill! I'm just... very, very confused!"

Toby set Anna aside, came to me, and put his now-strong arm around my shoulders. I sobbed into his chest. "I don't know many people who would be so upset at gaining a great honor from the emperor himself," he said.

Of course, I hadn't stayed to see what the emperor was going to do with me. "You all knew, and you said nothing. I'm not a child!" I straightened myself and blew my nose into my handkerchief. "What honor?"

A few hours later, after we'd all eaten Greta's wonderful roast lamb and potatoes and turnips, and Danior had taken great pleasure in teasing me to the limits of my tolerance—especially about my unexpected violence toward the captain—I found out everything. I was thereafter to be known as Freiin Theresa of Volkstadt. And I had a handsome living settled on me—enough to move my family to a larger apartment and give my mother the kind of life she'd always dreamed of.

That was all well and good, but I had one more matter to discuss. I had not told my friends and family why I was so angry at the captain, or the entire story of what he'd done to warrant my reaction. I determined that I would seek him out the next day and demand he tell me how he happened not to die when I had seen him do so with my own eyes, and why he had lied to me about the murder.

The next morning, I found myself once again at the Hofburg. Not in the royal apartments, but in one of the dozens of rooms set aside for officers of the court. This time, the captain had arrived first. He stood when I entered and gave me a curt, military bow. "Please, sit," he said, indicating the chair on the opposite side of the desk where he was seated.

"I prefer to stand," I said.

"Very well. I won't waste your time. As you see, the chevalier did not kill me."

"But I saw—"

"You saw what you were intended to see. After you left the chevalier's apartment the previous day, he and I reached an agreement. He recognized that my position in the Swiss Guard had become untenable because of my various acts, and that at any moment my subterfuge might be found out. He also understood that I had a powerful sponsor, and that to end my life would not go down very well with said sponsor."

"But what about his loyalty to the house of Orléans?"

"He is intelligent enough to understand that, although he is forced to play politics in order to achieve his artistic aims, that is a risky and uncertain gamble to take."

"I wonder if he knows just how risky it is," I said, as I reached into the pocket hidden in the seam of my skirt and closed my fingers around the duke's gold snuffbox. "You see, captain, I know you were lying, and not just to the chevalier, Sophie, and the other officers in the Swiss Guard." I drew my hand out closed in a tight fist, turned it over, and opened my fingers one by one to reveal the snuffbox.

The captain looked surprised. Shocked, even. He picked it up from my palm with two fingers and held it up to the light. "Where did you get this?"

I had thought that I would simply tell him. I had thought that morning that I would relate all my experiences of that evening once we talked. But I changed my mind. "It's a duplicate of another one I saw the day before the duel. I'm not going to tell you where I found it. You have not proven trustworthy enough for me to share that story with you. I will, however, call you to account for lying to me. You are no murderer."

He bowed his head, looking as close to sheepish as I'd ever seen him. "Don't hate me for it. Joseph—the chevalier—and I came up with the idea to help prevent you from trying to save me, and interfering with our plan."

I had recovered enough from my anger of the day before to know that I didn't hate him, and was unlikely to start doing so anytime soon. However, I said nothing.

"Which reminds me..." The captain strode over to a desk and opened a drawer to take out a sealed letter, which he handed to me. "It's from Joseph. Once he knew you were from Austria, and that your godfather is none other than Joseph Haydn himself, he placed one condition on participating in the charade that made it possible for me to leave Paris unnoticed."

"What was his condition?"

"It's no secret. I can tell you that the chevalier de Saint-Georges requests an introduction to Herr Haydn, because he would like to extend an invitation to him to come to Paris and compose some symphonies for the Concert Olympique."

I didn't open the letter. Not there. I wanted to be alone when I did so. Of course I would speak to my godfather, for whatever difference it would make. The chevalier's fame was surely enough in itself to guarantee that Haydn would go to Paris.

An awkward silence fell between us.

"I should—"

"So, Theresa—Mademoiselle Schurman. I understand there is a certain Hungarian baron who is eager to hear that you are safely back on Austrian soil."

We'd both started speaking at the same time, and I blushed. Somehow here, so near to home and the life I knew awaited me, all that had transpired in Paris took on an unreal, fantastic sheen. I accepted his words as meaning that our previous interactions were not to be taken seriously. I should have been grateful, but I felt foolish. I said nothing.

The captain rose, walked around the table, and stood next to me. I was about to move aside, since his face was close enough for me to feel his breath.

"It still stings," he said, pointing to his cheek.

"Do you wonder why I did it?" I asked.

He shrugged. "Since you clearly don't like me, you will be glad to know that tomorrow I will be going to London at the emperor's request." He took half a step closer to me. I still didn't move.

"How will you manage without my help?" I asked, lifting my chin so I could stare straight into his eyes. Their expression was dangerously familiar. Perhaps he had merely been teasing me about Zoltan.

With one finger, the captain traced the outline of my face as he spoke. "It's true that matters would not have concluded so quickly and in such a satisfactory manner if you had not been working with me. But I do have other resources. And you, I believe, have commitments that are likely to keep you in Vienna for good. Or perhaps, you will move to Hungary."

His face drew gradually closer to mine until I could feel the heat not just of his breath, but emanating from his skin. So many thoughts and emotions raced through my mind and heart. Every other time the captain had been so close to me, the times he'd touched me, his kisses. And then, fighting with those memories were the ones of the times he had tricked me, or misled me, or deliberately tried to confuse me so I would have to go along with his plan, whatever it was.

He drew closer and closer. I thought, he's going away. I need never see him again. Perhaps, just this last time...

The moment before our lips met, the door to the office banged open. We jumped apart as if a rat had run between us. I felt my cheeks go hot and turned away from the page who had entered with a message for the captain.

I put out my hand to the captain, all at once realizing how utterly foolish it had been for me to let him lead me so far down that path. And yet, the fact that I had allowed him to do so perhaps said something to me about how ready I was to tie my life to Zoltan's—that is, if he was still interested in having me.

"*Auf Wiedersehen,*" I whispered, and then, without hesitating, I followed the page out the door and made my way home, half in a daze.

As soon as I arrived, I went into my small room, sat on my bed, and opened the letter from the chevalier.

To my surprise, the letter contained not only the note about my godfather, but also an invitation to me, to visit Paris as his guest any time at my convenience, so that we could play chamber music again.

I promise you a less eventful time, he said, and at the bottom of the letter, very small, I saw a hand-drawn staff with a melody dotted on it. I hummed it to myself. It was the melody from the duet we had played together. Beneath it, in even smaller characters, were the words, *À mademoiselle Theresa Schurman, violinist, artist, and friend.*

I folded the letter and tucked it away in my desk. Yes, I was an artist. And I would be for my entire life, wherever I went—whether I stayed in Vienna or accepted Zoltan's proposal and moved to his estate in Hungary.

Or, if my travels ever took me to London...

Author's Note

My decision to send Theresa to Paris was based in part upon stumbling across the fabulous Joseph Bologne, Chevalier de Saint-Georges, the famous black violinist, composer, and music director who made a huge splash in Paris before the Revolution. Well, not literally stumbling, but I was researching something else at the time. As a mixed-race man he was unusual in Europe in that era, although not unique. What made him exceptional was his astounding virtuosity—in both fencing and playing the violin. How could I not find a way for my feisty violinist to meet him and get to know him? Especially when I discovered that it was Saint-Georges who invited her godfather Haydn to Paris, where he composed his gorgeous Paris symphonies.

Like many of the non-white people who came to Europe, Saint-Georges was from the Antilles, born on Christmas Day, 1745, in Guadeloupe. He was the son of a Creole landowner and a 16-year-old Senegalese slave who was maid to the landowner's wife. His father loved him, and apparently also loved his mother, which wasn't always the case when the wealthy procreated with their slaves. There's very little known about what Madame Bologne thought of this arrangement, but young Joseph was her husband's only son, and he was given every advantage of education and treated as well as any child who was the result of legitimate marriage.

Although Joseph stayed in France (Bordeaux) with his family for a year between the ages of 3 and 4 (there was a spurious murder charge against his father that had to be dealt with), Bologne brought his son to live in France for good under the care of his uncle when he was eight years old. Gabriel Danat (author of *The Chevalier de Saint-Georges; Virtuoso of the Sword and Bow*, Pendragon Press, 2006) conjectures that the reason for this early move to France was that, because of his race and the fact that he was illegitimate, Joseph could not inherit his father's property—and would thus need other advantages to make his way in life.

Joseph was educated in a Jesuit institution in Angoulême for a couple of years before his father and mother joined him in France, and the family moved to a handsome house in Paris. There, at the age of thirteen, Joseph was enrolled in the academy run by La Boëssière, where he learned the usual scholarly subjects as well as fencing and instrumental music.

Not a lot of information exists about Joseph's early education in Paris, but apparently he learned a kind of fortitude and patience that helped him weather the inevitable hardships of being a black boy in a white country. His exceptional skill, intelligence, and talent must have helped a great deal.

Although there are several reliable records that relate Joseph's prowess in fencing, there's comparatively little known about his early musical training. The first time he is mentioned as a musician was in a poem published in the *Mercure de France* in 1768, when he was a grown man. By that time he was sufficiently adept to have been invited by François-Joseph Gossec, a prominent French 18th-century composer, to join the Concert des Amateurs. By 1773, Joseph joined the more famous Concert Spirituel, and after that focused more on music than on any of his other talents. He was an accomplished composer, not only of violin concertos but of other orchestral works. He may well have encountered Mozart in the late 1770s, who was in Paris trying to further his career.

In 1776, Joseph was named co-director of the Paris Opera. But his mixed race proved a hindrance there, when a group of singers and dancers at the opera petitioned the queen, saying they would not take orders from a mulatto. Joseph bowed out gracefully (not much else he could do), but he was smitten with opera and began to compose works in that genre. His increasing renown as a composer led to his appointment in 1778 as the music director of Madame de Montesson's private theater. Although Sophie is a creation of my imagination, Madame de Montesson and the Orléans family are historical figures.

Around that time, Joseph survived a never-solved assassination attempt, although conjecture has it that it was provoked by one of his love affairs. He was an extremely handsome man—as the only existing portrait of him attests.

In 1781, the Concert Olympique was formed with Saint-Georges as its director. This is the position in which we find Joseph in this fictional narrative.

When the old Duc d'Orléans died in 1785, Joseph no longer had steady employment as a musician and instead became involved in politics with the young duke, his friend. He was on the side of the Republic, and remained committed to that side when others vacillated. He made two trips to England in the 1780s, and was an officer in the Republican army during the Revolution. He unfortunately found himself in Amiens in 1791 among an enclave of royalist émigrés. When he tried to give a concert there so he could earn a living, he was accused of trying to recruit people to the Orléanist cause, and ordered to leave the region.

Saint-Georges returned to Paris and survived the terror and its aftermath. However, he was not well for the last few years of his life, and succumbed to a disease of the bladder on June 12, 1799 in Paris. There's a great deal more to his remarkable history than I have space to share here, but if you can get ahold of Banat's book, you'll find ample additional information.

As to other historical figures in this book, Rose Bertin was indeed Marie Antoinette's milliner. She survived the Revolution and the terror and wrote a memoir in the early 19th century trying to rehabilitate the queen's image. The artists I mention in the scenes in the Louvre are also historical figures: Joseph Vien and Elisabeth-Louise Vigée Le Brun. And there was, indeed, a printer in the basement of the Louvre. No evidence whatsoever, though, that anyone was ever murdered there.

Acknowledgements

No writer ever works in complete isolation. I am very fortunate to have a community of writers I look to for support and guidance, and who have listened to and commented on parts of this book as it was being written.

I would like to thank the writers in the generative workshops at Writers In Progress in Florence, MA, run by the remarkable Dori Ostermiller and her prodigiously talented assistant director, Emily Lackey. Thank you both.

Thanks to all my fellow Wednesday evening workshop participants, who gamely listened to unfamiliar historical fiction in a workshop that was supposed to be about writing from life: Elaine Arsenault, Emily Everett, Roxanne Nieman, Amelia Perkins, Gaye Rheinhold, David Stevens, Liesl Swogger, Rocky Thompson, and Marie Westburg.

Wonderful writer and friend Nerissa Nields also helped to foster this book into being through her inspiring retreats.

Last but not least, I would like to thank my beta readers, fabulous historical novelist Stephanie Cowell and fellow belletomane and fiction writer Liesl Swogger, whose feedback helped me polish the manuscript.

And of course, my ever-present, ever-intelligent and witty partner in crime and in life, Charles Jackson.